Gunny Mac
Private Detective

Trouble in Chinatown

Steven Walker

Gunny Mac Private Detective
Trouble in Chinatown

ISBN 978-1-7357026-0-5

Acknowledgements

I want to thank God for giving us so many wonderful gifts, our religious freedom, my wonderful country and our forefathers who gave us the U.S. Constitution. The U.S. Marine Corps for protecting our country and allowing us to live in peace and harmony. My wonderful wife Susan, who has always been my cheerleader and supported me. Noah Regan who illustrated my cover and logo, what a talent, Ted Dilenschieder who was always ready to help me edit (day or night) my life-long friends (the skids) in Cleveland, what fun we have had, LTC Roger Furnival who I served with and has been my steadfast friend and encouraged me to write. Thanks, Rojo.

"In the Marine Corps no word is spoken with more reverence than the word gunny." Except the word God!

Prologue

September 12-14, 1942 Guadalcanal

Several hundred feet above the jungle floor, torrents of rain pounded and shredded the triple canopy of leaves. The drumming cadence of the rain drowned out the symphony of sounds usually heard on the jungle floor. Millions of raindrops splashed from leaf to leaf, flowing down wild orchid vines and cascading off big floating banana leaves. The wide-eyed monkeys scrunched under the larger leaves, just like a man might do, trying to keep from being washed away. Overflowing streams gurgled lustily, red water spilling over their embankments, hungrily eroding the stream beds.

Before the storm, the interior of the jungle had reached 115 degrees Fahrenheit. Now, the more cooling rain made the Marines pushing through the undergrowth shiver uncontrollably. They moved like old men before their time. They were bent at the waist, only their eyes darting to the left and right. They didn't wear their GI ponchos, those ridiculous contraptions that allowed more water in than out, made them sweat ferociously, and smelled like the result of an all-night drinking binge in Shanghai. They used them only as an overhead cover, to try and keep foxholes dry.

Every day, every single day, the rain came down in sweeping bursts like a gray curtain. Then the rain would stop, and steam would rise from the jungle floor like it did from the sewer grates in New York City in the winter. Then, in the next moment, all was lost in another cloudburst. The Marines called this time, "chills and pills," but they'd run out of quinine pills weeks before.

The wetness made the men miserable causing painful immersion foot. On patrol days, they prayed to the rain God to mask their movements in the jungle. If the downpours made their lives unbearable, they could only grin and know the Japs suffered also.

At the beginning of the battle for Guadalcanal, they had several hundred mules carrying supplies to the front quickly and efficiently. The Japs killed the mules off weeks ago, but they often joked that they were in the process of becoming more mule-like every day.

To a casual observer, the Marines seemed to slog across the jungle floor. But each movement they made was precise and planned. The jungle floor was a death trap. Gnarled roots would grab an unsuspecting ankle and snap it like a twig, leaving Marines writhing in pain. Swamps appeared like magic, swallowing the unlucky Marines whole. High, unfeeling winds, toppled over huge rotting trees, crushing unsuspecting men. Vines came out of nowhere to wrap themselves around hands, their nasty barbs ripping out chunks of flesh. Snakes and eight-inch centipedes feasted on them, inflicting poisonous bites, and sometimes, without warning, a Marine suddenly would keel over dead.

After months of close combat, they had learned to accept the brutal nature of their lives. The idea of driving a car, taking a girl out to the movies, or playing baseball with your friends seemed unreal. Oiling down your 03 Springfield lovingly with dirty, callused fingers, sleeping in foxholes filled with putrid water, and killing Japs were more real.

Even Marine Corps pilots flying with their cockpit's open, five thousand feet above the jungle, could smell the rot and death.

Jungle ulcers and scratching the itching, burning jungle rot, soon became part of second nature to all Guadalcanal Marines, just like spitting tobacco juice or scratching places that would make a woman blush. Over time, their senses sharpened like that of any jungle predator. When something was amiss, the sounds of the jungle told them. Combat honed their instincts; their eyes caught any unnatural movements.

Several months back, they had heard the booming of the navy's sixteen-inch guns that had lit up the sky like a summer heat storm. Throughout the night, they waited with anticipation to hear what happened. The next morning, as the sun rose over the Pacific Ocean, the United States Navy was nowhere to be seen. Word slowly filtered down to the Marines that the United States Navy had been defeated and had left the Marines alone to suffer their fate like on Corregidor months before. The navy abandoned them to face 20,000 well-supplied Imperial Japanese troops. The Marines possessed limited food, ammunition, and other supplies. They began to make signs that said no Poppa, no Mama, and no Uncle Sam!

Their uniforms hung in tatters, making them look like pasty green mummies. Caked mud and remains of dead insects covered their bearded faces. Their eye sockets were dark with exhaustion and a fiery sea of red surrounded their pupils that had seen far too much death. History recorded the birth of a new nom de guerre, 'The Walking Dead.'

President Roosevelt made a decision. The 1st Marine Division on Guadalcanal would never surrender and fight to the death. He calculated that the defeat of the First Marine Division would ensure the Hawaiian Islands would be invaded. He issued orders for the money in Hawaii to be destroyed and replaced by US currency with the word Hawaii printed across the back of each bill. Money useless to the Japanese to use against the United States. This true story is an interesting one. President Roosevelt ordered the millions of dollars burned. How much, if any, was stolen. The reader will have to think of the possibilities of this question during the bleak days of 1942.

Chapter 1

September 13, 1942 on Bloody Ridge.

Gunnery Sergeant Mac stopped on the reverse slope of Edson's Ridge to catch his breath and stared at the impenetrable prison of vines and trees that walled him off from the Japs. He turned his head to the right, gazing north, where the lagoon protected their flank. Last night the Jap's had waded across trying to outflank them and now their bloated bodies feeding the crocodiles for the past day. The gas escaping from their punctured bodies producing a wailing sound that sent shivers down his spine. He hadn't felt this disjointed from reality since his last three-day drunk in Panama.

During daylight hours, the trees were so green they looked black, which added to his feeling of intruding into some God-forsaken world. Triple canopy jungle surrounded Edson's Ridge, squashing out any glimmer of light twenty yards past the barren ridge, and defying even one ray of light to find its way into this hell.

His fever from a prolonged case of malaria made him shiver uncontrollably. He swiped at his brow, clearing the feverish sweat from his forehead. His eyes moved side to side, watching for the faint luminous light given off by decomposing vegetation on the trail ahead. He knew that he needed to move faster, twilight was his friend, but the Nips thrived like mushrooms in the dark.

The gunnery sergeant used the butt of his Tommy gun to stop from sliding off the ridge; the saturated ground more slippery than snot on a doorknob. He struggled to the next machine gun position, his fatigue bearing down on him like a suit of medieval armor.

He put a finger to the side of his nose and blew out a green wad of mucus and looked down the path. A hot, stifling mist rose a foot above the trail. *If any place in the world needed an enema, God could start with this place*, he thought. He felt some relief that his first machine gun emplacement was ready, but this last one worried him. The second squad machine gun team had endured the brunt of the attack last night. How they had held the rice -eating bastards back the previous night was a miracle.

Crawling on the reverse slope of the ridge, the gunny came up behind the last machine gun emplacement and slid into the muddy L-shaped trench. He whispered to his second squad machine gun team, "Throw a poncho over us." He flicked his flashlight on, revealing their faces. "You, boys are a beautiful sight to behold."

Their bloodshot fixated on him. One of the Marines ran his hand affectionately across Mac's bearded face. "Gunny, you're looking spiffy yourself." The rest of them in the shallow hole chuckled.

Mac continued. "The Japs cannot turn this flank." He searched each Marine's eyes, punctuating his concern with silence. "We'll lose this ridge if they do. Next, we'll lose Henderson Field and Guadalcanal. There's nowhere to go, boys, except fight or die in your hole. When the bastards attack, don't give away your positions until you must. Throw grenades, wait to fire until they are right on top of us. Get your Ka-bars out ready to stick the bastards, if they slide into your hole. I'll be with the first squad anchoring the right side of the lagoon."

Before they could reply, the gunny disappeared into the darkness. Mac swore as he heard the rain pound the foliage around him. More noise to mask the movements of the Imperial Marines. Mac brushed a large banana leaf, dumping the cold water it had collected down his neck. He slid into his machine gun position into ankle-deep water.

Thank God, he had sent Gunny Wojohowitz to the left flank knowing the boys there needed him. No use his best friend dying with him.

They heard the Japs before they saw them. "Today, Marrrrine, you die!" The grizzled veterans knew from experience that the shrill, high-pitched voices meant the Nips had been hitting the sake bottle. The Imperial Marines blew horns, beat empty coconut shells, and shot their rifles in the air. The sounds erupting from the jungle seemed to be all around them. He envisioned flying monkeys, carrying rifles, reminiscent of the Wizard of Oz, attacking them from the triple canopy jungle.

Then, an eerie silence seemed to float on the rising mist, along with a bile wrenching fear.

Mac strained to hear the slightest sound. All he heard were the jungle sounds. The steady hypnotizing drone of rain, crickets, tree frogs, and the happy clapper monkeys clapping high in the trees.

Twenty yards in front of the main ridge, Mac heard the thump of grenades and the deep barking cough of the Browning automatic rifles firing. He whispered into the field telephone, "Outposts coming in!" Then silence. He understood that the guys in the outposts were the canaries in the mine. An involuntary shudder went through him when he thought about dying alone, cut to ribbons by some Jap like a piece of fish bait.

Then he heard grunts, more yelling, the thrashing sounds of men fighting for their lives in the distance. His senses deepened with a rush of adrenalin and raw fear. More screams. He said a silent prayer. Wait till the Japs try to come in your hole boys, then cut them, stab them, kill the bastards.

He couldn't see the two Marines with him, but he could hear the breathing of Robbie, the machine gunner and that of his assistant gunner. The traversing mechanism under the .30 caliber Browning machine gun was zeroed in to fire its rounds at mid-thigh. The sweetest sound too desperate Marines was the throaty, coughing sounds of the .30 caliber machine gun. Corporal Robbie was the company's best machine gunner. He could hear Corporal Robbie whispering to Madeline, his nickname for his machine gun. "Don't let me down, baby, don't quit on me, no Dear John letters tonight." Mac reached out in the darkness and gave him a reassuring pat on the arm.

The rain came down even harder as if God wanted to wash away the transgressions of all men. Closing his eyes, he concentrated on sounds that might be unusual. His breathing seemed too loud. He held his breath: nothing but the swishing of rain hitting the leaves. Minutes seemed like hours. Mac could feel the tension as his jaw muscles clenched into knots. Water filled his foxhole up to mid-calf.

He opened his eyes, hearing an unnatural sound in the cacophony of natural sounds, a scrape against the ground. Was it a plant breaking or a twig snapping? They had to be close: he pulled the pin on his grenade, let go of the spoon handle, and counted to three. He lobbed the grenade down the slope in front of his position. The explosion was followed by the wafting smell of cordite wrapped up in the odor of burst intestines. More Marines threw grenades in front of their foxholes and bounced them down the ridge into the Japanese crawling toward them.

Mac yelled, "Now Robbie, open up on the bastards!" Corporal Robbie, with calm deliberation, traversed the .30 caliber machine gun, firing three and four round bursts to the left, and the right, and back again.

Mac heard the rounds smacking into the Japanese flesh like fists slamming into a carcass of beef. For God's sake, where are the flares? The company commander promised flares! The cordite from the gunfire stuck to the mist on the spine of the ridge and formed a fog above the machine gun. The Japanese began a ferocious assault on the position. Wave after wave welled up from the ground and attacked. Yelling "Banzai!" they ran straight into the train of slugs, which dealt out death with uncanny accuracy. Corporal Robbie's head shot back, a small hole between his eyes, but his dead hands refused to let go of the trigger.

Mac pushed him out of the way and kept up a staccato rate of fire. He swore as a bullet tore through the water jacket, which cooled the .30 caliber and precious water gurgled out. The Browning machine gun's barrel turned red; the raindrops made sizzling noises as they landed on the barrel. The whomp of mortars finally sending illumination into the night sky made him look up involuntarily. The flares made popping noises and lit up the night up and down the ridge. A flare lit up the sky directly above them, the only place where the sky was visible. Yellow uniforms surrounded the position. A wounded Japanese soldier fell on top of Jones, the assistant gunner, knocking him over. He rolled on top of the Jap and drowned him in the bottom of the foxhole.

Using his helmet, Mac scooped up water, leaned over the machine gun barrel pouring water over the red-hot barrel. A mustard-colored uniform rose out of the cloud and shot him in the left arm. He saw the flash of a rifle and fired his .45 toward it, and a body without form then bounced off his shoulder. He loaded the machine gun with a new belt and started hammering the shadows. Two Japanese Imperial Marines jumped into the foxhole. PFC Jones shot them point-blank, shoving the bodies out of the hole. The roar of the machine gun deafened him to any surrounding sounds.

Jones screamed, "They're all around us, Mac…keep firing, kill the bastards!" The Japs climbed over their comrades bodies, piling up on the forward slope in front of Mac's position. Without warning, the flare extinguished. Where are the goddamn flares! Mac yelled for more ammo, and Jones fed the last belt into the smoking breech. Mac pulled hard on the cocking mechanism and fired. The mortars boomed in the night sky, showering light over the ridge. The flares were floating downward, rocking like a pendulum, making shadows jump up and down. He could see that the assistant gunner had rolled out of the foxhole, wrestling with a Jap.

An Imperial Marine dove into the foxhole, Mac stabbed wildly, ripping him across the face and neck. Blood spurted over his hand with a wet, hot stickiness. He turned around quickly, startled to see a wall of dancing shadows like marionettes on top of his position. Mac kept his right finger glued to the trigger. The shadows toppled like bowling pins, and for the first time, he realized how many there were! More flares hissing and smoking lit up the night sky, and he murmured, "thank God... more light, please! Don't turn off the lights!" Blood ran down his arm and hand, dripping off the closed breach. He made Madeline sing a song of death... bam...bambambam...bambambambam! "More ammo... more goddamn ammo!" he yelled above the sound and fury!

His assistant gunner appeared at his side to feed the hungry beast. More flares appeared, and with his peripheral vision, he saw his best friend Wojohowitz, his big Polish guardian angel, dumping machine gun ammo and grenades at his side. He looked to his right again, and Wojo was gone.

Mac's neck snapped back and he grabbed his throat. His body slammed backward, into the opposite side of the foxhole. Warm blood spattered his face, and the metallic taste of copper flooded his mouth. Heaving himself forward, he grabbed the trigger of his machine gun and fired until the ammo was gone.

Jones, blood streaming from his face, quickly reloaded. Mac and Madeline administered Marine justice to the relentless enemy. Time was non-existent in any normal sense, it was measured by how long it took Madeleine to spit her rounds out, and the frenzied loading of ammo that she demanded. Rounds began to cook off in her, and Mac knew he had precious seconds left. Madeline barked for the last time, her red-hot barrel on the verge of melting. There was no time to change the barrel. He could see the Japs forming in front of him. He felt for the box at his right.

He stood up and threw grenade after grenade down the ridge, exposing himself to incoming fire. Rounds kicked up all around him like hard rain on a calm lake. The yellow-jacketed forms continued the never-ending assault on his position. The flares kept falling. Gunny Mac grabbed three grenades, putting one in his dungaree pocket. He gave one to Jones and he threw the other one as far as he could in front of his position. The thought kept going through his brain that Crockett and Jim Bowie must have felt like this at the Alamo.

He released the empty magazine in his .45, inserted a new one and shot each screaming uniform as they assaulted his position. He inserted another magazine and drew his Ka-bar. Two Japs jumped into his hole, the flares went out, and darkness left him helpless. He felt a knife go inside him. He grabbed onto the Jap's hand holding the knife and shot the shadow through the head. More orbs of light floated down. A hand grabbed onto his leg. The Jap screamed as Mac drove his Ka-bar through his hand. Another hand grabbed Mac's leg, trying to pull him down. He stomped a face with his boondocker. Jones was out of the foxhole and yelled at

Mac. Mac caught the grenade he threw him. He pulled the pin on a grenade dropped it at his feet.

He rolled out of the foxhole as the grenade exploded, red hot shrapnel peppering the bottom of his boots. Rolling over on all fours, trying to rise, a Jap tackled him. He stabbed upward, his Ka-bar sticking into a rib cage. Rising, he stepped on the writhing man's chest and he pulled until he freed it.

A Jap circled Mac. He appeared as a shadow as the last flare extinguished in the night sky. Where in the hell was the son-of-a-bitch? He couldn't see him, but he was so close Mac could smell him. Flares again lit up the ridge. Mac could see the glint of a knife in the Jap's hand. He rushed Mac. Mac took off his helmet and pitching like Bob Feller, smashed the bastard in the face. It gave him time to step forward and slice the shadowy figure across the side of his neck.

Japs seemed to be everywhere, like midges on a Cleveland summer night. He tripped over the body of a Marine and in the light of the flares, saw that it was Jones. An avalanche of grief overcame Mac as if someone was ripping his heart out. All the kid ever wanted… was own a house and to mow the grass in his yard.

The second he saw Jones' face, he turned into a snarling, growling heathen from hell. It was not enough just to kill them. He needed them to suffer! He wanted to rip their guts out and see them scream in agony.

He stuck his .45 into the neck of one Imperial Marine and pulled the trigger. He felt a pain in his right thigh, turned around, and shot another screaming shadow. Turning to the right, he saw several shadows running toward him. He threw his last grenade at the Japs coming toward him. He dropped to the ground shielding his body behind a dead Jap. With no time to reload before they were upon him, he threw his empty .45 at a rushing figure. Yelling,"C' mon, you sons of bitches!" He advanced toward the moving blobs of darkness with his Ka-bar, knowing somehow, he had to kill them all.

* * *

Colonel Edson, the Marine Raider-Parachute Battalion Commander, walked along the top of the ridge viewing the carnage. He stopped and looked at the doctor, "Where is he, Commander Ryan?"

"I moved him over to the best spot I could find, Sir. He is the third litter on the right."

Colonel Edson walked over to the litter and Dr. Ryan followed. Edson knelt next to the litter, his face contorting in pain. He looked down at the blood-encrusted gunny and placed his hand on him. He started to pray out loud causing Mac to open his eyes. The bullet wound through the side of his throat made him speak as if he was choking.

"My boys stopped them, Sir, didn't they?" Edson jerked his head up at the straggled sounds emanating from Gunny Mac. "No, you stopped them, gunny, a fight that will go down for ages! Edson yelled to the surgeon. "Get this Marine to surgery now."

* * *

Five days later, Lieutenant Van Deer sat in on a briefing with the head surgeon at the naval hospital in Oahu, Hawaii. She leaned forward, listening intently as her boss explained the injuries of their newest patient who had been flown in directly from an aircraft carrier.

The surgeon put on his reading glasses and glanced at the patient's medical records. "Gunnery Sergeant Mac sustained life-threatening injuries, and it is a miracle that he is alive. All total, he received thirty-seven wounds. His major wounds: shot in the side of his throat, gunshot wounds to his arm and leg, a deep bayonet wound in his side, knife wounds and slashes. The rest are minor shrapnel wounds. Medically, it doesn't look good…, but his Marines say he was the reason that they held onto Bloody Ridge. We must hang onto him. He will need extra attention, and I'm asking for volunteers to work their shift and to stay an extra amount of time throughout the night. He has given his all for us, and we must give our all to him."

Lieutenant Van Deer's hand shot up immediately, as she shouted out. "I'll care of him from midnight till my next shift begins.

The surgeon smiled and told everyone to sign up for their extra shifts and called Van Deer over to him. "I was hoping you would take the overnight shift and be with him. If anyone can help him, it will be you. Just remember there is an excellent chance he might die. I don't want you, heartbroken." The surgeon started to walk away and turned around to her. "I become amazed every day by these Marines; there is no quit in them."

At midnight Lieutenant Van Deer walked over to Mac's bedside, leaned over him, and gently brushed the sweat off his forehead. She sat in the chair by his bed, listening to the sounds around her. She heard his labored breathing caused by the drain tube in his neck, but his face was calm and peaceful. He needed something to hang onto. Earlier that morning, an idea came to her. She knew Mac could die within the next two weeks. She lifted a puppy from her shopping bag and placed him on the pillow next to Mac. His little pink tongue stretched out and licked Mac on the side of his face. As if the puppy understood, it curled around the unwounded side of Mac's neck and fell asleep. Van Deer watched the two sleeping, and a sad melancholy filled her soul. She prayed in silence for the Marine and waited for morning to come.

Chapter 2

Honolulu Naval Base

Lieutenant Commander John Kincaid rose, uncoiling his six-foot-four-inch scrawny frame and stood at attention, as the front door of the Quonset hut opened. Admiral Johnson strode in, breezing past him without bothering to acknowledge his presence. The admiral was trailed by ten men, all empty-handed, who each took a seat at the twelve-by-six, battleship gray conference table located in the center of the room.

Kincaid picked up his cigarettes and retreated to a chair at the far end of the table, as the admiral, the world's best bloviator, walked to the front of the table. Kincaid lit another cigarette from the one he was finishing and looked away from Johnson, whose military bearing was more like a king than an admiral. Maybe because, like a king, he wore an inherited crown, the stars passed on to the son from the father, who had been an admiral.

"Gentlemen," the admiral began, "we've picked up radio messages from the Japanese who have made their intentions clear. If they can't invade us, they plan to start an insurgency in Hawaii, tying up at least two to three Infantry Divisions." He paused, gesturing for one of the men to pour him a glass of water from the metal pitcher on the table. After taking a couple of sips, he cleared his throat and continued. "Because of this, President Roosevelt has put in place 'Operation Torch', a plan which you, gentlemen, are tasked with carrying out."

As the admiral yammered on, Kincaid's eyes glazed over, absently drifting over the three flags flanking the table-the U.S. flag to the right and the Navy and Marine Corps flags side-by-side to the left. At their meeting two days ago, Johnson had given him seven days to come up with a workable plan to collect and burn all the money in Hawaii while distributing two hundred million in new bills to the fine citizens of Hawaii. More and more, he couldn't figure out why Johnson had chosen him, of all people, for this job. Nonetheless, he intended to make the most of it. He stiffened up when he heard his name. "Lieutenant Commander Kincaid is in operational command."

As if on cue, Kincaid straightened and snagged the ashtray in front of him, grinding out the last of his cigarette. He stood up and waved to the people in the room, then quickly sat down.

He took a drag on his third cigarette in fifteen minutes while thinking what the admiral told him. The First Marine Division was hanging onto Guadalcanal by their fingertips, and the U.S. Naval ships supporting them long gone. Roosevelt and the bloviator were worried that the Japanese might visit them, take U.S. currency and pay off some Jap loving people in Hawaii to blow up building and ship repair facilities.

He shook his head. So, the idiots dreamed up this plan. Kincaid thought of the waste. Two hundred million dollars burned to ashes.

He watched the admiral as he continued speaking. The question still tormenting him. Why did the admiral pick him for this job? He knew the admiral hated his guts. The bloviator's wife told him while he undressed her, fondling her breasts until she let out a gasp.

He had no illusions about his wasted career. Most of his Annapolis classmates roamed the vast expanse of the Pacific Ocean hunting down Japs and future promotions, everyone but him. He had no chance for a wartime command.

He had learned of his new job two days ago when he was romancing the lonely wife of a destroyer skipper. When his leave was abruptly canceled, she grabbed his bottle of scotch, smiled sadly, and left without a word. Now, he found himself in a briefing room wondering how in the hell he was going complete this ludicrous mission.

Kincaid lit another cigarette from the one he was finishing and inhaled deeply. He suddenly noticed there was silence in the room. Everyone in the room was looking at him. He looked up to see the admiral staring at him.

A scowl replaced the admiral's bland look. "Lieutenant Commander Kincaid, I hope I'm not boring you?" The admiral continued. "The money will be burned at two locations: The Dole Sugar plantation and the Watonga Mortuary and Crematorium."

A small murmur arose from the group as they stared wide-eyed at each other and the admiral. He raised his voice to overcome the talking in the room.

"Gentlemen, please! Your responsibilities will be to develop a plan to collect the money from companies and banks where the Hawaiian people will drop their money off. They will be reissued new notes of legal tender with the word Hawaii stamped on each note's backside. Banks will be the only place to turn in the old money and be reissued the new money. Please look up at the projection screen, and you will notice the new Hawaiian bill with Hawaii stamped across the back of each note. This note will only have value in Hawaii. You will submit a plan to me within seven days or less, explaining in detail what you will need to accomplish this task. In the folder in front of you are my guidelines and detailed information to assist you in your planning. Now, cots will be brought in, a head with full capabilities to service your needs is behind the podium. Your work schedule will be from 0700 to 2200 hours. Breakfast will be at 0745 hours, lunch at 1300 hours, and dinner at 1700 hours."

He paused. "Gentlemen, we cannot allow any U.S. currency to be exploited by the Japanese or used against us in a possible Japanese-planned insurgency. I want your plan in seven days, and the money burned in fourteen days. Kincaid will pass out a legal document you must sign. Lieutenant Commander Kincaid is the only one authorized to leave. Anyone trying to take advantage of this situation or leaking about this operation will rue the day they were born. May God bless us all!"

* * *

Lieutenant Commander Kincaid sat at the "O" Club bar sipping his fourth Jack Daniel's served neat. His resentment simmered like a beef stew because the Navy Department had not promoted him to a full commander. Most of his Annapolis classmates earned promotions within three months after the beginning of the damn war, commanding battleships like the U.S.S Alabama. He commanded a gray, non-descript desk lorded over by Admiral Johnson.

He stared into his glass as if the answer was waiting at the bottom. Swirling the whiskey around, he inhaled the aroma of caramel and took a long drink. Finishing off his whiskey, he ordered another. He knocked the ash off his cigarette and stared at his tobacco-stained fingers. He tried not to think about his uneventful career and the butts he had to kiss to make lieutenant commander. Big white fat asses that hadn't seen the sun for twenty years.

He remembered how his classmates laughed at him when he received orders to the Shanghai Rose, a ship held together more by rust than steel. The Shanghai Rose was a former gunboat that was jury-rigged into a minesweeper. He earned his surface warfare officer insignia on that ship. His classmates earned theirs on destroyers, cruisers, and battleships.

Every day he left that ship smelling like he worked on a garbage trawler all day. When he walked into the Officer's Club, they looked at each other with smirks.

He never felt elite like his classmates. They wore their elitism like peacocks strutting their feathers. They ran the navy and only allowed their friends into the upper ranks of the elite, "Naval Academy this and Navy Academy that, and remember how we beat Army in '32' when you ran for that touchdown?"

Just thinking of them made him want to gag. The ring knockers gave him every insignificant assignment or billet, making his career a mockery of sorts. He was never allowed the same opportunities to achieve stardom as others. They never gave him a chance. He didn't have any blue blood running through his veins. Maybe the deep brown of bourbon, but indeed no damn blue blood! His father never finished the eighth grade. Hell, he never even met his mother.

But his brother had something none of the bastards had. Something called the Medal of Honor earned in World War 1, at a place called Belleau Wood. When the wheat field was cut down by German machine-guns and wheat chaff danced on the hot summer air, they never stopped advancing toward the Huns. When they couldn't walk, they crawled. Hugging and digging the brown earth between their fingers, they kept moving forward, where the Germans holed up, pouring lead into the tree line. When the battalion commander blew his whistle, they rose like devil dogs from hell and killed the Germans where they lay.

His brother's bravery got Kincaid an appointment to the Naval Academy. Officers commissioned by other sources called it Canoe U. Kincaid glanced at his academy ring and rubbed the ruby embedded on the top with his forefinger. He was proud of the Naval Academy, but he was no ring knocker!

He thought of his father and brother, who worked in the coal mines, never asking for special favors, never telling anyone about the medal. "Boy," his brother said, "The real heroes are those young lads who saved my life more than once in those woods! They fought like animals; those boys did. The Huns were right to call us devil dogs because when we reached them, we gave them no quarter. We killed them all. The boys would be proud you are going to the academy."

He buried his father during his senior year, coal dust still buried under his fingernails, and his father never got to see him graduate. His brother, who was his hero, died five days after he graduated.

His classmates never quite accepted the peasant amongst them. He smiled as he remembered the small ways he got back. Navy wives got very lonely. Wives that would not compete with the navy or refused to and ended up broken and drunks.

He reached for his new drink and spilled a bit on the front of his wrinkled uniform as he took a sip. He had to be careful how much he drank, one more for the road, and then head back to his BOQ.

He couldn't stop thinking about the money! His drunkenness changed nothing. He began to obsess about the greenbacks until he thought he would go crazy. He rationalized that his yearning for the money was not exactly stealing. It was just common sense. He was saving good old American currency from getting destroyed by a president gone mad.

His brand of common sense, in truth, was not typical; at least that's what his fitness reports stated. But he realized that when word leaked out that the money was going to be collected, and the new currency exchanged, millions of dollars would disappear. Anybody who was somebody was going to start grabbing a fistful of dollars and stuffing money down their trousers.

That's how the navy was. Hell, if you shouted, "Atten-hut" anywhere in Norfolk, Virginia, half the homes would collapse because of all the stolen U.S. Naval supplies appropriated by sailors. Couldn't anyone figure out why ninety percent of the houses were battleship gray? Any sailor who didn't steal was not legitimately a sailor of the U.S. Navy.

Gold-braided mucky-mucks would be licking their chops trying to figure how to save good American greenbacks from Roosevelt's stupidity.

His hands trembled when he thought of the opportunity that lay ahead. He needed money. His gambling debts at Gentleman Jacks' were now more than his yearly salary. He ran his hand over his face in need of a shave. All he needed was one short winning streak.

His face became taut and hard. He oversaw all the money, and they were not going to shoot anybody. He was the proverbial wolf in the chicken house. One thing he knew for sure; he was not stupid. With twenty years of practice breaking the rules and surviving, he was the master. He finished his drink and stumbled his way back to his BOQ, despondent over no promotion orders and for the terrible plan he was forming in his stupor.

Chapter 3

Oct 28, 1942 Chinatown

Mac was thankful for his apartment above the Bombay Alley and more grateful for Seadog. He filled the bathtub with lukewarm water and arranged the towels and soap where he could find them. He walked into the bedroom and called for Seadog. Out of the corner of his eye, he saw his buddy run under the bed. Mac got down on all fours and pulled Seadog out. Carrying him into the bathroom, he tried to put him into the tub. Like most dogs, he splayed his legs to avoid his bath. Seadog growled. Mac swore. Soapsuds flew. At the end of the bath, Mac had more suds on him than his dog. As he dried Seadog, he heard the door chimes in his office.

Mac peeked around the corner. A sailor stood waiting for him. He looked like any other sailor in the fleet, young and stupid. After eighteen years in the Corps, he knew immediately what the problem was before being told.

Seadog saw Mac leave and slouched away, looking for a hiding spot.

"The boys down at the hospital told me you were an okay guy," he said.

Mac put on his shirt and jacket and looked at him. "They could be lying." Mac found his tie and tightened it around his neck and sat down.

"They said you could help me…" He looked hopeful.

Mac looked at the ring on the boy's finger. "Look, kid, I'm not a marriage counselor. Just let her go!" said Mac.

"You don't know her, gunny. She's a swell girl!"

"Then, why do you need me?" Mac looked at him with a blank face and waited.

"She doesn't know I'm in port. I can't leave the ship at night. Someone on my ship saw her with another man. I thought--."

"It's your money, son. Ten dollars, one night, and a picture, if possible. I need Mr. Hamilton upfront."

The sailor got up slowly, reached in his pocket, and pulled out a ten. He gave Mac his wife's name, address, and a photo. Mac handed him his card with his phone number.

"Call me tomorrow night. Stay on your ship until then."

He thanked Mac and left. Somehow Mac felt sorry for him and the whole damn world.

* * *

The next evening, Mac parked across the street from her apartment and waited. The sailor called and said she got off work at seven p.m. and didn't know what time she left the apartment to go out. Mac had arrived at six and checked her mailbox. He got back in his car and slumped in his front seat and turned on the radio. Tommy Dorsey's band was playing, "I'm getting Sentimental Over You." He couldn't stop thinking about the boys at the Pearl Harbor Naval hospital in Ward D. He looked at his watch and saw it was almost 2130 hours.

The full moon shone through his front windshield. Mac blew smoke rings around it. "Could've used a few of these bright moonlit nights on the canal." He frowned at the thought.

Most men his age would have been thinking about holding some girl's hand in the moonlight. Maybe someday he'd think that way.

A door slammed. It was the lovely war bride, on her way to meet her boyfriend at her favorite haunt, the Black Orchid, two blocks from her apartment. Mac got out of the car and followed her. A few minutes later, she went into the bar. He followed her in. The place was packed. Several B-girls gave him the once-over and he could see why. Most of the men present were old enough to be their fathers.

The sailor's wife had taken a seat at the bar. He sat two seats from her and ordered a whiskey. A brunette came over and asked him to buy her a drink, Mac couldn't miss the wedding band on her finger. He bought her a drink. She sat next to him.

"Thanks, handsome," she cooed.

"Scram, sister."

She shot him a puzzled expression.

"I bought you a drink. Beat it!"

She gave him a killer look, took her drink, and walked away. Mac shook his head and sipped his whiskey. As he sat the glass on the bar, someone poked him in the shoulder. It was the sailor's bride.

"Do you have a light?" she asked. Mac flipped out his Zippo. She took his hand in both of hers and lit her cigarette. Her touch was like mink.

"Thanks. You know you didn't have to be so mean to her. She's probably lonely."

Mac looked at her closely, pretty hair, shiny and curled in all the right places, full lips, dark red and luscious. She wore a black skirt with a checkered black and white coat.

Very nice. He spoke. "Half the world is lonely right now, sister. What makes her so special?"

She looked at Mac and smiled.

"Tough guy, aren't we?" She ran her hand over Mac's black flat-top. "I like tough guys." She turned and walked back to her seat.

Way too much woman for that deck ape, most likely, the marriage was a fraud. She probably was using the poor kid for his insurance money, in case he got knocked off. Mac pulled out a cigar and ordered another whiskey.

He watched as she teased the men around her. Then, they all seemed to freeze. Their eyes followed a man as he entered the room, he had a slight but noticeable limp. A scar ran down his left cheek. He looked quite suave with an Errol Flynn mustache, and he was on top of the hit parade, dressed in black trousers with a white sport coat, finished off with a pink bowtie. He strode up to her and kissed her on the lips. They both laughed. She put her arm around him. Mac saw the bulge in his back, where her fingers traced the barrel of a pistol. Mac moved down several seats and asked the bartender if he knew of the gentleman.

He smiled. "Yeah, that's the boss." As he turned to leave, Mac grabbed him by the arm. "What's your boss's name?"

The bartender glared at Mac's hand on his arm and pulled away. He put both elbows on the bar and leaned forward toward Mac. "You been living in a cave, mister? That's the owner of this establishment!"

Mac's hand pushed against the man's forehead. "You're crowding me. What's his name, wise guy?" asked Mac

"What's your problem, buddy? His friends call him Gentleman Jack."

"What do his enemies call him?" Mac asked.

He laughed. "He hasn't got any enemies." Five minutes later, he came back and gave Mac a drink.

"What's with the drink?"

"Compliments of Gentleman Jack!"

To the right, at the end of the bar, the man in question waved at Mac. The young bride whispered sweet nothings in his ear. Mac waved back, unable to believe his luck. He was tracking down a cheating broad enamored with the biggest gangster in the city. On top of that, he had to take a picture of them doing whatever the hell they were going to do. Mac gagged on his drink as a shiver went down his spine. He realized his luck started going bad when Guadalcanal became part of his Marine Corps resume.

Around eleven in the evening they got up to leave and so did Mac. They walked arm in arm toward a Cadillac parked kitty-corner to Mac's jalopy, but one block up from Hotel Street. He crossed the street and waited for them to leave, except, they didn't. He walked down to his car and got his camera. He checked the flashbulb, put the strap around his neck, and walked in the building's shadows. As he got closer, he couldn't see anyone in the car. The sidewalk was barricaded from foot traffic because of scaffolding. It was so dark; he could only see the outline of the vehicle.

He looked for an avenue of escape, just in case he had to run for his life, broken body and all. There was an alley off to his left. After waiting a minute, he slowly walked toward the car. After having several whiskeys, his judgment was suspect. Crouching along the rear fender, he noticed that the car was moving up and down. Mac peeked in the back window and saw nothing but darkness. Mac knocked on the window, and then his flash from the camera seemed to light up the entire block. In that instant of flash, he swore he saw Gentleman Jack with his pants around his knees, and he was a smiling Jack. But at present, all he saw were blinding white orbs of light. He laughed. Poor Jack was seeing them too. He sprinted through the alley, running several blocks around and across to his car. He looked down the street and Gentleman Jack's car was gone.

Chapter 4

Guadalcanal, September 22, 1942

Lieutenant Alan Burke maneuvered his way through the mud in the most agitating way trying to find the S-3 Operations tent. At fifteen hundred hours, he was supposed to meet with a Gunny Wojohowitz leading the patrol. He grabbed the arm of a passing Marine. "Where in the hell is the Operations tent?"

The Marine frowned as he looked down at the navy officer holding onto his arm. He yanked his arm away.

"Lieutenant, head down the ridge about a hundred yards or so, until you come to the Battalion Aid station, make a left and head toward Hill 123. When you get there, follow the trail down into a copse of trees."

Burke looked at the Marine and said, "You better not be lying to me. The last Marine sent me to the crappers."

The Marine smiled. "Lieutenant, that was just some Marine having some fun."

After fifteen minutes of wandering and wondering where he was, he finally saw the S-3 Operations sign outside a

GP tent, thankful he wasn't late. He introduced himself to the sergeant at the desk and was told to make himself comfortable until the patrol leader showed up. He noticed a field radio, M-1 carbine, large reels of comm wire on a large backpack, and assorted other gear stacked neatly near the sergeants desk. Last night the quartermaster had him sign for a bunch of items and told him the patrol leader insisted the gear be delivered to the operations tent, so he could personally inspect the gear.

He sat on one of the cots and smoked a cigarette, thinking about his bad luck. He wondered how Laura was doing-probably married to someone richer than him. He pictured her in a Saks Fifth Avenue party dress, with a bottle of 1938 Moët & Chandon Champagne Dry Imperial on the table ready to be sipped and enjoyed while waiting for a prime filet cooked to perfection. She was the winner; he was the loser. As Napoléon said, "Champagne! In victory, one deserves it; in defeat, one needs it." Later she would be dancing and drinking more out on the balcony at his country club. Well, she was beautiful, but also a gold digger. Let the son of a bitch have her!

He threw his cigarette on the muddy floor of the tent. At that moment, a rather large gunnery sergeant entered the tent. He stood up, knowing this was the patrol leader. He watched the gunny slowly look around the tent until his eyes fixated on him. Burke interpreted a modicum of disdain in the man's hard, cold, gray eyes. He had several days of black heavy stubble covering his face. His dungaree shirt was cut off above the elbows, one arm displaying a tattoo of the Eagle, Globe, and Anchor. He filled Burke with a sense of awe and raw fear. The Marine was a cross between a Neanderthal and a man who had fallen on hard times. The only thing clean, shiny, and well-oiled was the shotgun that appeared to be a normal appendage to him as an arm or a leg. Held in place by a leather sheath across the gunny's chest was a Ka-bar, it's handle was a rusty, reddish color. Burke gulped when he realized it must be bloodstained.

He extended his hand out to the gunny. "I'm Lieutenant Burke; you must be the patrol leader."

Ignoring Burke and spreading his map on the table next to the cot, he motioned for Burke to come closer to the map. "We will be heading northeast on a compass heading of 189 degrees for three hundred and fifty yards from our front lines." He ran his filthy finger along a creek line to a ridge approximately thirty yards from a cave entrance indicated on the map and stopped. "We will be in Jap territory." His eyes bored into Burke's.

"You and your field radio will be in an overwatch position on this ridgeline, where you will have a good position to see and understand what takes place. Your equipment, EE-8 field radio, and double reels of W-30 light assault wire on dual spools are on your backpack. Enough wire to get you to our location. Your ammo, M-1, and canteens have personally been checked by me. Your batteries are fresh and ready to go. The battalion radioman has instructed you how to use the radio and lay the wire. If you have any questions, now is the time to spout them out."

Burke spoke up. "Who is going to carry the wire, gunny?"

"We are not on an African safari, lieutenant. You carry your own gear. Your equipment never leaves you! Understand?"

Burke was about to ask the gunny how he was going to carry the field radio, wire, M-1 carbine, canteen, and ammo, but he decided he better not. "Ok, gunny."

Gunny Wojo continued, "You will radio messages to battalion headquarters and keep them up-to-date what is going on and if we run into trouble. If we do run into problems, make sure support gets to us in time. On the way, if you make too much noise or fall behind, I'll leave your ass to the Japs. School is out!" Without any fanfare, he simply said. "We will attach your wire to the switchboard which is on our way out. Follow me," and walked out of the tent.

Flummoxed, Lt. Burke picked up his radio, assorted other gear, and his carbine, then ran after the gunnery sergeant. Loaded down with more gear than a mule could carry, he tried to keep up with the Marine who appeared to blend in with the jungle, becoming part of the dappled shadows.

After one hundred yards, he paused. Within seconds he lost sight of the gunny. Burke stood transfixed in his spot, trying to see any movement ahead on the trail. A hand reached out and grabbed him. His heart nearly stopped. The hand fastened on the scruff of his neck and pulled him within inches of gleaming white teeth. "Lieutenant… let's go. Keep me in sight at all times."

Burke took a deep breath, and with renewed determination, followed the shadow in front of him, trying not to crash through the brush like an orangutan in heat. Burke kept thinking how scared the Japs would be seeing this crazy bearded fucker in combat. Just looking at the gunny scared the shit out of him.

Lieutenant Burke, had poor grades at Intelligence school, along with a recalcitrant attitude, so the navy decided to retrain him as a Forward Artillery Observer, where his life expectancy was shorter than Mickey Rooney. He was briefed on this mission two mornings ago by a Marine officer possessing an incredible red handlebar mustache. Later that morning a Marine with the radio section had given him training on the EE-8 field radio and its use. He hoped that he remembered how to use all the dials and how to put it on vibration. If he didn't, this gunny was going to kill him!

After forty minutes of travel, Gunny Wojohowitz dropped him off at his position with a direct view toward the cave. Burke, wincing with pain, peeled the backpack with near-empty wire spools off his back and the EE-8 by squeezing his shoulder until one of the straps slipped off his shoulder. He swung the radio off his right shoulder and placed it on the ground. He then unslung his rifle and leaned it next to a tree. After uncoiling the last of the wire off his spools, he cut the wires and stripped off one inch of insulation and attached them to the posts.

He swore as a six-inch thorn ripped across his arm. His brain refused to accept that he was in the stinking jungle, fighting his way through thick jungle foliage like a dirty, scared monkey. He winced at the bite of a mosquito and slapped it, leaving the bloody insect still sticking in his neck. *"What's a little malaria,"* he thought? Soon he would be like the crude Marine grunts who sliced the seams out of their dungarees, so they could hastily squat and discharge their bloody mess upon the ground. Toilet paper was the nearest creek or some putrefied water from their canteens.

Months earlier, he had taken his alcohol-infused body into the recruiting station and summarily flunked his physical. But his dad, God bless him, had talked to his senator friends, and soon he was on his way to Intelligence school. He did so poorly and had shown so little motivation that the navy sent him to Forward Observer school and shipped him off to the United States Marine Corps. The rest was bad history. There would be no lunches at the Officer's Club and no scotch and sodas. Only crawling around the jungle like a common enlisted Marine.

His commanding officer was a naval mustang officer who chewed tobacco and drank coffee like a stevedore. Burke could not help himself. His dislike for this ruffian boss became quite apparent. Without much effort, Burke soon detested his boss's hatred of Harvard blue bloods. He rode Burke hard and put him away wet... every day.

This assignment only cemented Burke's dislike of him. Turning on his radio, he went through his checklist. He rubbed his shoulders where the strap had chafed the first layer of skin off his shoulder. How Marines could carry their heavy packs, day in and day out, in all this heat was beyond him.

The low humming of the field radio handset made him feel a trifle safer, especially when he completed his communication checks. He waited for the radio to vibrate, and when it did, he smiled. "Communications check complete," he whispered. He leaned back against a tree and waited, cursing softly as the sweat ran down and burned his eyes. He leaned his M-1 carbine across his legs and tried to keep awake. He remembered what the gunnery sergeant said, "Son, we run into trouble, get on that damn radio and send us some help;

chop, chop!" Then, Gunny Wojo had turned without fanfare and walked down the ridgeline with his men and disappeared.

The sun burst through the jungle foliage, with rain falling intermittently. The bright rays created a palette of various shade of greens, reminding Burke of the paintings by Wilfredo Lam. A while back, one of his girlfriends talked him into going to an art museum in New York City, a big mistake. He had asked her if they had a bar. She didn't understand his question. How a Harvard grad did not understand or appreciate art left her speechless. Two dates later, she was history. He remembered her calling him uncultured and lacking civility. "Well, you ought to see me now, babe," he thought. The field radio vibrated, he picked up the handset knowing they were asking him for sitrep. He complied and realized he had been daydreaming.

The gunny positioned him about forty yards from the cave entrance, with a good view of all the trails leading to the cave. Without much effort, he could see the Marines approach the cave. Two riflemen moved to the left and right of the gaping entrance to the cave.

Gunny Wojo looked up at Burke, waved his arm and pointed to his eyes, indicating for the lieutenant to watch. The gunny, armed with a pistol, moved into the cave, along with his translator. He thought the gunny must carry his balls around in a wheelbarrow because going in that dark cave seemed like suicide. Burke felt his heart start to hammer with fear.

He looked at his watch; five minutes had passed with no sounds, no noise, no nothing. Burke gripped his M1 carbine tighter. He was afraid to blink because it might cause him to miss something small.

Suddenly four shots rang out! Burke practically jumped out of his skivvies. Two more shots rang out. The sounds echoed and reverberated deep inside the cave. He saw the Marines on each side of the cave aim their rifles toward the cave entrance. Burke glanced at his watch, the secondhand ticking around the face of his watch. Sweat dripped from his forehead down his cheeks and onto his collar. Where in the hell was gunny?

He stared at the entrance and saw movement. He saw someone half in the shade of the cave and half in the sunlight. The translator moved into the full sunlight, followed by the gunny. Burke leaned his head against his carbine and let out a huge sigh. The gunny stared up at him and waved. Burke waved back, a smile across his face. He watched while the gunny opened a bag.

He grabbed his binoculars and watched. Out of the bag tumbled diamonds, rubies, sapphires, and emeralds. The sun made the jewels effervesce in an explosion of sparkles. He watched the gunny put the jewels back in the pouch. He swung his binoculars to the left and noticed some movement. He saw yellow uniforms coming down the trail. He stood up and tried to get the attention of the Marines. Their backs were to him. He screamed. "Japs to your right, gunny!" Wojo grabbed his shotgun and looked at Burke who was pointing to Wojo's right.

The Japs opened fire as the gunny fired two rounds toward them. Burke could see two Japs fall even as two more approached. He searched to his right and saw more movement. Two U.S. soldiers were watching from concealment on the gunny's left flank. Burke watched in astonishment as they opened fire on the gunny and his Marines. Burke stood up and fired his carbine at the soldiers, emptying his magazine. He slapped another one in the magazine well. The soldiers fired at him, the shots snapping around him, sounding like freight trains. One round hit him in the leg, buckling him to his knees.

He remembered what the gunny had said. "Get help!" He flipped the knob to speak and back again to listen and repeated his message, getting no response.

He fired at the soldiers again, trying to keep them occupied while the Marines fought off the Japs. He watched as a soldier came around to the gunny's side and fired directly into his back. Burke screamed out, "What the hell are you doing!"

Still, kneeling, he fired his entire magazine hitting one of the soldiers several times, staggering him backward. The remaining soldier peeked around a tree and fired, hitting Burke's helmet and knocking it off his head. He was slammed to the ground, a fine red mist exploded behind his eyes. He bounced off his radio as he tumbled to the ground. He remembered his training, if you can't talk, turn on the speak knob and off again three times in a row - three shorts and a long - and the battalion will know you need help. Blood dripping into his eyes made it hard to see.

His hand searched for the handset until he found the cord. He turned on the knob to speak. "one actual send help…casualties" He counted to three and spoke into the handset. "one actual send help, casualties" His strength was ebbing. He willed himself not to pass out, he spoke over and over again, asking for help. A stupid thought crossed his mind. He should be saying *SOA. . . save our ass.* He breathed a sigh of relief when he heard,

"Roger that… we will follow the wire to your site with corpsman and help, out" Help was on the way. He felt himself smiling as a calm he had never experienced before overcame him. It was all right, for the first time in his life, he had done his duty.

* * *

The remaining U.S. soldier grabbed Gunny Wojo's shotgun as a plan formed in his mind. Somehow the Marines had beaten them back to the cave. Now they had the jewels, and he was going to get them hell or high water.

He realized for the first-time blood was spurting from his leg. That bastard on the hill had shot him. He fastened a tourniquet around his leg and used the shotgun as a crutch. He walked toward his companion, lying still and quite dead. He ripped off his dog tags, replacing them with his own. He then aimed the shotgun, closed his eyes, and blew his head off and walked toward the big bearded Marine that he had shot.

Wojo's hand searched around his waist till he found his .45. He gripped the familiar weapon in his hand and placed it on his chest. The warm, welling of blood against his hand made things slippery. A face appeared above him, hidden in darkness. He tried to raise his .45 and shoot the obscured face, but his arm wouldn't move. A hand checked his wounds. The person grunted and began searching his body. The ghost of a man rolled him onto his side.

"Where in the hell are the jewels?" he grunted.

Wojo knew he was hit bad, and as he was falling into a dark abyss, he grabbed onto an arm and ripped off a wristwatch. Thanks to God's tender mercies, all went black.

Chapter 5

Bombay Alley

The Hawaiian morning sun was streaming through Mac's office window, dust particles dancing in the air, and warming the back of his neck. He touched the sensitive area where the bullet had exited, now just a lump of scar tissue.

It was a beautiful Sunday morning and the streets below him were quiet and peaceful. Momma Leone owned the Bombay Alley. When Mac had approached her about available rentals in the area, her eyes had sparkled with amor.

"Why not rent with me and make an old woman happy? I will give you a special rate. A big man like you will make it his business to take care of Momma Leone!" She placed both her hands on his cheeks and smiled like a grandmother. She then kissed him on both cheeks and a deal was struck. Not only did he get his office, he got the whole top floor. He watched out for momma, and she became one of his favorites.

He looked around the room and tried to figure out the color of his walls. Some sort of tropical yellow, a cross between

41

a robust, rising sun and a fiery sunset. Or one might simply say, the color of a Jap tank on fire. The floors were dark mahogany and unevenly worn. The desk and chairs were navy surplus, battleship gray, most likely stolen by a sailor who needed money before payday. Clamshell sconces lined the walls every four feet; at night casting a pinkish glow. The worn sofa covered in a Hawaiian flower design graced the wall to the left of the desk. The door directly in front of his desk led to a reception area, and to the right of that door, led to four other rooms and two bathrooms.

Momma Leone served him a breakfast on Sunday mornings that made his eyeballs pop out with joy. Scrambled eggs and cheese with two slabs of fried Spam, two fresh biscuits slathered with fresh butter, and a large slice of pineapple. She would always laugh when she asked, "How many eggs would you like, Mac?"

And he would say, "Six, Momma Leone."

He took turns drinking his cup of sweet Hawaiian coffee, scratching Seadog's head, and at the same time, trying to read a month-old Cleveland Press that Father Gibbons had saved for him. Good ole Bobby Feller had pitched for the navy in an interservice game that drew sixty-two thousand fans at Cleveland Municipal Stadium. The ace threw against his former teammates. The Cleveland Indians won, and the game raised much-needed money for the war effort. The Cleveland Indians had finished in fourth place this past season. Poor Lou Boudreau did the best he could with the likes of Chubby Dean, Buster Mills, and company. He remembered with pride when Bobby Feller had joined up in December 1941, as did so many ballplayers. The Japs were going to pay double if anything happened to Feller. What he would pay to be sitting in Cleveland Municipal Stadium, the sun shining on him, munching on a hotdog with that beautiful stadium mustard slathered over it. But that was not about to happen.

He stopped scratching Seadog's head, and his big black paw came out of nowhere and almost slapped the cup of coffee out of his hand. His pup was growing quickly and now weighed thirty-two pounds. He wiped the coffee off the top of Seadog's head and reminisced.

While in Ward D, still bedridden, he had woken up one night with something warm on the unwounded side of his neck. A small pink tongue stretched out to lick him on the side of the nose. Sitting in a chair at the side of his hospital bed was Nurse Van Deer smiling. "I brought you a friend."

Whenever Lieutenant Van Deer would lift Seadog off the bed to take him home for a while, he would whimper, struggling to get back to Mac.

So many people helped him, Van Deer, Seadog, and Gunny Jones. Late at night, he would beg for water, and Jonesy would hobble out of bed and place ice chips on his lips and wipe the sweat off his face. Jonesy would talk to him and tell him that everything would be all right. Now he was so attached to Seadog, Jonesy, and Van Deer it scared the willies out of him.

He had become so afraid of losing the people that he cared about; he was broken into tiny bits. Like Humpty Dumpty. When they put him back together again, some pieces were missing.

Maybe he was fooling himself, trying to be a private detective- studying a three-dollar book, passing a test, and paying for a license. Lieutenant Van Deer said that the world needed good men to be good detectives. He had to do something when they medically discharged him.

All the money he had this month went into renting Momma Leone's top floor. Soon he and Seadog would be eating out of the same bowl. He could picture Seadog holding onto a steel cup with a sign around his neck, "Please donate because my best buddy needs money."

Then he made a huge mistake and ran into a stupid sailor and for ten bucks ran into a man who wore a two-hundred-dollar suit. He had no clue what Gentleman Jack was going to do, but he never had much of an imagination.

The chimes went off in his outer office, where one day, he thought he might have a receptionist. He yelled, "Come on in!"

A young Lance Corporal walked in with his cover in his right hand.

"Are you Gunny Mac?"

Mac stared at him, wondering why the hell this young Marine needed him.

"Yes."

"I need you to find someone for me."

Mac reached into his desk and pulled out a piece of paper.

"I need all the pertinent information."

He looked at Mac as if he was asking for absolution.

"I love her. I got her pregnant. She said she didn't love me, but she's going to have my baby. I don't know where she went."

"What do you want me to do, son?" asked Mac.

"The chaplain said that I need her personal information, and the baby's so that I can legally set up a fund for the baby. You know, send some money to a bank in her name."

He became pensive. "In case I get killed. I want to set up what the padre called a trust fund with my insurance money for the baby."

"How do you know that you got her pregnant?"

"She told me."

"Is that your only proof?"

He nodded, yes.

"How old are you, Marine?'

"Seventeen."

Mac felt a major headache coming on quickly, starting at the base of his neck, a crescendo of pulsating and rushing blood, desperately trying to exit through his eyes.

"Write down everything you know about her: height, weight, eye color, hair, beauty marks, if she has one, an address, where you met her, and your unit address. I want the name of your commanding officer."

Five minutes later, he handed the sheet to Mac.

"How much do I owe you, gunny?"

"How much you got, Marine."

"Three dollars…"

Mac felt like a father taking money from his son. "Get the hell out of here, Marine. I'll get in touch with you as soon as I find out what the hell is going on."

After he left, Mac read the information and set out to find this girl before she got her paws on the kid's money.

Three hours and nine bars later, he found her. She was drinking with a sailor and having a great time. He sat down next to the sailor and told him to beat it. The sailor looking at Mac's size decided his new date wasn't worth a stay in the hospital.

Mac ordered a drink and bought her one. "Rebecca Downs?"

"How did you know my name?"

"It's written on half the bathroom stalls in Chinatown."

She laughed. "I hope it also said for a good time!"

"I see you have a sense of humor," said Mac.

Her laugh disappeared, and a sneer replaced it. "You smell like a cop. What do you want from me?"

"You have a job?" asked Mac.

"Buy me another drink, copper. Maybe if you are nice to me, I'll let you take me home."

"You have a job?" he asked again.

"Yeh, it will cost you five bucks."

"You're on the expensive side."

He grabbed her purse and found her wallet. She reached to grab it back. Mac closed his hand over hers and squeezed.

"Stop, or I'll break your fingers."

"Who do you think you are, you big lug. I'll report you to Captain Chin, and he'll take twenty dollars out of your ass!"

Mac squeezed her hand harder. She let out a loud "ouch!"

"Just another ass-wipe to hate me. Shut up," said Mac.

He looked at her license and saw her name and address. She had one hundred and twenty dollars in her wallet. He took out a twenty and put it in his pocket. He handed back her wallet and purse.

"You want to know why I took the twenty?"

"You're a rotten copper like the rest of them," she snarled.

"I took it for my expenses. I spent one dollar on your drink and mine, three hours looking for you, and another wasted ten minutes talking to you. And as you said, twenty dollars in case Chin wants a piece of me."

"And I suppose you want a freebie too?"

'No, but I'm going to give you some free advice. Lay off the Marines and sailors. I'm going to submit your name to the military authorities as a scammer. I know where you live and your name. Don't let me hear of you scamming again! As far as I'm concerned, you can fuck for a living, but don't fuck over any servicemen. Do you understand what I'm talking about?"

She blew smoke in his face. "You coppers are all the same. Always bothering the working woman."

He left the bar and walked back to his office. He reached in his drawer and pulled out the phone number the Marine gave him. He called the commanding officer and left his phone number, asking for the captain's help. Seadog put his head on Mac's lap.

"We did a good thing today, Seadog. We helped one of our young Marines. Maybe this new job is going to be all right."

Chapter 6

Naval Base, Pearl Harbor

Lieutenant Burke left Admiral Johnson's office confused as hell. He shook his head, trying to clear the ringing in his ears. Since wounded in the head, a ringing came at the most inopportune times, like when the admiral gave him instructions. The arrogant bastard reminded him of Captain Bligh of the HMS Bounty. He could picture the admiral ordering him to the main deck and passing a sentence of fifty lashes of cat-o-nine tails across his backside.

Last night he had received word from the Pearl Harbor Office of Intelligence (S-2) to report to an unknown admiral's office located at Naval Base Operations Center no later than 0900 hours. Upon arriving, he was ushered into Admiral Johnson's office after signing some non-disclosure documents.

He knew that he was in trouble; as soon as he walked in and stood at attention. The admiral stared at him like he was the creature from the black lagoon. After several seconds, he spoke up.

"I reviewed your service record file, and I'm not impressed, Burke. It says here you barely graduated from Harvard, and you made it through Intelligence school with the lowest grades in your class. Because of this, you were attached to the Marine Corps as a Forward Observer. You made it through that school with high grades after what your instructor said was an intensive one-on-one remedial training. If I weren't in need of an Intelligence officer for this assignment, I'd ship your ass back. Don't think your Purple Heart and Silver Star will save you, if you fail in this assignment. I will snip off your panties and send you back to the Marines. Furthermore, you will report your findings at least every other day to me personally. You will only report to me! Is that clear?"

Burke tried hard not to show his disdain at the admiral's condescending looks and comments because the son of a bitch couldn't hold a candle to a Marine private. "Yes, sir, quite clear."

"Read the file, given to you on the way in. It contains five pages outlining what is going to happen with 'Operation Torch' and the assignment given to Lieutenant Commander Kincaid. Included are the directions and orders needed to follow him. When you are done reading, please ask me any questions you have, and I will try to answer them. Is that clear?"

Burke nodded and started reading. Ten minutes later, he put the file down and looked up at Admiral Johnson. The admiral slurped some of his coffee and noticed that Burke was through reading.

Burke spoke up. "It seems to me you think Kincaid is going to steal the money that he is collecting. Why use him if you can't trust him?"

The admiral walked over to his coffee pot and poured himself a cup. He did not offer Burke a cup.

"It is not your job lieutenant, to analyze me or my orders. I have limited resources, and that means even with personnel. Most of my good officers are out on the ocean doing what they get paid to do. Kincaid is a below-average officer. I don't know Kincaid. I don't have to know him. I don't want to know him. His fitness reports document his poor performance. I don't trust him to do the job correctly, and I need to have someone watch him, so that he doesn't make mistakes that make me look bad. If I had other choices, Burke you would not be the Intelligence agent I would pick to oversee this individual. Your record shows you are not up to this job. But I have no other choice."

"I'll do the best job I can, admiral." He quickly surmised Kincaid was going down the shitter, and most likely, he was going to follow Kincaid in the same flush. The admiral was going to get both of them with minimal effort. Two worthless officers punished for having the audacity to be a part of his navy.

Burke glanced down at the floor, knowing his face was turning red. The admiral did not mince words. He looked up and saw the smirk on the admiral's face. The thoughts running through his mind right now were fighting to erupt from his lips. Just a few short months ago, the admiral would have been right. He knew that his service record was below average. He also knew redemption was every man's right. He pushed his smart-ass comments back down his throat.

The admiral knew that he made his point and said, "Kincaid is in charge of the actual implementation of

'Operation Torch.' His job is to plan the collection of two hundred million dollars and the distribution of the new currency with Hawaii printed on the back of the money. Your job is not to stop him from stealing the money, but simply to document what he has done."

Lieutenant Burke tried to discern the expression on the admiral's face. It appeared that Kincaid might have trouble surviving a devious, cunning bastard like the one sitting before him. Certainly, Johnson had a hard-on for the guy; venom dripped from his voice while he explained in detail what he expected Burke to find and write in his final report.

"When you are done studying the file, please return it to my secretary. This is a need to know only operation, and you have signed away your rights and agreed to the obligations as listed. No one will know of your assignment and you will only discuss any information you have with me. Whatever assets you need, let me know. I have already told your BOQ manager to move you to a room next to Kincaid's. You will have total access to all locations approved for Kincaid. If he spots you, he will be told you are working with a Treasury official monitoring the situation. Do not let him even begin to smell you on his trail. Now, what questions do you have?"

"How long is this assignment?" asked Burke.

"Until I relieve you of this assignment. Any more questions? If not, you are dismissed."

Burke saluted in the most arrogant way possible and left. He paused outside the front of the door of the Naval Operations Center and lit a cigarette. He was selected to monitor the Officer in Charge of 'Operation Torch' because he happened to be available. Burke smiled, he had it all figured out. The admiral thought he could control him…threaten him…and use him. Like the admiral said while pointing a stubby finger at his chest, "You better stick to Kincaid like glue; when he takes a shit, you better be in the stall next to him!" What the admiral didn't understand was that you didn't do that to a Burke man! He'd have to do two things at the same time. Watch Kincaid and find out where in the hell Wojo was and get him transferred back to Pearl. The admiral could kill him, but he couldn't eat him. Burke smiled as he put his Camel out on the bottom of his shoe. Life was getting exciting, and he was right in the middle of it all.

Chapter 7

Chinatown

Gunny Mac walked toward the Bombay Alley maneuvering through the crowds of people, feeling like a salmon swimming upstream. He didn't feel like a detective. Two days ago, he saw the movie Charlie Chan in Rio. Charlie Chan is on the trail of a singer who kills the man she loves in Honolulu and then is killed. The movie made him feel less a detective and more of a nursemaid. Since the base chaplain found out that he was in the private investigations business, all he was doing was chasing down lovesick kids: no jewel robberies, no murders, no crimes, just boring matters of the heart. Right now, he was exhausted, spending useless hours trying to find a young missing girl who didn't want to be found. He wanted to do nothing but sleep, eat, drink, and spend some time with Seadog.

He leaned against the wall next to his office door, trying to find his key. He paused outside his office door because he heard a noise from inside. It was the sound of a file drawer being closed.

He pulled out his .45, tried to turn the knob, and found it locked. He slipped in his key and opened his door a crack. He slid silently into his office. Seadog stood wagging his tail next to the thief. Mac waited a few moments until Seadog spotted his daddy and slid over to Mac with his tongue hanging out one side of his mouth. Mac kept his gun pointed and steadied on the female guest bent over his filing cabinet. After Seadog announced his presence in the room, she swung around, showing Mac a silver-plated derringer.

"My gun is bigger than yours," Mac wisecracked. He leaned against the door frame and smiled, "I liked the other view better."

Her red hair framed a redder face as she tried to hide her rage and embarrassment. Mac's eyes moved from her face down to her black blazer, then further down to her black and white checkered skirt that covered her splendid skeletal system. Her lips turned into a pout as she slid her gun into her purse.

Mac stared at her, and she stared at Mac. His .45 also stared back at her. Seadog broke the ice as he trotted to the unknown lady and sat at her feet. His nose and eyes went up her skirt.

"He's your dog, that's for certain!" she said as she pushed Seadog away. "But the dog is better looking and much more charming." She watched Mac gauging his reaction.

Mac worked a smile at the corner of his mouth as he sniffed the air. Her perfume invaded the room like a fireteam of Marines. All his senses were working overtime.

She walked toward him, her black-and-white high heels making soft clicking sounds as her hips rolled to and fro like a battleship. Mac continued to point his gun at her. The barrel was soon touching her bosom. She stuck her finger inside the barrel and pushed his pistol down and off to his side. Her tongue slid over her red lips that were full and inviting. Her arms soon circled his neck. Her lips brushed his cheek; her breath was warm on his cheek.

"Bulldogs are my favorite," she whispered. She kissed Mac below his ear working her way down his neck. "Thick neck, pug nose, big broad shoulders, hard body. . . You make me want to pet you."

"I'd rather you feed me some table scraps," Mac said.

She scrunched up her face, walked to Mac's chair, and sat down, exposing the top of her stockings and garter belt. She pulled out a gold cigarette case from her purse and waited for Mac to give her a light. He moved closer to her and lit her cigarette. He sat in a chair next to his desk and pulled out a cigar and lit it.

"You have anything to drink in this rat hole?"

Her insolent comment and facial expression hurt Mac's feelings.

"Now, now, if you insult me, you'll have to drink out of Seadog's water bowl. If you're nice, I'll get you a glass of bourbon."

"Make sure it's clean; I don't want to catch a disease," she said.

Mac pulled the bottle of bourbon and two glasses out of his filing cabinet. He poured two fingers in each and handed her one.

"You got a lot of explaining to do," Mac said.

Before he could say another word out, she threw an ashtray at him. Seadog ran for the hills.

"Why you slimy pervert. You're the one who has a lot of explaining to do. Why don't you gumshoe's work at a decent job like the rest of us instead of trying to ruin people's lives!"

Mac put his drink on the desk. He took a puff of his cigar and sent a cloud of smoke that enveloped her. She raised her hand to hit Mac, but stopped when he said, "You crack me, I'll break your pretty arm, and I'm hardly fooling!"

She slowly put her hand down.

"Now sister, tell me why you're giving my office the once-over while you're sipping my cheap bourbon. And don't lie to me."

"You know why."

"I gave up mind reading a few years back. Start talking."

"You don't remember me?"

"Maybe I do, and maybe I don't. Some parts of you do look kind of familiar."

"I was looking for some pictures you took. And if you don't give them to me, you are one dead palooka!"

Mac was used to wise guys threatening him, but now it was starting to irritate him that lately, everyone was doing it. Soon it would be little boys popping off at him. Then little girls. Where would it end?

"You and your little popgun don't scare me. And if you don't quit threatening me, I'm going to do something I've never done before, and I'm going to enjoy it," said Mac.

She smiled. "I'm not the one threatening you, pervert; it's a guy by the name of Gentleman Jack."

At the very mention of Gentleman Jack, Mac frowned, grabbed his drink, moving to the window. Gulping down his drink he poured another.

"While you're at it, dummy, pour some more of your cheap bourbon in my dirty glass. You know I could make it easier for you. Give me the pictures and fifty dollars, and I'll beg Jack to let you live. He is enamored with me."

Mac swirled the bourbon in his glass, took a sip, and thought of his next move. He thought about all the sailors and Marines scared, lonely, and dying with wives cheating on them.

He pulled a chair closer to her, ran his fingers slowly down her cheek, then slapped her hard across the face. He grabbed her jaw in his hand and squeezed.

"Look, lady, your husband, paid me his hard-earned money to find out if you were a cheating whore. I took some pictures of a cheating whore. Yeah, I remember you. Mostly I remember your legs straight up in the air, and Gentleman Jack was Smiling Jack! Just remember that Jack has bunches of whores waiting on him hand and foot. You give him more trouble with bad photos and publicity, and you might find yourself fish food."

Mac got up, went to his filing cabinet, grabbed the photos, and threw them at her.

"Your husband has the other copies. Tell Gentleman Jack that he knows where I am, and I know where he is, and I know where you are. Now get the hell out of here before Gentleman Mac becomes Gunny Mac and throws your ass out in the hallway!"

She gathered the photos and paused at the door. "It's a shame he's going to kill you. I just hope I get to watch!"

Chapter 8

Naval Base Pearl Harbor

Admiral Johnson was at his desk at Pearl Harbor, drumming his fingers on his desk while waiting for the man who had been screwing his wife up, down, and sideways. Yessiree, navy justice the old-fashioned way. The admiral smiled as he took a small sip of the coffee brought in by the mess steward. In his capable hands, navy justice made him a God over the careers and lives of his officers.

He spoke into his speaker. "Please have the lieutenant commander report to me."

The secretary looked up at Kincaid and said in a nasty voice, "Commander, the admiral will see you now."

He stood at attention while he watched the admiral sign some operations orders. The admiral handed the orders to his Chief of Staff and pretended to just notice Kincaid. He looked up and forced a smile.

"Have a seat Kincaid and grab yourself a cup of coffee." He reminded himself to throw that cup in the trash. "How is our plan coming?"

"Sir, with minimal problems, except for the time element. We have enough people, but not enough time. Unfortunately, we will need another two or three planning days and another week or so to collect, burn, and hand out the equivalent dollars back to the people."

The admiral leaned back in his chair, folding his hands on his ample stomach. A navy ensign had more leadership skills than this fool, he thought. He smiled an asshole-tight smile and said, "That's why I chose you, commander, and why I'm giving you full control over the security measures to ensure the mission gets completed and nothing is misplaced as one would say...." The admiral gave Kincaid a look of a hound dog treeing a fox. "This could be a feather in your cap and help you finally make full commander."

When he said that, he could see Kincaid's hands tense into fists and then relax. He enjoyed emphasizing the word *finally*.

"Full security measures, admiral?"

The admiral knew he had him now; he could see Kincaid's face turn bright red with excitement. The loser was already counting the money that he was going to steal.

"I thank you for having faith in me. I shall not let you down, Sir."

The admiral leaned forward and said, "Kincaid, is that a stain on your jacket?"

Kincaid looked down at the front of his uniform. "It looks like a stain, yes, Sir."

The admiral shook his head in disgust.

"Before I dismiss you, commander, make sure you keep me informed every other day how our plan is coming together.

Roosevelt is on my ass over this issue. My endorsement on any promotion will hinge on your success." An unfriendly smile crossed his face.

"Dismissed, commander."

Kincaid mouthed an "Aye-aye Sir," about-faced and practically ran out of the office.

Admiral Johnson mentally put a checkmark next to the second part of his plan and began planning the third part that ensured that the miscreant of a lieutenant commander would soon be descending to Davy Jones' locker.

* * *

When Commander Kincaid had first walked into the Admiral's office, pangs of jealousy crawled his up his throat and choked him. The bastard dry humped him at every opportunity. It had taken all of his military posture learned in his decades-long service not to show his disdain. The worst part was the stars on the collar-a gift from his elite friends. Standing at attention, he had faced the window, and the sun's rays reflected off the stars and made him wish he had worn sunglasses. The admiral probably shined them every morning. He knew the admiral was playing him; he didn't know to what extent. He would have to be careful. He would have to be very, very careful.

One thing was certain; the admiral could have his stars; he would have the money.

Chapter 9

Bombay Alley

Mac was in the bathroom when he heard his office door open. The moment he took a leak, somebody walked into his office. He could be sitting in his chair for hours, waiting for Mr. Hap to grow in stature and voice his disapproval. Mr. Hap was the nickname gunny gave his esteemed hemorrhoid that had been with him since the end of his days on Guadalcanal and who showed his affection periodically. Mac stepped into his office and stopped at the sight before him.

"Are you Gunny Mac?" the woman asked. "I hope I didn't need an appointment?"

His gunnery sergeant's intuition raised the hairs on the back of his neck. In fact, they weren't just rising, but standing at attention. Her hair was the color platinum and fell seductively over her ears, coyly covering the right side of her face from prying eyes and ending a few inches past her shoulders. The style that made men think of Rita Hayworth and started their hearts pumping, creating sinister thoughts.

She took off her white gloves and put them in her purse. The rest of her screamed money; so much money that he smelled the greenbacks over her perfume. Mac squinted at the woman's face and could see a slightly masculine jaw underneath the heavy makeup. Her shoulders also seemed a bit too large for a woman her size, but they could be the padded shoulders so prevalent in women's fashions. A Marine with too many drinks would probably not have noticed, especially in the dark lighting of a bar.

"Do you mind if I sit down?" she asked.

Mac went over to a chair in the front of his desk and pulled it out so that she could sit.

"I need the services of a good private detective. I've heard from various people that you're my best bet. That you're tough and fair to everyone."

Mac frowned. "I don't know about that, since I have no clients, and I doubt that many people have nice things to say about me. To be truthful, I'm new at this game. You might be wasting your money. I wouldn't hire me to be quite frank with you."

Her smile was radiant. "I think you will do fine."

With long tapered fingers and clear lacquered nails, she pulled out a black enameled cigarette case and set her dainty black velvet purse on Mac's desk. She opened the brass clasp on the case, withdrew a Parliament cigarette, held it toward Mac, and waited for him to give her a light.

He reached into his pocket and pulled out his Zippo lighter. She touched his hands with tips of her fingers as he lit her cigarette.

"What's your name, sister?"

She sat back in her chair and took a quick drag on her cigarette.

"Thank you so much," she murmured. "It's nice to be around a gentleman. . . and a handsome one at that!"

She took another puff on her cigarette and looked Mac in the eyes.

"Caroline Mathews."

The smoke escaping her lips with each syllable made her appear even more exotic to him.

"What do you do for a living, and where do you live, Miss Matthews?"

"I insist you call me Caroline."

Mac nodded.

"I own a dress boutique shop on Canal Street and live above my store."

Mac drew hard on his cigar and turned his head away from her to exhale.

"If you aren't concerned about my experience, how can I help you, Caroline?"

"I'm sure what I need you to do is within your level of expertise."

"What is it exactly you want me to do?" Mac asked again. He shifted in his chair and tried to take in the whole scene. Somebody this good-looking ought to be in the movies.

"My boyfriend is in trouble, bad trouble. He owes Gentleman Jack several thousands of dollars. Gambling debts. Yesterday, I received a phone call from him, begging me for money. He said Jack kidnapped him and was going to make him work off the money he owed him by forcing him to service male clients in Chinatown at five dollars a crack."

Mac grimaced at the prospect.

She picked up her purse, opened it, and pulled out a small feminine hand-tooled wallet. She handed him a card.

"This is the address where he is being held against his will. He has somebody guarding him outside his door. Please get him out of there and bring him to me."

"Why don't you go to the police?" Mac asked.

"Mr. Mac, this town is run by Gentleman Jack. Secondly, Captain Chin is a partner in crime with Gentleman Jack along with a man by the name of Joe DeVito. They protect each other while they rob all of us blind. If you take this job, you will be pissing on Gentleman Jack's leg and Captain Chin's."

Mac knew she was telling the truth, but he would piss on King Kong's leg to make some money. "Once I get him to you, how are you going to protect both of you?"

"Thank you for your concern, but I will worry about that when the time comes. We'll be safe."

She withdrew two U.S. Grants and placed them with care on his desk.

He looked at the money for several seconds as if she was offering two one-carat diamonds. Real money! He looked up from the money, amazed at her deep blue beguiling eyes, and felt sorry for her. Her whole get-up, her perfume penetrating his senses; her sensual qualities made him light-headed. He knew that when he began to overthink, he got into trouble. He understood his instincts better than his feelings. His instincts screamed, "Don't do it!" but the U.S. Grants told him to get on with it.

"Keep bringing out the U.S. Grants, Caroline; this will take at least five."

Caroline quickly laid three more bills on the desk.

"I like the way you do business," Mac said as he scooped up the money and stuffed the bills in his pocket. "Let's discuss how to rescue your boyfriend, shall we?"

For the next ten minutes, she gave Mac all the information that he needed to make a battle plan and rescue her boyfriend.

"There might be a bonus if you're a bit rough with the men watching over him," she said with mischievous eyes.

She stood and demurely put her white gloves on. She turned to leave and smiled at Mac. "You know, we all love Marines because you're the only real men left!"

Her dress was the color of salmon, the plumeria flower above her left ear put an exclamation mark on her ladylike qualities. With the small velvet purse dangling from her arm, it was hard for him to believe she was a man.

* * *

The Milky Way stretched across the Hawaiian sky, not as impressive as the Southern Lights, but made Mac appreciate it all the same. He hoped that he would see a shooting star, could make a wish for Wojo to come home soon.

He suddenly felt as small and insignificant as a pimple on a Parris Island boot's ass. The salty humid air pressed in on him as he sat and watched the Hubba Bubba Bar entrance from ten feet away. Sweat rolled down his chest and back. People said he could sweat in a frozen meat locker. He took a pull on the Primo Lager beer, compliments of a passing drunken Marine. The label said that they had been brewing beer since 1900 at the Hawaii Brewing Company. Good enough for Mac. It tasted just as good as his POC beer back home, The Pride of Cleveland.

He had been watching the comings and goings of the people in Chinatown for the last two hours--wharf rats, police, merchant mariners, soldiers, sailors and Marines, military shore patrols, Chinese, Japanese, and every seedy element that prospered following armies with their loneliness, walking or staggering on the sidewalks of Chinatown. And he couldn't forget the prostitutes; they had propositioned him no less than three times in the last hour. The smells of fried foods and the grease of a thousand woks permeated the air. French fry and hot dog wrappers rolled down the sidewalks pushed by unseen winds, piling in the corners of storefronts. Food and beer puke were scattered on different street corners waiting to be stepped on and cleaned up in the early morning hours.

Most people who came to visit Chinatown wanted to get drunk, gamble, get a tattoo or spend five minutes with a lady of the night. The Marines called it stewed, screwed, and tattooed. Decadence and people's problems were putting money in Mac's pocket, so he wasn't that upset. He didn't understand certain people who lived underground or around the edges of society, especially in Chinatown. He knew they were somewhat like him, misfits who didn't belong in a well-mannered and ordered society. He experienced a tinge of sadness for them and himself and quickly shook off his thoughts.

Just a few months ago, he would not have entered the bar and hotel across from him unless a platoon of combat-hardened

Marines accompanied him. But civilian life was changing him faster than the grueling weeks at Parris Island.

Yesterday, Caroline gave him a picture of her lover and told him where the local poofters hung out. He learned from an Australian soldier on Guadalcanal what poofters were. A man, who liked to have sex with men but loved to dress like and hang around women.

The second night Mac had identified the guards and what time they left for breaks or dinner. He knew that he had to go in quickly without a fuss, retrieve Caroline's boyfriend, and then escort him down the street to her place. He watched the relief arrive at the hotel and waited until the other one left.

Mac waited five minutes and walked up to the hotel clerk.

"What room are they in and how many guards up there?"

The clerk looked at Mac and ignored him. Mac asked again. He stared at Mac with a bland face.

"I don't know what you're talking about."

Mac leaned over the counter, grabbed the guy's tie, and pulled it down so hard the guy's chin bounced off the counter.

"I'm hot, tired, pissed off, and sober. The next time you don't answer my question, I'm going to drag you over the counter by your necktie."

The clerk rubbed his chin where a large red bump was forming.

"Room 22. Only one man," he said.

Mac mouthed, "Thanks for nothing" and wondered if he should take the stairs or the elevator. He took the stairs and got to the second-floor landing and peeked around the corner. The guard was half-asleep. He quietly walked up to the guy by the door and whacked him across the head with the butt of his pistol and slowly lowered him to the floor. He stood outside room number two and waited for the phone to ring. He smiled as he listened to the conversation.

He figured the voice on the line was telling them that someone was on his way up. He heard a voice say, "Thanks." That's when he made the big mistake and decided to walk into the room.

At the last moment, he saw the glint of the brass knuckles in his peripheral vision, but it was too late. The only thing that saved him was his years in the boxing ring. Enough of a duck to avert a solid blow to his brain housing group. He didn't think; just reacted. Mac flipped the attacker over his back and chopped him in the throat ending that immediate threat. A second man, probably weighing a hundred and sixty pounds soaking wet, attacked Mac like he was trying to steal his six-inch stiletto heels.

He had come out of Mac's blindside, attaching himself to Mac by wrapping his legs around his waist while still pummeling him as they both fell. The son of a bitch had brass knuckles and hammered Mac five times before he could get his bearings. The last right to his temple dropped him to all fours. The attacker scrambled to his feet. The pissed-off feather merchant grabbed Mac by his ears, jumped on Mac's back, and rode him like he was Trigger, Roy Rogers' horse.

Mac groped wildly and dragged him off his back onto the wood floor. He stood up on shaky legs trying to clear his head. He saw two of everything. That's when the little pervert kicked him in the balls. Mac let out some expletives from hell itself and grabbed his pride with both hands.

He knew he couldn't last much longer under the present circumstances and had to stay on his feet. With his left hand holding onto his coconuts, he raised his right hand to stop the next brass knuckle attack. The brass knuckles hit head-on to his knuckles, and he let out a scream that stopped the guy in his tracks. The little guy laughed uncontrollably.

"You dirty bastard," screamed Mac. He grabbed him by the throat and hit him between the eyes with his forehead. The guy went limp. Mac let him thump to the floor. He kicked until he heard ribs crack.

He should have known better. Years ago, a salty corporal had told him to stay clear of the homosexuals; they'd stick a stiletto between your ribs and then piss on your grave. But two hundred and fifty bucks was two hundred and fifty bucks, especially when money was as scarce as a Marine on payday.

This wasn't what he had imagined weeks ago while lying in the hospital, thinking of becoming a private detective. He had pictured himself sitting at his desk smoking a pipe or fine cigar with a beautiful receptionist setting appointments with the rich and famous, all of them waiting with bated breath to hear how he solved their cases. Charlie Chan would praise the brilliant Detective Mac and ask him how he put the pieces of the crime- puzzle together. Trailing some guy into a disgusting flophouse and fighting for his life was not what he had imagined. He reminded himself that a new Charlie Chan movie was now playing downtown.

Mac bent at the waist, blood dripping from his hand as he went through the guy's pockets for his wallet. He checked the driver's license. There were two, each with different names. In a side compartment were four twenty-dollar bills. Mac pulled out the eighty bucks.

"Twenty for my surveillance, asshole, twenty for getting whacked with those brass knuckles, another twenty for my fingers that now look like hot dogs with nails, and twenty more for getting whacked in the family jewels."

He walked back to the unconscious first attacker and emptied his wallet of ten measly bucks and kicked him in the ribs once more so that he could earn his bonus.

He walked over to Caroline's naked boyfriend and untied him from the bed.

"Put your clothes on. I'm getting you out of here. Hurry, before an army shows up."

He walked out the door dragging Caroline's half-dressed boyfriend, then pushed the man ahead of him down the stairs.

Mac grabbed onto the handrail while descending the stairs so he wouldn't fall. Every bone in his body ached. His head ached like it was a baseball walloped over the fence by Joe DiMaggio. It throbbed with every beat of his heart. His head, like his hands, dripped blood. He stopped at the counter and eyed the hotel clerk, who wore a small smirk at the corners of his mouth.

"I'm coming back. I won't forget. I'm going to find the biggest, meanest faggot in Hawaii who needs some dough and have him kick the shit out of you!"

Before Mac could stop him, Caroline's boyfriend bolted through the door and down the street. Mac looked down the street and hoped he could make it back to his office.

Chapter 10

Mac struggled up the stairs to the Bombay Alley. Somehow, he made it to the top and staggered to his desk. He dropped into the chair, almost fell over, and turned on the desk lamp. His fingers were swollen like Vienna sausages; one knuckle had a split at the joint. He tried to make a fist but stopped halfway because it hurt too damn much. His head felt like his swollen testicles, and his left cheek throbbed. He didn't want to look in the mirror.

Bogey made it look so easy; get busted in the chops, bust some chops back, light a cigarette, pull out a gun, mouth a few wisecracks, and all was okay.

He pulled out his bottle of booze. Mac drank more than his fair share of whiskey because he liked it. All the places that he had ever served in the Marine Corps, cigars and whiskey were easy to find, but round-eyed women were scarce as hen's teeth. Bourbon and cigars were mated together like Bogey and Bacall; Gable and Lombard. One didn't quite taste the same without the other. He was no different; he was mated to the Marine Corps. The Corps was branded into his very being, burned into every fiber of his body and mind. He lived and breathed the Marine Corps. Seventy-hour work weeks were ordinary and unnoticeable. It was a way of life, like a monastic monk working for the glory of God. His workday started before the sun rose and ended long after sunset. He was no longer just Mac. He was Gunny Mac. His three stripes up and two down made him hard as steel that had been forged in fire and pounded out on an anvil. A man who showed men how to live and die. No word was uttered with more reverence than the word gunny.

He had cut his teeth in the Banana Republics, Nicaragua and Panama, hatching from a polliwog to a shellback more times than he remembered. He had protected the mail trains from gangsters in the states and lived the life of Riley in Shanghai, China. He added more salt to his dungarees with sea duty. Along the way, Wojohowitz was right by his side.

His new title now was going to be shamus, private dick, private eye, private detective, private investigator, gumshoe, inquiry agent, sleuth, bird dog, peeper, snoop, and flatfoot. He stared at his diploma and license hanging on the wall and toasted to them. "Congratulations, peeper." He downed his bourbon and poured another.

He sat back down letting, out a grunt of pain. Seadog came up to him and put his head on Mac's lap. Maybe next time he'd bring him. He needed somebody to watch his behind. He hugged Seadog, who immediately went for the ice cubes by trying to grab them from Mac's injured hand. He kissed Seadog on top of his head. It seemed like yesterday that he had opened his eyes right after surgery to find a small puppy with big brown eyes staring at him. At that moment, a little tongue snaked out and licked him on his nose. In the background of his memory, he heard Lieutenant Van Deer telling him that he had a new buddy. He didn't know it at the time, but Van Deer worked an extra shift from 2400 to 0440 hours every evening just to watch over him. Every evening she would bring Seadog and place him on the edge of the bed. He would fall asleep with his puppy. Sometimes he would wake up, and Lieutenant Van Deer would be sleeping in a chair by his bed.

He gently pushed Seadog off his lap. He owed so much to so many.

He opened the windows on each side of the big arched window to feel the breeze that he loved. He bent down and grabbed his glass of whiskey.

He sat back down in his chair, swiveled it around, and looked out his window. He put his feet on the sill and was beguiled as the palm trees swayed back and forth by the wind coming off the ocean. If he listened carefully, he could hear the gentle swishing of the palm fronds.

He watched the lost street people pushing and shoving their way through the teeming crowds. His prying eyes captured the street scene below him amid the exploding light from all the different colored neon signs, each beckoning the drunken attention of all. To his left across the street was the Coconut Grove, a sizable neon-green palm tree gracing its front. Located next to that bar, displaying his favorite neon work of art, the undulating Hawaiian Hula girl that welcomed men to gawk at her sensual delights. To the right flashed the open sign for the "no-tell motel" where women of the night plied their trade for three dollars a trick. Next in line was the Windjammer Bar and Grill, where the whiskey and blood flowed like water.

The lights seemed to have no beginning and no end. They twinkled down the street like the stars in the night sky, reminding him of the Aurora Borealis.

He liked to turn off his lights and view the greens, reds, and blues that reflected off his walls. This evening was no different. The honking of horns, loud catcalls, and drunken laughter assaulted him through his open window. The smells of Chinatown, curried fish, chicken with spices unknown, and cooked Hawaiian pork made his stomach growl.

He was so damn tired.

His neck wound had healed; his bayonet wounds hadn't fully healed. Drinking whiskey didn't help. He knew he could die at any time, collapsing on some side street on a pile of pigeon shit and croak.

As a Marine, he had a purpose; now, he didn't know what his purpose was. He was being left behind. He was a nobody, not part of any whole, a small, insignificant cog in the wheel of life. What was happening to him didn't make sense. There was more honor in fighting for your country and killing Japs. People who didn't wear uniforms were threatening to kill him. This was new to him, and he was starting to take it personally. If all this nonsense continued, a savage demon inside him would be released; giving no quarter, no mercy, and no justice. The war had taught him to kill humans like cockroaches.

He threw his empty whiskey bottle in the trash. Mac used his feet to wheel his chair to the refrigerator. He pulled out two six-packs of beer and wheeled back. He had trouble opening the bottle and used the edge of the desk to pop off the top. He drained the bottle in less than a minute, erasing his thirst. He placed the empty on his desk. He finished the second bottle soon after, burped, and set it behind the first. He left just a little in each for his dead Marines. Within forty minutes, he finished six beers. He pointed to the first bottle. . .you're Sergeant James. He pointed to the second bottle... you're my Jonesy... you're Corporal Walker... you're Sergeant Windham. . . Corporal Robbie. . . and the bottles formed a long line- Corporal Robbie--the best damn machine gunner in the division.

He opened his seventh beer. Tonight, he would drink to every dead Marine he knew. He frowned.

"I'll kill a beer for every dead guy," he whispered.

He would have to drink a lot of beer and order more! Cases of it! As he stared at the bottles, they morphed into the heads and faces of his dead buddies. Legs and arms grew out of each bottle. They marched in perfect cadence, silent, but for the thump of boots hitting the deck. Each bottle marched past Mac. They did eyes-right and saluted. They continued walking off his desk and over the edge until only one was left. The last bottle turned around and looked at him with sorrowful eyes.

"You're the last one left, Mac!" Then it walked off into oblivion. Mac shook his head. The room was dark except for the reflection of the colors of the flashing neon sign across the street, rooms for three dollars. He took a deep breath; the smell of stale beer and cigar smoke surrounded him. To the left of his desk, glass fragments littered the floor. Seadog was watching him from the corner of the room. Mac wondered if he was going crazy!

Chapter 11

September 30, 1942 Naval Base, Honolulu

Lieutenant Commander Kincaid had one major problem. That was how to handle the Treasury agents verifying the money being put into bags and keeping the rosters of those bags. But this next agent was critical to him understanding the amount of money each bag might contain. He walked into the Quonset hut along with the agent and walked to the podium.

"Mr. Williams, you are the money guy. Please tell us what we need to know so we can start planning and collecting the money for Operation Torch."

Mr. Williams moved to the podium.

He turned toward Commander Kincaid and half bowed.

"Thank you, commander. I have researched some specifics relating to the volume and weight of two hundred million dollars. This is important because we will need to understand the number of bags needed to haul such money to the burn locations and amount of money each bag might contain."

Kincaid moved his chair closer to the podium and leaned forward.

"The first item on my agenda is the need for you to understand what money amounts are in circulation in all of the United States." He looked out at the interested faces before him. "There are approximately seven billion dollars in one-dollar bills which, if my calculations are correct, represents 50% of all money. There are 1.6 billion dollars in five-dollar bills or 10% of the currency. There are approximately 1.6 billion in ten-dollar bills, representing 10% of available currency and 4.4 billion in twenty-dollar bills, representing 20% of the currency. The other currencies, fifty dollars, one hundred dollars, and so forth, represent the final percentages. There is no reason to suspect that these percentages are any different in the territory of Hawaii than the mainland. These percentages will become important later in my briefing."

He surveyed the audience to ensure he had their immediate attention.

"Now let's discuss currency bills. Each bill is 75% cotton and 25% linen."

Williams smiled at his audience, knowing he had their rapt attention and enjoying the spotlight.

"A dollar bill weighs one gram and a five-dollar bill, though worth more, weighs the same."

The men at the table chuckled.

"For our purposes today, let's say we have two hundred one-dollar bills. They would weigh in at .44 pounds total. So, we can conclude that $500 in one-dollar bills weighs about a pound. Our bags will hold sixty pounds of weight. Therefore, if we multiply five hundred one-dollar bills times sixty, we get about $25,000 to $30,000 per bag. Gentlemen, that is only one-dollar bills. Now let us look at the different denominations and percentages that I mentioned before in my briefing and see the potential worth of each bag. Thank God, we aren't required to separate the bills by value because we know it would take forever. Anyhow, it doesn't matter because the money is being burned."

Kincaid felt the blood rush to his head. He hadn't thought about each bag having a different worth. He turned his head back to the briefer.

"Using my percentages previously mentioned, what is the possible worth of each bag? I'm passing out a sheet to assist you in following my computations. I have included the math calculations explaining the possible worth of each sixty-pound bag. These calculations will give us an indication of how many bags we might need for transporting two hundred million dollars, no small feat. In each bag, 50% of the weight will or could be one-dollar bills, which will be around 13,500 individual dollar bills. 10% will or could be five-dollar bills, or 2,700 bills. 10% might be ten-dollar bills or 2,700, and 20% might be twenty-dollar bills for 5,400. This will come to 27,000-one-gram bills, equaling around 55 pounds. That will be the approximate weight of each bag. Now, what might be the worth of these 27,000 bills?"

Kincaid's pencil flashed across the paper in front of him. He didn't hear what Mr. Williams was saying at this point. He didn't have to. He circled the figure he wrote down. Each bag was worth at least $162,000. Maybe a little less, perhaps a little more! The figure at the bottom of the paper stated they needed 1,235 bags to transport the money to the burn stations. Kincaid looked up when the room became silent.

Each man had a stunned look on his face as if for the first time, they realized the magnitude of their mission.

Kincaid stood up and walked to the front of the room.

"Mr. Williams, I can say without equivocation you did an outstanding job. I just don't understand what the hell you just said."

The group broke into applause with hoots and hollers.

"Our job is going to be difficult. I think we now understand the enormity of our task. At our meeting tomorrow, we must talk about the collection points, supervision of those collection points, securing the bags, transportation, and security moving the bags to our two locations. I will find out how many bags we can burn during an eight-hour shift at each location. Mr. Williams, place your file and notes in the safe; the rest, please put your notes in the burn bag. Meeting adjourned."

Kincaid sat down in his chair and wished he had a bourbon. He had no idea how much of the two hundred million would be turned in. If he had any money saved, he probably would hide what he had and wait for the damn emergency to end. He suspected that's how most people thought. One madam was making thousands each month and had saved over $40,000. She had sent most of her profits back to the states. No way she was going to turn those greenbacks into him or anyone else. After Williams' talk, he now understood it would take at least five to ten bags per million. He thought of that beautiful figure for a moment. His monthly pay was around $375.00 per month. Doing some mental calculations, he figured it would take him over two hundred years to make that much money. Why be greedy; even one bag would set him up for life; one measly bag! He put out his cigarette and headed out to the "O" club bar. He had to drink some bourbon and dream of how he was going to spend all that money.

Chapter 12

The Royal Hawaiian Hotel

Mac walked into the Royal Hawaiian Hotel, turned right, and walked through the archway down to the courtyard. Caroline stood up and waved to him. The first thing that Mac noticed was her dress. Sunrise yellow with buttons going up from the waist to the neck. Around her waist was a belt, the same color as the dress. She wore black gloves with a gardenia on the front of a wide-brimmed black hat.

She stretched out her hand for Mac to shake. He stood there looking at her.

"Is there something wrong, Mac. I mean, with my dress?"

Mac felt his face turning red. He stammered. "I'm sorry for staring; it's just that. . . you look like an actress. . . well, I mean, nice outfit."

Caroline blushed. "Thank you. It's one of the new dresses I designed. Simple, elegant, and very ladylike. I hope it will make a splash. I want to thank you for accepting my lunch invitation."

She ran her gloved hand over his scabs. "I'm so sorry, Mac, about what happened to you. I had no idea it was that dangerous."

Mac laughed. "Neither did I. Let's grab some lunch."

"If you don't mind, Mac, I thought we would have lunch right here. It's so lovely. I also took the liberty of ordering you a drink."

The waiter placed a drink next to Mac. "Very fancy, Caroline. What am I about to inhale?" he asked.

She laughed and clicked glasses with him. "A Manhattan up... made with their first batches of Five crown whiskey flown in from the states."

Mac took a sip and then another. "Thanks. I'm a man used to drinking rotgut, and now I have you trying to civilize me. Shame on you."

She let out an infectious giggle. "Remember, lunch is on me. I have so much to thank you for, and I have some information for you."

She moved the menus off to the side.

Caroline spoke up. "I hope you don't mind, but I ordered you lobster and steak. Medium rare. Is that O.K.?

"Not only do you design great dresses, but you are also a mind reader."

She smiled. "Some of my friends who keep their ear to gossip relayed some information to me that makes me worry about you."

"About me? Why would anyone be interested in me?"

Caroline took a sip of her Bloody Mary. "You have come to the attention of Gentleman Jack and Captain Chin. My friends have told me that they may have to make an example of you."

"Just because I helped you?"

"No."

"What else did I do to get on their shit list?"

Caroline stirred her drink and took a sip. "You put a dent in the head of a police officer in the employment of Captain Chin."

"When did I do that when I was sleepwalking?"

"He was the individual you clobbered guarding the door of my boyfriend's room. Then you beat up two of Gentleman Jack's boys inside. Then, you put a knot in the guy's head in the hotel. Jack owns the hotel. And don't forget about the pictures!"

Mac grinned. "How do you know about that?"

"Jack's people aren't the brightest, and a little money makes their tongues wag. That's why I hired you. I thought you were fearless, and I was right."

Mac sipped on his Manhattan.

"You are a national hero, Mac, and we all owe you. You have to be careful, or the bastards will get you. They control Chinatown and everyone in it."

The waiter brought their lunch, and they changed the direction of their conversation. They spent a lot of time laughing and sharing memories of their lives. After lunch, he ordered another Manhattan.

"I have a favor to ask of you, Caroline. There is a navy nurse who was responsible for saving my life. She took extra shifts to care for me. She gave me Seadog, who also helped me recover. I would like to buy a dress for her, like the one you are wearing now."

"What is her name?"

"Lieutenant Van Deer."

Caroline put her hand on Mac's and smiled. "What is her first name…."

Mac hung his head. "I don't know."

"I'll tell you what Mac. I will visit her at the hospital and figure out her correct dress size, and you shall have your gift. I promise you. I think you are in love."

"I'm not much of a catch Caroline and rough around the edges."

"I disagree, Mac. I know a good man when I see one."

"How much do I owe you for the dress Caroline?" Mac asked.

"No charge Mac. I hope I get to watch love blossom between you two." She smiled. "That will be payment enough." She picked up her gloves, put them on, and thanked Mac again. "We must do this again soon. If I hear anything, I will call you. Please don't stand up. Finish your drink and enjoy the rest of your day."

He watched her walk away and began to think about what she told him. She was a classy dame who wasn't a dame and had a code of honor that coincided with Mac's. She had a big heart, but a flawed heart. He guessed Caroline tried to make a life for herself in Hawaii because her kind was accepted as a part of the Hawaiian culture. Mac knew more friendships were needed in a world gone crazy. He believed her when she said if he ever needed help that she would be there for him, which meant she would tell him every time Gentleman Jack, or anyone moved against him or anyone in Chinatown.

He walked up Hotel Street to Bombay Alley, put his .45 away in his desk, and knew that Seadog had taken a dump somewhere because he was in hiding. Mac shook his head. It wasn't Seadog's fault. He knew his buddy was embarrassed. He found the turd and deposited it in the toilet and called Seadog to come out of hiding. Mac sat down at his desk and saw a furry head peek around the corner. He rattled Seadog's leash, and he came running. Mac rubbed Seadog's head and promised to spend more time with him.

He could hear the sounds of the bar below--men and women drinking and having fun, and he thought of Momma Leone. She asked him to watch the bar for her and to find out if anybody was stealing money from the till. She had reminded him that detectives were trained in that matter. Mac pulled out his private detective manual and tried to find a chapter on how to watch shysters stealing money from a till. He threw the book on his desk and figured out quickly he'd wasted a dollar.

He rubbed his sore temple. Thankfully, the scabs were growing smaller and smaller. He was a mess, shot to shit, stabbed, scabs all over his face, and a hemorrhoid from hell. Mr. Hap became very unhappy with him because, after lunch, he had walked around Chinatown for nearly three hours looking for another wartime bride. Mr. Hap must have grown a couple of inches in that time and was feeling his oats.

A few days ago, the base chaplain had called him and offered him a contract to run down and investigate all the enlisted men and women getting married, which sometimes caused them to go missing. Mac laughed. What did the navy expect during a war?

He was still feeling the effects of getting his ass beat, and it felt like a bowling ball hung between his legs. If he ever saw that homo in room 22 again, he was gonna rip off what he didn't need. Mac gingerly moved in his seat, poured himself some hot coffee, and added some very high-octane hooch a friend had given him. He said it was 100 proof and made from the finest Hawaiian sugar cane. Mac knew he seemed to be drinking more now, but hell he had been drinking his whole life. Civilians might not approve of him drinking in the early afternoon; he didn't approve of it himself. But it was evening now. Mac turned around and peered out his window. He felt melancholy, a feeling quite uncommon to him. His spirits would rise when he visited the boys in Ward D, sometime, maybe even tomorrow.

When they wheeled him into Ward D two months ago, he'd asked what the D stood for and they told him "Death." Ward D held the most of the severely wounded. More of his friends died there than Mac wanted to remember.

He glanced up at a Hawaiian ceremonial mask with a clock where the mouth should be. It was approaching 2130 hours. Mac figured he'd sleep at his desk in case Gentleman Jack visited. He opened his top drawer. He couldn't wait to see who might want to kill him for doing something. Just get in line, boys, no need to push, you'll all get your chance....

Chapter 13

Mac's office Bombay Alley

Mac couldn't believe how fast the day went. He spent all afternoon waiting to see the doctor at the naval hospital only to be told his wounds were healing slowly, and they would be reviewing his request to stay on active duty. Mac needed some time off and decided to spend the rest of the day at the beach with Seadog. The little pecker head was becoming a beach bum. He must have thrown the ball into the ocean over a hundred times, and his arm felt like it was ready to fall off. Seadog wasn't tired at all and was next to his chair, waiting for a belly rub.

He had a great dinner with Momma Leone. He noticed during dinner that she hadn't said much. He asked her if everything was alright. She patted his hand and said everything was okay.

It was late, and Mac decided to sleep right at his desk with his .45 on his lap. After yesterday's lunch date with Caroline and her warning, he wasn't taking any chances.

He was just getting comfortable in his chair when someone knocked on the door. In one quick motion, Mac whirled around and grabbed his .45.

A little guy came in walking like a pigeon, head bobbing up and down, straightening his tie with his left hand. He kept clearing his throat as if he had a feather caught in it. He wore his hat at a jaunty level, low over his right ear and high over his left ear. A cool autumn brown jacket covered his light brown shirt. His pants were a canary yellow, and his brown wingtips glowed as if the shoeshine boy had just polished them. He smelled like the barber had just given him a haircut and shave. Mac felt a little jealous and sniffed under his armpits to check if he smelled like he probably looked. He concluded this wop boy had to be on some official business. The feather merchant gave Mac the evil eye as if the sight of Mac offended him. He wrinkled his nose as he bobbed his head, straightened his tie, and cleared his throat.

"What's that smell?" he rasped in a Brooklyn accent. He whipped out a silk handkerchief from his jacket pocket and placed it over his mouth and nose and swatted a few flies that suddenly descended upon his Old Spice shaving lotion.

"What the hell is going on? It smells like someone died in here. This is a hellhole!"

He swatted at a fly the size of a B29 bomber. Mac turned his eyes to the fly swatter on his desk and handed it to him.

"Here, this works better."

The dandy walked up to the desk.

Mac looked into the man's eyes and noticed that he had tears running down his cheeks. He was dabbing at his eyes.

"You okay?" Mac asked.

"Yeah, yeah, I'm alright. I got allergies. The air in this room is not so desirous." He swatted another fly that landed on the desk.

Mac pushed it over to the growing heap of carcasses.

"What's your name, shyster," Mac asked.

"Tony Coniglio."

"Now, what can I help you with, Tony C?"

The visitor glanced at Mac and walked around as if he was looking for something.

He stared at his feet and then at Mac. "I got a problem. I don't know if you can help me. You don't look so prosperous."

"Don't look at my surroundings," Mac smiled. "I'm investing all my money in stock." With that, Mac pulled out the wad of bills from his pocket. "I don't need your money."

The guy's eyes rolled in the back of his head like a cheap slot machine.

"Have a seat."

Mac pulled his handkerchief from his jacket pocket and wiped off the seat. He put a cigar in his mouth and started to light it.

A look of shock came over his visitor's face. "What's it you're doing?"

Mac lit the cigar drawing in deeply several times. Plumes of smoke filled the room and drifted towards the strange little man. He batted the smoke away.

"Cigar smoking is such a filthy habit."

Mac pointed his cigar at him.

"I'll tell you what's a filthy habit and that's being broke! Now how can I help you?"

Mac was thinking of a nickname that fit this character. His nose was his most outstanding attribute. It was a honker. A big schnoz. Marines always had nicknames for people. He decided to name him Schnoz.

He watched as he reached into his jacket and withdrew a brown envelope. With great care, he put it on the cluttered, dusty desk.

Mac stared at the envelope and glanced up at the Schnoz. Mac smiled and bobbed his head in unison with him. The Schnoz's face became a huge question mark.

"Aren't you going to open it?" he asked.

"Let me guess. It's a package of money."

The Schnoz nodded his head up and down.

Mac laughed out loud. He was on a roll, baby.

"Let me see," Mac continued.

"The money is for doing something."

His head bobbed at a faster rate like he was approaching the last furlong of the Kentucky Derby.

Mac was really getting good at this detective business.

The Schnoz took out a photo and handed it to Mac.

Mac looked at an older picture of a pretty woman somewhat resembling Virginia Mayo, wearing a simple plain dress with no jewelry.

Mac looked back at Tony C. alias, the Schnoz. He looked back at Mac with widening eyes.

"I need your help to protect her."

This is getting pretty interesting, Mac thought. Mustering his best private eye voice, Mac asked him to please continue.

"She's been threatened. I'm worried about her. Someone follows her every day. Well, not every day, mostly on the weekends. In the last seven days, she has seen the same men hanging around her place. They follow her most of the day. She doesn't think it's a coincidence."

"Have her give me a call, so that I can get all the details; I don't want her to come to my office just yet." Mac scribbled his number on a card and handed it to Tony.

Mac leaned back in his chair and unconsciously rubbed the stubble and scabs on his face.

"Is she your sweetheart?"

The Schnoz's face scrunched up, and a look of horror crossed his face.

"I've been her friend since she was a little girl. She hung around the racetrack where I worked. I don't know much about her; just helped her. She calls me Uncle Tony. I got no family, but her. She sort of adopted me and I sort of adopted her."

"That's a very sweet story. What do you want me to do, adopt her? Or maybe I could adopt both of you. We could be a family," Mac said sarcastically.

"Maybe I should go somewhere else." He started to get up, grabbing the money.

Mac snatched the money and looked into the envelope--a large wad of one-dollar bills. "Where did you get all this money?"

The little man squirmed in his seat and turned sideways. "It's all the money I got."

Mac threw the money on the desk.

"What do you do for a living? You a shyster?"

"What's it to you what I do for a living?"

"Answer my questions or go somewhere else."

The Schnoz looked at Mac solemnly and stopped bobbing his head.

"I muck stalls."

Mac drew on his cigar and blew smoke circles aiming for his visitor's big schnoz.

"What did you do before that?"

"I was a jockey."

That's why his head still bobbed up and down like he was heading for the finish line.

"Tony, what's your address?"

He turned his head downward and mumbled.

Mac leaned forward on his desk, his hands clasped as if in prayer.

"What did you say?"

"I live at the racetrack."

"Where at the racetrack?"

"I live in the stall next to Painted Warrior."

"I hope that's not a horse."

He looked at Mac with those soft, big brown eyes. "It ain't an Indian."

"And you're telling me my office stinks? You have a lot of nerve, buddy!"

Tony dropped his monogrammed handkerchief and bent to pick it up. Seadog came out of nowhere and smothered him in a thousand bad breath kisses.

Mac hoped Seadog hadn't been licking his balls.

He got up, turned and glanced back at Mac saying, "I got to go now. I'm not feeling so well." "Please protect my friend."

When he was almost out the door, Mac yelled to him, "How did you know to trust me?"

"She told me to go to you, and we could trust you with our lives."

"Get back here!"

"Does she know me?"

"Not personally. Her brother knew you on the Canal and now is at the naval hospital. He told her to go see you if she ever had any problems."

"How about an address and phone number Tony? And make sure you swing by tomorrow and have a little talk with me."

"There is a note with an address and telephone number along with the money. I'll see you tomorrow." He ran out as if he was chasing Painted Warrior for the best spot in the stall.

Mac looked at the picture. He now had two actual clients. Business was picking up and he was starting to feel like a private detective. Move on over Charlie Chan; a new man is in town.

He snuggled in his chair and soon fell asleep with Seadog underneath his feet. In his dream, he was on a stretcher with two corpsmen carrying him and another one holding onto a bottle of plasma. One looked behind him and shouted, "Start running, boys; there is a mortar shell right behind us!"

Mac raised his head and read what was on the side of the shell. "Kiss your ass good-bye, Gunny Mac."

He looked at the corpsman holding onto the plasma. "If you find something round and hairy, it's my asshole!"

He woke up staring into the barrel of the biggest .45 he ever saw.

Chapter 14

Pearl Harbor BOQ

Kincaid looked in the mirror hanging on the bathroom wall in his BOQ. The image in the mirror scared him. He saw the circles around his eyes, dark circles like a fucking raccoon. Sleep came in spurts, one hour here, one hour there. He was drinking a fifth a day and working as an indentured servant for that pig of an admiral. Every other day he was invited into the bloviators office and grilled mercilessly. The only thing missing was the bright white light shining in his eyes with his hands tied behind his back. The admiral was having the best fucking time, slowly taking his pound of flesh. He dreamed of choking the shit out of him, watching him turn blue, and his tongue protruding grotesquely from his mouth.

He sat on his bed and poured himself a drink. Last night he had lost and lost big at the gambling tables. He had gotten so drunk that he couldn't tell the difference between a spade and a club. He stuck out his tongue at the mirror and noticed it was covered in a deep layer of white shit. He rubbed his hand over his face in need of a shave. He decided at that very moment, his life had to change, or he would end up dead.

His visit from Gentleman Jack in the form of two men that looked like they just got out of Sing Sing prison scared the shit out of him. They followed him out to his car after another night of losing at the poker table. They grabbed him as he attempted to get into his car. Kincaid was drunk, but not stupid. He knew who these gangsters were and did not attempt to fight back. The bigger one smiled as he smoothed down the commander's uniform. "I'm so sorry, commander about manhandling you, look at all those pretty ribbons!"

"Yeah," said the other one. "But I don't see no 'V' devices. It seems like he's a desk jockey to me!"

The bigger one smiled. "Look, commander, Gentleman Jack is getting worried about you losing and doesn't want nothing happening to you. It seems like you owe him some money, and he just wants to see you about settling up. He has bills to pay just like you. Now, what is a good time for you to visit Gentleman Jack?"

Kincaid seemed to sober up real fast and waited for his brain to unfreeze along with his tongue. Without missing a beat, they patted him on the back and told him Jack would be expecting to meet with him at his club tomorrow night around 8:00 p.m. They opened his car door, half pushed him in, and closed the door for him. The bigger one leaned in the open window and said, "Remember, commander, 8:00 tomorrow night!"

Kincaid leaned his forehead on the top of his steering wheel and let his heartbeat get down to normal. He lit a cigarette and leaned back in his seat. He made $379.64 per month and he owed Gentleman Jack over $3,800. He had to convince Jack that his money was forthcoming and soon. He made a mental note to push 'Operation Torch' personnel a little bit harder. His only consolation was that he was a U.S. Naval Officer and gangsters didn't usually go around knocking off ranking members of the navy, or at least he prayed so.

* * *

The next evening Kincaid wore civilian clothes and walked through the casino. He turned right down a hallway and up to Jack's door. A big gorilla was standing to the right of the door. He was at least a head taller than the commander, towering over him.

"Hands up, commander," he commanded. He checked Kincaid for any weapons, smiled, and opened the door.

He walked into the office, and Gentleman Jack rose to meet him extending his hand to shake.

"Nice to see you, commander. Please make yourself comfortable."

Kincaid searched the smiling face looking for anything that could give him a clue as to what was going to happen next.

Gentleman Jack walked behind his desk, opened a file, and handed it over to Kincaid.

"In that file, commander, you will find all your gambling receipts and payments. The amount owed is at the bottom of the last page."

Kincaid took the file and looked through the receipts and felt a sense of doom. He looked up from the file and stared into Gentleman Jack's cool black eyes. They reminded him of a German Shepherd's eyes, alert and unforgiving. Kincaid's mind was quickly analyzing a proper response, while he lit a cigarette, hoping, it wasn't his last cigarette before the firing squad. Jack remained silent, his eyes watching Kincaid without betraying his internal thoughts.

"I guess I'm not a very good gambler. I seem to have forgotten how much my losses have been. I can pay you half my monthly salary until I'm paid up."

Gentleman Jack leaned forward in his chair, pulled out a cigar, and waited.

"Commander, why don't you light my cigar. The lighter is on the desk."

Kincaid felt a flush starting at his neck and ending at the top of his head. Now it seemed he had two asses to kiss. He picked up the lighter leaned forward and lit Gentleman Jack's cigar.

"John, I can call you John, can't I?" he asked.

Kincaid wondered how he knew his first name.

"Yes, of course."

"You know how much this Cuban cigar costs, John?"

Kincaid just stared at Jack, curious where in the hell this was going.

"This cigar costs one dollar. And the Napoleon Brandy I drink cost twelve bucks a bottle. This Italian suit cost me two hundred bucks, and I possess twenty-two of them. Believe me, Kincaid, I am not bragging. I am just trying to show you that my expenses as a businessman are different than yours. Now, commander, even though your gambling debts are over $3,800, you must realize there are costs associated with debt.

There are some interest charges attached to the amount. The interest charges come to another thousand dollars, and that brings the total charges to over or close to $5,000."

Kincaid felt the blood surge behind his eyeballs and felt his heart pound against his rib cage. He rose half out of his chair, trying to get some words out, but failing. He slowly collapsed back in the chair and stared at Gentleman Jack speechless.

"Let me pour you a drink. You're no good to me dead. You are worth more to me alive than dead…."

Kincaid grabbed the bourbon and downed it. He took a deep breath and extended his glass toward the bottle.

Jack placed the bottle on the desk in front of Kincaid. Gentleman Jack watched him as he downed two more shots in succession.

"Now, John, let's talk some business together, shall we? I've done some research on you. You are a man with discriminating tastes, much like me. I also know that the navy's idea of fairness concerning your career, well, let's say politics intervened, and that is unfortunate. A man of your caliber should be commanding at the minimum a cruiser, but we know that is not in the cards. There's a saying that I kind of like, all's fair in love and war. You've made a lot of husbands angry, and they're all lined up to take a shot at you. You're looking at me with a bewildered look on your face; what seems to be the problem?"

"How the hell do you know so much about me?"

Jack smiled, "Let's just say, I know people, people know me, and the people that know you, know me."

"How much do you know?" asked Kincaid.

Gentleman Jack sipped some of his bourbon before answering. His eyes bored into Kincaid's eyes with an all-knowing look.

He walked over to his liquor cabinet and poured two fresh drinks of Napoleon Brandy and gave one to Kincaid.

"I know enough that you and I are becoming business partners." He clinked his glass against Kincaid's and smiled. "To our partnership!"

As Kincaid drank the brandy, two thoughts came to mind, "What the hell?" and "Couldn't anyone keep a secret anymore?"

Chapter 15

Bombay Ally, Mac's Office

"Don't look so surprised, Gunny Mac, it's only a little .45. By the way, Mac, you look like shit war hero. The word with all the tough guys is you got your ass beat by a homo. On top of that, you got no business and no money!"

The man and his sidekicks laughed.

"Little from your end, big on my end," Mac said. He looked down at his desk. "And it was two homos."

All three glanced at each other and let out howls of laughter.

Trying to talk between gasps of laughter, Big Gums said, "Didn't anybody tell you the civilian world is for hardworking men? This ain't the Marine Corp, Mac; this is the real world!"

Mac ignored the smiles and stared into cold hard eyes that had seen death before. The tiny, beady black eyes that got his immediate attention.

The thug kept laughing and put his pistol back in his shoulder holster.

Mac's eyes gravitated to his mouth.

"What are you staring at?" he asked.

"I'm wondering."

He looked at Mac with a question mark in his eyes. "About what?"

"Do you have tall gums or small teeth?"

Big Gum's smile slowly faded.

"How would you like to have all gums and no teeth?"

The men with him snickered.

He remained silent. When Mac had opened his eyes, he noticed there were three of them. . . Larry, Curly, and Moe. His gaze soon centered on Big Gums as he waited.

"My client is offering a business proposition for you," Big Gums said.

Mac reached for his coffee cup. In unison, as if from a gun turret, all three guns pointed at him. Mac forced a big smile, showing all his teeth.

"I can't kill you with my coffee unless you drink it. Would you guys like a cup?"

Big Gums reached inside his raincoat and threw an envelope on the desk. "In there, you will find ten C notes. My client wants to make you happy. All you have to do, Mac, is do nothing."

Mac sipped his coffee and stared at the envelope. He thought about what a bright man might do. He wasn't the brightest bulb in the world, but right now, he was really confused. He looked up at Big Gums.

Big Gums spoke. "You're frowning, mop head. Do you need my boys to explain something?"

"No, I understand completely. So, I'm doing something for nothing."

Big Gums smiled. "Something like that."

"So, I'm not doing nothing, Big Gums, I'm doing something for the ten C notes."

Big Gums leaned over the desk showing his teeny weenie teeth and rapped Mac on the noggin with the barrel of his pistol.

Mac rubbed his head where the barrel struck him, bringing tears to his eyes. He started to move out of his chair to respond when one of the mugs put his pistol to Seadog's head. Mac sank back down and stared up at Big Gums.

"You ever touch me or my pup again, I'll be doing something for nothing all right. I'll break all your gums." Mac picked up the envelope and tried to give it back.

They turned their backs and walked to the door.

Cocking his head to the side, he asked Big Gums what he was not supposed to do.

"Oh yeah."

Big Gums paused, turned around, and smiled. Walking back to Mac, he threw a picture of a dame on the desk.

"If she wants to hire you, you know what not to do." He looked at Mac long and hard.

"Let me give you another piece of advice, jarhead. Be careful who you pick for clients. You have interfered too much in my bosses' personal interests, and you don't want to see me again. Gentleman Jack told me to give you some health advice; be careful who you pick for clients. The faggot owed him some money and you're lucky Gentleman Jack has decided to forgive you. Remember what you are getting paid for gunny . . .to do nothing. Nasty looking face, gunny, you don't need more scabs."

Mac was beginning to understand he shouldn't play games with Gentleman Jack. The next time he crossed good ole Jack, he was going to be in deep trouble, and it was nice that Jack at had least gave him a warning. Maybe that was the reason he was called Gentleman Jack. What made Mac grab his stomach with instant indigestion was that he had already crossed Jack twice. He knew Big Gums would come around again because Jack and Mac were not going to get along. Mac picked up the photo and gave a low whistle. Good-looking dame, he thought. Light wavy, shoulder-length hair that framed a Virginia Mayo face. In fact, she looked more like Virginia Mayo than Virginia Mayo. He looked closer and realized it was the same woman that the Schnoz had shown him.

Things were beginning to make sense. It was a shame that he was supposed to do nothing when she came knocking. He wondered if that meant he couldn't ask her out for a drink. It would be worth getting shot to spend an hour with her. The only problem getting in the way was the palooka in the photo--a swarthy looking fellow with a slight scar running down his cheek. It was his buddy, good ole Jack, once again coming into his life. He knew at that moment that his job was to make sure Jack was always unhappy, and just maybe he needed to find out more about this son of a bitch. He picked up the envelope and smelled the greenbacks. The smell of money made a guy smile.

Gentleman Jack was going to be out ten C notes and more if he had anything to say about it. He turned to Seadog.

"How can we not help a damsel in distress?" He reached down and rubbed Seadog's ears. The gentle soft mouth gently bit his hand.

"Well, partner, you are my sidekick; I'll need your vote. Do we help her or not?"

The alert brown eyes seemed to smile, and he gave a woof. Mac smiled. Seadog knew a good-looking dame when he saw one.

Chapter 16

Pearl Harbor BOQ

Burke drank his sixth cup of coffee, waiting for Kincaid to leave the Quonset hut and then follow him to his BOQ, not more than a five -minute drive. He had mentioned to the admiral that following Kincaid so closely and often might allow the commander to notice he was closely watched. The admiral followed that statement, by getting him a room next to Kincaid's, at the expense of a pissed off navy commander, who was forced to move all his stuff to another room.

The displaced officer had given Burke a once-over, staring at his rank, and gave him a look that said. "I'll fuck you later, ole man!"

Kincaid wasn't staying too long in his room these days. Burke sat in his car watching Kincaid disappear into the BOQ. It had been arranged last night that the desk clerk would step outside the BOQ's front door if someone asked for Kincaid by telephone or visited him.

His hand reached down and rubbed where the bullet had gone through his leg. Stretching his leg over the transmission hump helped some. The round had missed his femur tearing through the muscle before continuing out his leg. The surgeon told him how lucky he was that the bone was not taken away by the bullet. If that had been the case, his leg would have been an inch shorter than the other one.

He kept looking at his watch, hoping another two hours would not go by without some movement by Kincaid. The inside of the car smelled like stale coffee, cigarette smoke, and beer farts, which were coming every few minutes. He prayed Kincaid left soon, because a MABs was coming on, and this *massive anal blowout* could cause severe structural damage to his asshole.

The BOQ building was a long, two-story "L" shaped brick building with a flat roof. The small windows made it seem like what it was during wartime, a transient building devoid of any architectural elements. The double hatches were open with closed screen doors to let the evening breezes blow through the bottom floor desk area and reading room. All the trim painted in a lovely olive drab named, "The most popular color of the year," for 1942. Burke turned his head toward the noise coming from the dining facility and tried to guess the evening meal by the wafting smells heading his direction. What scared him was he couldn't identify the odors as food cooking.

His eyes riveted to the front screen door as he heard it open and banged shut. The clerk put a match to a cigarette throwing the match to the side. Smiling, Burke whispered, "Thank God!" and slowly got out of his car and limped over to the clerk.

"What you got?"

The older man handed him a piece of paper.

"A man named Jack called him from the number I wrote on the paper."

Burke asked him if he heard anything else.

"I tried, but the man named Jack made sure I hung up."

Burke rubbed his eyes and said, "You got a crapper nearby?"

The clerk said, "You can use mine."

He jerked his thumb to a door behind the front desk.

Burke mumbled thanks and quickly walked behind the desk and disappeared. Burke had no sooner pulled his pants down and squatted before he practically jumped off the toilet seat from the urgent pounding on the crapper door. He pulled up his pants, using words he learned from the 1st Division Marines and opened the door to see a guy by the front desk. He was a portly fellow, looking like he was eating his cigar rather than smoking it. A pork pie hat covered his head; the sides of the man's black hair glistened from hair lotion.

The clerk started to speak, as Burke stepped next to the desk clerk.

"Frank, why don't you take a break while I handle this gentleman?"

The clerk, looking tired, said, "Thanks, boss; I will."

Burke smiled at the fat head, sitting on an even fatter body.

"How can I help you, Sir?" he asked.

"I'm here to visit Lieutenant Commander Kincaid."

"Well, Sir, can I see some ID before I sign you in?" The man's jowls took on a life of their own.

"What the hell I showed my ID when I entered the gate to get in here. Why do I have to show it again?"

"Sir, there are many high-ranking officers who visit and live here. We must ensure their protection; a war is going on, and we are under martial law."

He gave Burke a withering stare. The fat hand pulled out his wallet and showed him his ID.

"Thank you so much, Sir. I'm sorry for any inconvenience I may have caused you. Please sign here, and you may go upstairs; the commander is in room 65."

The man grunted and waddled up the stairs.

Burke saw the name on the license and compared the signature on the visitor log. Fat boy's name was Joe DeVito, and now Burke had another guy to follow tonight. Burke called the clerk back in and finished his unfinished business. He then walked to his car and waited for Kincaid's playmate to leave the building.

Chapter 17

September 2, 1942 Pearl Harbor, Naval Hospital

Mac drove past the naval hospital three times before he found the courage to swerve into the parking lot. Turning into a familiar area, he put his car in park. His heart was beating out of his chest. Second-guessing himself, he put the car in reverse and started to leave. He slammed on the brakes and almost caused a Ford in the back of him to rear-end him. He hit the steering wheel with both hands.

Mac stared out at the ocean and clenched the cigar between his teeth. The breeze had picked up, whipping the surface of the ocean into little ridges and further on whitecaps. In the distance, he saw the silhouette of a navy ship, seemingly standing still. He breathed in the ocean's briny, seaweed fetidness, as it washed over him like a summer downpour. The ocean to a Marine is like water to a duck. He feared the expanse of the ocean; at the same time, he loved it. He smiled as he remembered his first time sailing from Hampton Roads with the 10th Marines. Venturing south through the Panama

Canal, he had smelled the diesel fuel and felt the vibrating of the deck caused by the powerful churning of the ship's propellers. He was hooked. He soon learned to respect the sailors in the fleet, who worked hard and were always ready to fight a Marine. Some of the toughest guys in the fleet were chiefs. They'd drink all night, work all day, and then go and kill Japs. In between, in their free time they would box twelve rounds and play poker all night.

Guys like Wojo, thought Mac, who grew up hard, joined the Marines and were happy to eat at least one meal a day and have a warm place to sleep. Most didn't need guarantees, just an opportunity. While in the military they became mighty grateful. They had money to send home to their mothers, sisters, and brothers. In between visits home, they fought wars, insurrections, drank, and tried to live up to the Marine's expectations—God, Country, and Corps.

The Corps didn't like married Marines. They said that if they wanted married Marines, a wife would be requisitioned by the supply sergeant. Most of the old Shanghai veterans thought of their families as their mother or father, baby sister, or brother.

Somebody honked at him. He waved him around his car. The driver appeared to be a shave tail ensign. He gave him his best Errol Flynn smile, put the car in drive, and drove into a parking space at the Konawa Bay Naval Hospital. Mac gathered the cartons of cigarettes and cigars under his left arm and carried a heavy canvas shopping bag in the other while at the same time holding on to Seadog's leash.

He walked up the stone stairs and stopped at the heavy brass doors. Deep inside, he knew that without help from these inside those corridors, he would have been underneath a white marble cross like so many of his friends. Good, decent boys who never made it out of their teenage years. He wiped his nose and walked through the hatch. A different world existed here. A world filled with pain, hope, and death. It had been his home for far too long. Often, Ward D was a final destination.

The hallway was filled with the hustle and bustle that war brings. Old Ben, the security guard, waved at him and smiled.

Mac threw him a cigar. Ben yelled, something he couldn't hear. Turning right, he headed down a hallway that was almost fifty yards long, went through two hatches, and walked outside to a sidewalk. In front of him was building after building containing the wrecked bodies of thousands of sailors and Marines. He passed wards A, B, and C. He hesitated as he entered Ward D. Ward D was two stories high and long as a football field. It contained Marines and sailors with massive body damage.

He strode through the front doors.

"Well, well, if it's not Gunny Mac."

His first impulse was to about-face and walk out. But it was too late for that. Lieutenant Van Deer was already on her feet, skirting around the nurse's desk to meet him.

He smiled as she approached. "Hello, Lieutenant."

She studied his face, her green eyes awash in concern, and said, "Is everything okay?"

Standing before him in her crisp white nurse's uniform, Lieutenant Van Deer was even more attractive than Mac remembered. Her hat sat neatly, as always, atop her wavy red hair, cut shorter these days, he noted, to just above her ears.

"I'm okay," he said. "Just brought some smokes for the guys." He held her gaze for a moment longer before looking down the corridor. "So, how is everyone?"

"Not before you answer me, Mac!" She tapped her clipboard with her pen. "How are you feeling?"

"Young perhaps." he thought, *"but plenty wise beyond her years."*

In a further attempt to deflect attention, he pointed toward D-Ward. "A lot better than the boys in there."

Seadog jumped at her and wanted some loving.

She bent down as Seadog gave her a thousand wet kisses. She laughed and hugged him.

"Your wonderful dog has come home to visit his friends." She looked up at him with a forlorn gaze. "And so, have you."

"I figured I better before the boys forget they are appreciated."

Van Deer smiled. "Same old Gunny Mac! The boys have really missed you. I've missed you too."

Mac's eyes bulged out unblinking like a deer caught in the headlights of a car. He shuffled his feet and murmured that he had missed them all. She reached over and gave him a hug.

"Welcome home, Mac! The boys will be thrilled!" Her face erupted into a warm smile.

"I don't know whether the boys missed you or Seadog more!"

Seadog knew he was home. He wiggled out of his collar and ran through the double doors, woofing and yelping down the row of beds. Marines started yelling and laughing.

"Hey, it's Seadog! Hey, Seadog boy, we missed you! Over here, boy!"

Mac walked through the door as Seadog did spins and slides, trying to visit every one of his pals at once. Mac wore a grin from ear to ear. His smile left as the smell of the ward hit him.

It was something a person never forgot. It was a combination of alcohol, body fluids, raw wounds with drain tubes, smelly body casts, bleach, and death.

He grinned at the Marines on each side of the aisle. It was nice to be home! Mac walked down the center of the passageway, laughing at the catcalls and name-calling. "Why, it's Gunny Mac!"

"Hey, guys, who let that crummy civilian in here?"

"Who is Gunny Mac?" yelled another.

He continued until he came to Gunnery Sergeant Herbert A. Jones' bed and sat next to the gunny. Bending down, he whispered into the gunny's ear. Gunnery Sergeant Jones' eyes fluttered open, and a smile slowly turned into a grin.

"Hey, Jonesy! How are you doing?" asked Mac.

"Doing all right for a shot-up ole gunny. I was wondering if I'd ever see that ugly mug of yours again. Where's that handsome ole mutt of yours?"

At that very moment, Seadog came up and leaped onto Jonesy's bed. His grin went from ear to ear and back again. Mac started to yell at Seadog when Jonesy waved him off.

"Boy, nothing like the kisses of ole Seadog. Better kisser than any woman I ever done kissed in my life!"

Seadog's whole body was shaking with excitement. Mac had forgotten how much of Seadog's life had been mixed up with the Marines of Ward D. Gunny Mac glanced at all the tubes going into and out of Jonesy. Mac let out a long sigh.

Jonesy stopped rubbing Seadog's ears and spoke up.

"Now, don't get your shorts all bunched into a ball, Mac. It looks worse than it is."

Mac swallowed a hard lump forming in his throat. He glanced away and then back into Jonesy's eyes.

"Jonesy, I need your help."

Jonesy chuckled. "You always needed my help, pecker head. What's the problem?"

Gunny Mac pulled out the photograph of the Virginia Mayo look-alike and handed it to Jones. "Her name is Rose; her brother was on the Canal with us and he's somewhere in this hospital. I need to talk to him. Also, have you heard anything about Wojohowitz?"

Jonesy felt a slight rush as he checked out the photograph. He looked up at Mac and nodded.

"I was dreading this moment. I've got some bad news. Wojo got hit really bad on the Canal."

Gunny Mac's face turned a light shade of gray like a cadaver.

"All of us here have been keeping it from you because we all know that he's like a brother to you. We've been trying to get more information. I'm sorry, Mac!"

Mac spoke up. "Wojo's the last of the best. I don't know what I'd do without him or you. When did he get hit?"

Jonesy's eyes moved away from Mac.

"A few days after you were hit. We were waiting 'til we got confirmation, but it's been hell getting news on casualties, too many of them. We know he's in a hospital and is not listed KIA. Mac, remember he's a tough guy. You two will be trading sea stories soon enough!"

Mac winked at Jonesy. "I would do him an injustice to think he's not alive and kicking. He's probably staring at the picture of him knocking me out!"

"I'll pass the word around, Mac, and see if we can find some information about this gal's brother. Especially if he served on the Canal."

Mac stood up and handed an envelope to Jones.

"Put this in the hospital fund for the boys."

Jonesy took the envelope and whistled. "The detective business must be good, Mac."

Mac looked down at his friend. "How are the guts and legs?"

Jonesy let out a half-laugh.

"The good news is there's not much more slicing and dicing they can do!"

Mac rubbed Jonesy's crew cut. "I'll leave Seadog here overnight and pick him up tomorrow. Tell the boys not to spoil him too much. He gets the runs on hospital chow."

Gunny Jones watched Mac until he disappeared from view. Something was wrong, he thought. Gunny Wojo was in trouble or maybe dead. Mac was going to get in real trouble. He was more of a Marine than a civilian private eye, and because he was hard-headed, he never knew when to back off.

He would have to find out what the hell was going on. Funny, he heard rumors after Wojo was hit. Rumors, if true, that would only lead to people dying, and nobody was better at killing than those two. The gunny laid back on his pillow. Seadog snuggled next to his neck. Too many Marines were dying. He closed his eyes and dreamed in olive drab.

* * *

Gunny Mac tried to leave Ward D with little fanfare but was caught by the ever-present Van Deer.

"You trying to sneak out without saying goodbye, Mac?"

Gunny Mac gave a half-smile. He couldn't get his lips to move. Lieutenant Van Deer grabbed his sleeve.

"You okay, Mac? Your face is all flushed?"

Mac nodded his head. "Just hot in here."

She grabbed Mac's hand and put a piece of paper in it.

"My phone number, Mac. . .call me some time." She turned away and walked back to the nurse's station.

Gunny Mac didn't look at the number. He couldn't think of anything, except wondering how in the hell the big Polack was doing.

Chapter 18

Pearl Harbor Naval hospital

Gunnery Sergeant Wojohowitz sat in the doctor's room, aboard the heavy cruiser, waiting to get discharged from sickbay. He picked up a magazine and guess who was on the cover? He read the title. *Gunny Mac saves Guadalcanal on Bloody Ridge.* He stared at the picture of Gunny Mac splashed across the whole cover. He shook his head. Bad picture of the gunny. He finished reading the article about the heroic exploits of a certain Gunnery Sergeant Mac, United States Marine Corps and threw the magazine back on the small end table. In fact, every child in America had read of Mac's bravery on Bloody Ridge. Hell, he thought, maybe they were building a statue to him in Washington DC at this very moment! The article said when they found Mac, and they only found him by luck, his hand was still holding his Ka-bar which was embedded in a Japanese torso. When the graves registration Marines had stumbled upon him and tried to remove the knife from his hand, he had started to fight them. They say they're still running from the shock!

Wojo grinned when he thought about the article and knew that much of the tale was true because Mac was one tough Irish-Slovenian. The bastard had gotten himself the Navy Cross for what he did on that ridge on Guadalcanal and the very thought of Gunnery Sergeant Mac getting the Navy Cross and all that attention made his blood pressure shoot up like a star cluster. All those many times, he thought, the bastard got the best of me while they served together in Shanghai, China.

Sure, in their past, he had gotten drunk on some occasions, and in fact, he even disobeyed a few petty orders, but he didn't deserve what the bastard did to him. Gunny Mac had him reduced in rank from staff sergeant to sergeant. He rolled his hands into fists as he remembered that day. Then there was the time in 1934 that he began dating a navy nurse, scarce as hen's teeth, the only female round-eye that could be found in China. Mac had zeroed in on her like he was at the rifle range. Mac made sure he had some sort of duty on her days off, so that he could date her himself.

He still turned into a raging bull every time he saw the picture of the title fight in '37' against Gunny Mac. But remembering the title fight for the Seventh Fleet heavyweight championship in 1936 brought a smile to his face. He had beaten the hell out of Gunny Mac. The fight went ten rounds at Camp Baylor, and in fact, both men beat each other bloody and senseless, but he landed the final punch that staggered Gunny Mac for the fleet championship! He carried the framed photo of Mac crumbling onto the canvas wherever the Corp sent him. It was the first thing that he unpacked and put on his dresser.

But he grimaced when he remembered defending his crown the next year. The entire navy was talking about the title fight. He faced a leaner, meaner and more determined Gunny Mac. Mac attacked Wojohowitz like he hadn't eaten in a week, and he was a sixteen-ounce sirloin steak. Mac pounded him in the ribs and shoulders for the first three rounds like he was a punching bag. After the fourth round, he saw all the bruises starting to form under the bright red blotches on his skin and knew he was in trouble. He worked like a surgeon on Gunny Mac's face starting in the fifth round, opening one cut over and another under his eye, blood and sweat flying over the boxing ring as he pounded away at Mac's face, which started to look like raw meat. In the sixth round, he hit Mac so hard his mouthpiece went flying into the crowd. But the seventh round started badly for Wojo. Mac slipped in a haymaker underneath his arms and cracked his rib. He still remembered Mac's bloody face as he bore in and continued to work the ribs. In the ninth round both blasted each other. One of Mac's eyes was completely closed and the other looked like a tank slit. Wojo had a cut over his right eye and one over the left cheekbone caused by a tremendous punch that had driven him into the ropes.

At the start of the tenth round, both dazed fighters stumbled toward each other. Thousands of sailors and Marines stood and cheered them on! They touched gloves and clenched onto each other, both hanging on for dear life. Gunny Mac pushed him away from the clinch and as he was falling backward, he reached out and managed to connect with Wojo's broken rib causing him to bend at the waist because of the incredible pain. Mac saw his chance and staggered forward quickly and connected with a combination to Wojo's head that sent him flying to the canvas. He was still on the canvas and out when the bell rang. When Mac was declared the winner, both met in the center of the ring. He remembered what Mac said to him. Mac smiled at him through a broken mouth and asked him how in the hell had he managed to make staff sergeant again?

Wojo had worked hard to run his rank back up to gunnery sergeant. His new orders sent him to the U.S.S Arizona, as part of the Marine Corps detachment. The U.S.S Arizona was stationed at Pearl Harbor, Hawaii. His mind wandered back to that wonderful warm evening when, after putting in a hard day drilling the Marines aboard the battleship, he went out on the town to celebrate the date of his knockout punch of Gunnery Sergeant Mac. He relished this day even more than celebrating his birthday. In fact, this day was like Christmas, Easter, and the Marine Corps' birthday all rolled into one. After having many drinks and visiting all the bars around Pearl Harbor but one, he dashed off to that last bar where he had one drink, and then pounded the bar with a shot glass and yelled out, "Survey, survey, can't a Marine get a drink?" In the Marine Corps lexicon survey meant, "I'm finished with this drink; get me another one quick!" The Sunset Beach Bar and Grill was packed shoulder to shoulder with Marines at the bar. He bumped into the Marine next to him and both men wheeled around to face each other. It was on this particular day that Gunnery Sergeant Mac had reported aboard U.S.S Arizona as the NCOIC of the Marine Corps detachment on the U.S.S Arizona. No one knows who threw the first punch, but the Marines around the two men stated that each contacted the other's jaw at the same time, and both dropped onto the sawdust floor in spectacular fashion.

On the morning of December 7, 1941, both men were in a naval brig in Pearl Harbor, sleeping off the worst hangover each had ever experienced. They woke up when the explosions and anti-aircraft fire disturbed the peaceful Sunday morning. Later on, both ended up on a transport ship to a place called Guadalcanal.

He would never forget how Gunny Mac had kept him on the right flank, where the least of the action was anticipated. When he told Mac, he needed to be with him, Mac just smiled and told him that the boys needed his leadership on the right flank. But he knew why. He could see it in Mac's eyes… Wojo couldn't wait 'til he got to see his best friend in the whole world.

Chapter 19

Royal Hawaiian Hotel

The evening held one surprise after another. Lt. Van Deer had surprised Mac by wearing the dress that he had Caroline make for her. Good ole Caroline came through. The dress accentuated Van Deer's feminine figure, in a subtle way, telling everyone that she made the dress. The second surprise occurred when he picked her up at the BOQ. She had grabbed his hand and kissed him on the cheek. The third surprise was how tired she looked. He hadn't seen her since he visited Ward D. Weeks and weeks of fatigue were etched across her face like a Marine on Guadalcanal. Her eyes were not dancing with their usual mirth and the color of her green eyes lacked their usual clarity and sparkle. But if fatigue had a color, her eyes would be that color.

"I hope you don't mind that I made our dinner reservation at the Royal Hawaiian. This hotel gives me a sense of peace. It's a beautiful place in a very ugly world right now," she said.

Mac said, "I keep forgetting, lieutenant, that you see the war close up and personal. Every single day."

She took his hand in hers. "My name is Kathleen, Mac."

He frowned. "It's sad. You saved my life. Gave me my buddy, Seadog, and I didn't even know your first name." He leaned into her. "I'm sorry."

"Don't be sorry, Mac. It's not your fault. Not after what you have been through. It's hard right now to think of anything but our duty. But not tonight, Mac. Let's forget about everything and enjoy this night like two human beings."

After a quiet but talkative dinner, they took a walk along the beach. She said she was not interested in dancing. After saying that, she smiled and said. "Just a couple of drinks, a slow walk in the sand with you. That's all I want."

Thirty-seven days straight days working in Ward D was too much for any human being to withstand. She was ordered to stand down and rest. The doctor who saved Mac's life gave him a call. He suggested he call Lieutenant Van Deer and ask her out on a date. Mac's silence on the other end of the telephone told the doctor exactly what was going on in Mac's thought process.

"She likes you, Mac. She asks about you all the time. You both need each other. You're exactly the prescription she needs!" When he had called, she immediately said, "What time, Mac?

She held his hand as they walked along the beach while avoiding the strung-out barbed wire stretching the length of the beach, put there in case the Japs invaded Oahu.

He couldn't remember the last time he had a date with a woman of her caliber. Just holding her hand made him feel clean and new again. The same emotion that he got when he went to confession. He hoped that she felt the same way. She pulled back on Mac's hand, stopped, and stared out to sea. She put her head on his shoulder. He put his arm around her.

They didn't speak. Nothing had to be said. The sunset across the water was splashing the clouds with fiery orange.

She turned to Mac and said, "I'll buy you a nightcap at the Royal Hawaiian. If I remember, bourbon is both our drinks."

"My type of girl," Mac said.

The last time that he talked so much was when he was eight years old.

At the bar he learned that she grew up on an Iowa farm raising cattle with two brothers and a sister. Her older brother, Floyd, enlisted in the Marines in 1940 and was sent to Wake Island where he was killed. Every time a wounded Marine came into her ward, she thought of Floyd, and her heart was torn open again.

In early 1942, she was a nurse at the hospital in her hometown. After Floyd was killed, she joined the battle along with her brother. Her other brother was at Parris Island at this very moment. Mac found out that she was a Catholic and she laughed at Mac's stories about being raised by Father Gibbons, a Catholic Cleveland Diocesan Priest, and a bevy of Catholic nuns who fretted over him like clucking hens.

"You know, Kathleen, when you suggested I get my PI license, I thought you were crazy! I miss the Marine Corps. I read in the newspapers about my Marines hitting a new beach and my insides curl up. This new life at least keeps me in the game. Keeps me from feeling sorry for myself. Keeps me busy."

She stopped walking for a second and faced him. "This war has taken so much from us. None of us will ever be the same. All we can do is try not to let the war steal our hearts or souls." She put her arm around his and they continued to walk the beach.

"The whole ward is happy that you are now a Private Investigator. You have shown all the Marines that a strong person can get on with their life, start over and achieve. Believe me; they need you as much as you need them. And I need you."

She kissed him lightly on the lips and he kissed her back trying to hold on to her kiss just a bit longer. He touched her hair and gently ran his hand down her cheek. She rewarded him with a sparkle that flashed in her eyes. She pushed him away, but the look in her eyes told Mac all he needed to understand.

As he dropped her off at the BOQ, she put her arms around Mac's neck.

"I also want to thank you for this beautiful dress. I will treasure it, Gunny Mac, and the beautiful note you sent with it."

Mac didn't remember writing a note. "I have to tell you that I was practically ordered to take you out by your boss."

She put her finger to his lips to silence him.

"I have something to confess to you. I was ordered to go out with you. But I wanted to go out with you. We just needed a push."

Mac kissed her and whispered in her ear. "I'm going to buy our doctor friend the best bottle of bourbon on the market." He said goodnight and quickly walked away.

He couldn't believe it was midnight. As he approached his office door, that third sense that combat experience gave you, a third sense that often had saved his life, kicked in strong. He pulled his .45 out of his shoulder holster and opened the door and entered the office. Seadog didn't rush him like usual, sliding on his belly to roll over at his feet. He tensed as he turned on the light. Tony Coniglio, alias the Schnoz, was sleeping with Seadog on the couch. Next to the couch on the floor was an empty bottle of bourbon. Seadog yawned and smiled at Mac. A toothy smile that told Mac that he had been recently replaced as a companion. Mac surmised that Tony must have been kicked out of his stall by something more important, like a stallion. Seadog came over to him and nuzzled him. He rubbed his face and hugged him. He smelled Tony's aftershave all over Seadog's head.

Mac sat behind his desk and thought of his evening with Kathleen. Every day she went into Ward D and witnessed the destruction of war on human bodies, bathing them, writing letters for them, and comforting them while they died. Tonight, when he looked into her eyes, the dark circles made him worry. Yet, she had that kindly smile and only thought of her patients. Where do we get such people? He buried his head in his hands and prayed as Father Gibbons had taught him as a young man. He reached into his drawer and pulled out a bottle of bourbon. He sipped on his drink and watched the second hand on his wristwatch move slowly around.

It took a bullet one second, one small tick, to travel vast distances and kill a man's millions of seconds of life. Seconds were like grains of sand, small yet so significant. They added up to make a man's life. How was he going to spend all those seconds he had left?

His thoughts turned back to Father Gibbons. He would write to him tomorrow and tell him about Wojo because he loved the big Polack.

He missed the man who raised him. Father Gibbons would introduce Mac to new parishioners as his son, and it often produced curious results. Mac's parents had left him in Father Gibbons' church with a note attached to his coat when he was four years old. They could not take care of a small child properly and they loved their son too much for him to suffer. His parents were returning to the old country. Father Gibbons talked to his bishop and told him about the young lad left in his church and he was told to take him to an orphanage. Father Gibbons said, "no." He added that he would resign as a priest if he were forced to do that. Father Gibbons was a Cleveland Diocesan priest and given special dispensation to adopt Mac. So, Father Gibbons raised him. Sister Rosalima and the other nuns looked out for him like they were his mothers

He slumped his shoulders and took a deep breath, his weariness consuming him. He sat quietly in the dark and his thoughts kept circling back to Kathleen Van Deer. Falling for a girl right now would cause him problems.

He knew if, given a chance, someone else would cause him problems. His .45 was on his desk, ready for Gentleman Jack to come shooting through his door. All he wanted was some peace, but he knew things would just get worse over time. Wojo dying would be the event that would send his world crashing around him and make him an outsider to this world forever.

The only reason he wasn't dead now was because killing a war hero orchestrated bad publicity. Mac shook his head, stretching his eyes to keep awake. He looked over at the sleeping form on the couch and thought war brought strange people together. He couldn't help it. He liked the funny little man. He slowly closed his eyes and went to sleep.

His dreams were fast and hard. Tonight, his dreams were in technicolor. Most times, he dreamed in black-and-white. When Mac was under great stress, his dreams were painted in vivid colors. This time he was back on the Canal, the jungle was he greenest he could ever remember! He screamed at the sight of Wojo lying in a pool of blood and his bloody arms were reaching for Mac. He moved his lips, but Mac couldn't hear. He moved closer and Wojo grabbed him and whispered in his ear. "I waited for you Mac. . . Japs were everywhere. . .what took you so long? . . Mac. . . I. . . ."

He woke up with Tony standing over him. Tony gingerly wiped Mac's face with a cold cloth.

"It's okay, boss; you're all right," he said.

Mac closed his eyes, trying to forget the very first thing that he saw was a big schnoz. He pushed Tony's hand out of his face and sat up, drenched in sweat.

"You had a bad, bad dream," he said.

Mac ran his tongue around the side of his mouth. His mouth felt like a thousand Marines had marched in his mouth, singing The Marine Corp hymn. Little drops of sweat gathered at Mac's temples and marched down past his ears. His face was one big question mark.

"What the hell are you doing here?" Mac asked. He brought his hand up and brushed the sweat away from his jaw. Mac stared at the Schnoz and said, "It's against the law."

Tony had a look on his face like Seadog when he stole some food off the table.

"I had no place to go, Mr. Mac."

"No, not that. You drank my whole bottle of bourbon."

His big round eyes looked at Mac.

"It was only half full!"

Mac picked up the empty bottle. "You drink like Wojo."

Mac walked over to his sink and splashed water on his face. He pulled out a clean t-shirt and put it on.

The Schnoz followed him to the sink.

"I got kicked out of my stall. Dandy Boy took it. I have nowhere else to go!" he said. He opened his wallet and showed Mac it was empty. "Anyway, I can earn my keep until I get back on my feet. I could clean your office. I could act like your receptionist. I could hunt down people for you. I know a lot of people in this town, some good, and some bad. I could keep you out of trouble!"

The little man sat on the couch next to Seadog and waited for Mac's response.

"If I let you stay for a while, buy your own bourbon!" He looked at Tony and Seadog and wondered which one was better looking. He couldn't decide whose schnoz was bigger.

"Well," said Mac. "I have to ask my partner."

Seadog jumped on Tony's lap and gave him a big lick. He then ran to Mac and put his head on his lap. Mac grunted in disgust.

"Looks like my partner agreed to let you stay."

Mac scratched Seadog's head and looked at the Schnoz.

"How did you get in here?"

Tony's head bobbed up and down. His Adam's apple was going up and down like an old elevator. He pulled out a small case.

"With these," he said, unzipping the case.

Mac looked at Tony and his fine set of lock picks.

"You good with those?" Mac asked.

He smiled. It was the first time Mac saw his teeth.

"I got in here, didn't I?"

Mac walked over to Tony and gave him his hand. He shook it.

"I have your first assignment. Find out all you can about a guy named Gentleman Jack."

Tony got up, straightened up his tie.

"I always have known about this guy. Always hung around the racetrack. He's dangerous people. He looks good, smells good, but is rotten to the core. He'd knock off his own mother. But I got my own contacts. I'll need some money. People don't talk for free."

Mac nodded at him and handed him fifty bucks.

"What should I be looking for? I got no detective training."

Mac began to think this was a bad idea. The little guy needed help and so did he. "Nothing seems to happen in this town without his involvement. I know he will be coming to visit me. In fact, I think he doesn't like me. I might not be exactly right all the time, but I'm never wrong. I need to know where he works, what he does, how many people work for him, and who his friends are. Watch your friend Rose and let me know who is following her and when. You need to talk to her. If you phone her, remember someone may be listening over the switchboard. I need this information ASAP! Write down all your expenses and give them to me, including meals. You can live here until you can make it on your own without living in a stall...."

Mac walked to his desk and took Tony's money and gave it back to him.

"The money you gave me to help Rose is yours."

"I'll make us some coffee," Tony said. He turned to Mac and said, "Thanks for helping me, boss; I feel like a member of the family!"

Mac sat down on the couch and rubbed Seadog's head and said.

"Quit calling me boss," said Mac.

Tony smiled at him. "Ok, boss."

Mac was getting that feeling again, and when he got that feeling, something bad would happen. But right now, he was going to drink a cup of coffee with Tony and Seadog, take a shower and get ready for whatever misfortune came his way

* * *

Gunny Wojohowitz fingered the wristwatch between his forefinger and thumb. When they shipped his personal effects, somehow, by a stroke of luck, he still had the wristwatch. He always knew it was both his salvation and his ticket to hell. The inscription written on the back of the dial. "To Jack Calamari graduating class of George Washington High School," was still readable. He fastened the watch onto his wrist for safekeeping. It was a constant reminder of what happened to his men. Someday he would find him, and then he would die.

Chapter 20

Bombay Alley, Mac's office

Mac placed his .45 in his shoulder holster, put his jacket on, and started for the door. His newest assignment for the day, given to him by the base Chaplain, was to find a teenage girl who had been missing for four days. The war was not yet a year old, and young people were falling in love every day. Most probably, the young girl fell in love with a sailor or Marine and, at the moment, was sharing nuptial bliss as a young lovely war bride. His first step was to check with the marriage bureau and see what marriage licenses were issued in the last two weeks. Then he would go to the base chaplain's office and see if she turned up. That would eat up most of his early morning.

He almost made it out of his office when three men approached him from the front. One was holding a pistol. Mac first looked at the pistol staring at him and then looked at the three mugs in front of him. One of them was Big Gums who would not look at him and stared down at the floor. The older fellow holding the pistol was a nobody. The taller, heavier-set man standing to his right was somebody to be reckoned with, his face scarred below and above his eyes. His nose was flattened, most of the cartilage gone. The look of a prizefighter who took home a few prizes in his day. His eyes were so cold it sent shivers down Mac's back. The big man jerked his head to the right, indicating that Gunny Mac should go back to the office.

"Keep your hands in front of you, shamus, and no sudden moves."

Gunny Mac raised his hands, turned around, and walked back into his office. He turned around, saying nothing. He just watched. The prizefighter talked first.

"You the shamus with your name on the front door? Your name Mac?"

Gunny Mac nodded his head up and down. The prizefighter walked closer to Mac.

"The cat got your tongue. When I ask a man a question, I expect him to look me in the eye and say yes or no. Answer the damn question!"

Gunny Mac had a feeling this would be a very bad morning indeed.

"Yeah, I am the shamus."

"You like taking pictures of people? Like taking pictures of people minding their own business. Where's your camera?"

Mac looked at the prizefighter and didn't say a word. The big man's hands moved like a cat. Before Mac could react, he was struck in the stomach, once, twice, then the face. He went down to his knees, holding his stomach. Pain engulfed him. Blood came dribbling down his mouth. He knew he was in trouble. The thought ran through his mind what his sergeant major once said, "pain is good; extreme pain is extremely good." It made him half-smile as he watched his blood drip on the floor. Something opened up in his gut.

He heard his bedroom door bang open and Seadog came flying out growling with teeth bared. His pup, all thirty-seven pounds, launched himself at Big Gums and knocked him down. The one with the pistol aimed it at Seadog while he was chewing on Big Gums. Seadog was in trouble. While still in the kneeling position, Mac drew his .45 and fired at the nobody with the pistol. The .45 caliber slug slammed him backward. He slid down the wall leaving a trail of blood like an abstract painting before crumpling in the corner.

Mac pulled himself into a sitting position, his back up against his desk, and pointed the pistol at the prizefighter. He yelled at Seadog to stop. Seadog trotted over and sat down next to him at the desk. Big Gums got up, holding onto a bloody arm, slowly backed out the door and was gone. Big Gums was smarter than he looked. Mac indicated with his pistol for the prizefighter to sit down on the ground.

"On the floor!" Mac commanded. He wiped the blood off his face with a handkerchief.

"Sit on the floor now, or I'll shoot you in the balls. I like people to be able to look me in the eye," he said. "I am going to ask you just once, as I don't have a lot of time. Who sent you?"

The prizefighter just smiled.

Mac struggled to stand up. Seadog growled, advancing on the big man.

"You better tell that damn dog of yours to leave me alone or I'll kill him."

Mac started to feel the numbness that combat brings. When the heart doesn't ask permission to leave your body, it just does and gives permission to do what you have to do to survive, to kill people who need killing. He struggled to get up while Seadog stood guard.

Walking over to the tough guy, he slammed the pistol across the man's temple, opening a gash and dropping him onto his back; then walking around him, Mac kicked the man square in the head. Two more swift kicks in the ribs and the man was groaning in pain.

He ripped open the man's pocket and his wallet fell out. "So, fuck face, your name is Sam, is it? I'll beat you to death if I have to. You'll end up like your friend in the corner. Except, yours will hurt just a little more. Now I'm giving you a little more leeway than normal, tough guy. I will ask you one more time who sent you?"

Silence except for some groaning.

Gunny Mac slammed the butt of the pistol on the big guy's kneecap and the sound of it cracking reverberated through the room. The man let out a muffled scream. Mac wiped at more blood flowing out of his mouth and down his neck. The big guy just looked up at Mac, his hand rubbing his cracked kneecap. Mac was still feeling the effects of the big guy's punches, and he figured that he had little time left before he passed out. He was busted up bad inside. He was getting dizzier and more nauseous. If he passed out, the son of a bitch would kill him and Seadog. He kept his eyes affixed on the bastard as he backed up to his desk and grabbed his letter opener. He drove it through the tough guy's thigh. He looked up at Mac with disbelief in his eyes and from his throat came a guttural sound. . . a choking sound, not exactly a scream. His face turned bright red and blood ran from his mouth, where he had bit through his lip. Mac withdrew the letter opener and wiped it off on the guy's shirt. He looked into Sam's face.

"I didn't start this, but I'm going to end it. You won't talk to me, I guess now I'm going to have to kill you."

He cocked back the hammer and pointed the .45 at his heart.

"Gentleman Jack sent me. Don't hit me no more!"

With his last bit of strength, he kicked the prizefighter in the head and the man went unconscious.

Mac fell down and dragged himself back to the front of his desk. He grabbed the phone cord and pulled the phone off his desk. He dialed Kathleen's number at the naval hospital. He told her he was hemorrhaging badly and to bring some MP's with her. He leaned back against the front of his desk, watching the unconscious form. Seadog licked the blood off his face and whimpered. He put his arm around Seadog and gave him a hug. He didn't know how long he could stay conscious, but the son of a bitch in front of him would never lay a hand on Seadog. He pulled back the hammer on his .45 to shoot the unconscious figure in the head, but a paw touched his arm as if to say no. The dark brown eyes stared into Mac's and a message passed between them.

"Ok, buddy, just keep me awake 'til help comes."

Seadog kept licking him so hard he figured his eyebrows would be licked off.

He heard the ambulance and people rushing up the stairs.

Mac watched his Kathleen, as she gave orders to the ambulance crew to start a transfusion. She loosened Mac's tie and wiped the blood off his lips, and her teardrops splashed on Mac's face. Mac was already in a faraway place, searching for Gentleman Jack.

* * *

After three days in the hospital, Mac felt better than he looked. He had been under the constant supervision of Kathleen, Jonesy and all the rest of the Marines in Ward D. One more day being showered with all that attention and he would've gone stark raving mad. The doctor told him his deep bayonet wound was still trying to form scar tissue and because it was internal would take more time to heal. He was ordered to drink a lot of the thick white liquid that they gave him as many times as he needed a day. It tasted like liquid chalk. It was the first thing he threw away as he walked to his car. He looked up from the trash can and saw Punta Point. His heart quickened at the sight of the navy destroyer, slowly making headway out to sea. He could see the sailors walking the decks and the lookouts in their positions watching out for Nip activity. He felt homesick, yearning to be part of a group of guys proudly doing their jobs. Now his job was to visit a piece of civilian shit and teach him a lesson he would never forget. All he had to do was sneak into the bastard's office and somehow spend some alone time with him. That was going to be worth the price of admission to a Charlie Chan movie ticket.

He smacked his lips at the thought of a drink of bourbon. As he approached his car, he let out a half-smile. Seadog was hanging out of the window giving him one of those smiles that made Mac blush. In the driver's seat was the Schnoz. Mac opened the door and sat down as Seadog jumped on his lap and licked him until Mac was giggling like an eight-year-old girl.

"Welcome home, Mac. We missed you!"

Mac looked at the Schnoz and smiled. This was the first time Mac left and someone missed him. He felt humbled at his reception.

Tony spoke up. "I got some of that information you needed. Gentleman Jack owns a bar called the Black Orchid. He has owned it for thirty-one days. His office is in the back and to the right of the bar. Two goons watch it at all times. His frequent guests at his bar and gambling tables are a guy named Joe DeVito and a Chinese cop called Captain Chin. His bodyguards are scattered throughout his bar. I found out that my friend, the young Rose was hired by Gentleman Jack seven days ago. Does that help, boss?"

Mac looked at Tony with a curious look on his face.

"Didn't know you had a driver's license, Schnoz," said Mac.

"I don't have a license, and I don't know how to drive. We barely made it here without killing ourselves, but I'm getting better now."

Mac turned to face the Schnoz, trying to understand exactly what the hell he had just told him when he took off like a Marine who had a bad case of Montezuma's revenge.

* * *

Gentleman Jack sipped on a Nun's Island Distillery Pure Pot whiskey and thought of poor Sam. The toughest bastard he ever met except for himself. Now, most likely crippled for the rest of his life. If it weren't for Sam's ruthlessness, he would not be in the position he was enjoying presently. They had come a long way together. Sam followed him from California, bringing DeVito with him. In just a few short months, he formed a team capable of doing anything and everything. He took another sip, leaned back in his chair, and smiled. It was DeVito that ferreted out Chin and the fat Hawaiian. Chin's real worth was finding the greediest of men. With the help of Captain Chin, DeVito, and the fat Hawaiian, they blackmailed, beat, or killed the unlucky people who had what they wanted. Since his medical discharge he had made a fortune, and he wasn't about to take shit from anybody. Especially a fucking ex-fucking Marine. He hated Marines. They would be on his shit list forever.

This shamus Gunny Mac. . . the son of a bitch did not seem to fear him, which made the shamus very stupid. He seemed to thrive on his stupidity which made him more dangerous. He could kick himself for letting him get away with the first two events. He should have ripped off his arm. But he realized knocking off a Navy Cross winner during martial law might come back to bite him. Now that didn't matter; payday was coming fast and soon this piece of shit would die. Maybe Sam could not do the actual killing, but DeVito would kill anyone he wanted under any circumstance. Pouring himself another drink, he closed his eyes and mentally checked off his growing shit list.

Chapter 21

Oahu National Bank

Kincaid had the lead Treasury agent meet him at the Oahu National Bank so that they could get a grasp on the money exchange. They walked to the interior central vault with the bank president.

Kincaid had sent out an official notice after his meeting with Williams that froze major accounts of businesses and individual savings accounts. Checking accounts were being monitored and only certain amounts could be withdrawn for personal use until the new script was released.

The good news was that Williams' second in command brought in a planeload of the new script and the process of distributing it could begin as soon as needed. The first planeload consisted of one hundred million dollars with the word Hawaii printed across the back of the bills.

"How many Treasury agents did you bring with you?" asked Kincaid.

"Not very many, commander. Most agents joined the military. We recalled retired agents to fill spots. I brought twelve with me. Most are old enough to be my grandfather, but they are professional and will do their jobs."

Kincaid smiled. This was going to be easier than he thought. Hopefully, they were blind and deaf also. "How do you want to use them?" asked Kincaid.

"The admiral made it quite clear to me we were not to get in your way and allow you to run the show. That is okay with me. Concerning my men, I do have a suggestion. It would be to station them at the largest twelve banks so that they can monitor the distribution and collection of the money. Tomorrow, one of my men will be here at this bank vault to collect all monies from the bank. By this time, each bank is supposed to have given us a list of accounts with the amount owed to each depositor."

The bank president spoke up. He showed Kincaid a clipboard.

"If you look at this tally, commander, you will see the names of each depositor with the amount of their deposit. This last page has a total figure of $7,456,345. The Treasury agent will check that final figure against the vault money and sign for that amount of money that he actually counts. The bank deposit money will be verified and matched with the total money in the vault and put into bags with a wire seal."

The agent showed Kincaid the wire seal and how it would be time stamped.

"Each bag will be weighed, and a time-stamped lead seal wired to each bag. Once everything is verified, signed by my men and bank officials, we will dispense the Hawaiian script immediately. Then you can collect the money from the other banks and secure the money at the sugar cane factory and do what you need to do," he said.

Kincaid asked the president of the bank to leave.

"I don't want our time schedule compromised if there are amounts of money not agreeing with depositors and such," said Kincaid.

The Treasury agent agreed with him that a certain percentage of the money was going to be unaccounted for by his people.

"Let's get this damn thing over quickly," said Kincaid.

"We have been instructed to give some leeway, approximately 10% to 20% difference, between the depositors' amount and the bank amount. We are doing this quickly and under wartime conditions; mistakes will be made."

"Do the banks know this?" asked Kincaid.

The Treasury agent frowned and shrugged his head to indicate he didn't know.

"Let's say, commander, that certain people have been told, and they tell certain other people, and before you know it, the whole fucking world knows it. Ten to twenty million dollars is a figure hard to pass up. The attitude is that burning all that money is a sin and if you take some, it is not actually stealing anything, and that attitude is contagious. It won't be us stealing it, commander; we are too low on the totem pole, but it may be a way for Roosevelt's friends to make some change."

Kincaid looked at the Treasury agent with total disbelief. Stealing this money was going to be as easy as stealing candy from a six-year-old. What he had going for him was that everybody was going to be stealing from good ole sugar daddy Uncle Sam. He was no low guy on the totem pole. That's for sure.

Kincaid interrupted his personal elation.

"So tomorrow I will have a truck with three Marine shotgun guards delivered to each of the twelve banks on your list. They will assist in delivering the script with your Treasury agents to the banks. They will guard the money while it is unloaded and then proceed to guard the entrances and exits. Bank officials will unload the script and secure it in the vaults. The weighted bags of money to be burned will be loaded onto the trucks and driven to the sugar cane factory. They will be met by my guards and the money will be unloaded into our secure space. The Officer of the Day and a Treasury agent will sign for the bags. They will receive a receipt and I will give a copy to you. Your agents will stay at the bank that they are assigned for three days to allow any more money to be turned in and script to be deposited to the customer's accounts. You can pick up more bags from the Quonset hut and sign for them. I will need you to give me a figure of how much money has been deposited and the value of the script handed out at the end of this process. What is your estimation of how much money will be turned in to be burned?"

"We estimated that around 20 to 30 percent will be hidden by people. Another 10 to 20 percent unaccounted for. So, I guess on the high side between $140 million and $160 million. On the low side, $100 million and $120 million turned in."

"I guess people don't trust their government," Kincaid said.

"Especially in Hawaii. We really don't have any idea if most of these people are loyal to the US. Most are of Japanese and Chinese descent and the rest Hawaiian. And I can tell you we are not loved by these groups. They feel like we caused the war and again we are outsiders. If we get twenty-five percent, I would be surprised. Again, we will find out how patriotic they are when the final tally comes in."

Kincaid offered a cigarette to the agent.

"The object of this exercise is to get as much money burned quickly as possible in case the Japs attack us," said Kincaid.

The agent agreed. "Since we have delivered the new banknotes, the military can commence paying the troops on payday in the new script and the banks will have the script. So, employers will be paying all their employees with the new money; as soon, as you give us the word."

"Do it now," said Kincaid.

Kincaid shook hands with the lead Treasury agent and told him he would see him tomorrow morning and if there were problems to give him a call at his BOQ.

He shook a Camel cigarette out of his pack while thinking about what just had transpired. High-ranking government officials, military officers, and members of the civilian government would be expanding their hidden bank accounts. He thought how unfair it was; they got to steal the money without much chance of being caught and he had to steal the money with an excellent chance of getting caught! Truly unfair.

He was glad the Treasury agent also realized that Roosevelt really didn't care what happened to the money. He just wanted it away from the Japs in case they invaded. He smiled as he had confirmation that he would be stealing actual full bags of money. He also realized that he might have to change his plans on a dime if something or someone came onto the scene. He had what he considered a straight flush. He had a plan and what a plan it was!

Chapter 22

The Black Orchid bar

Mac knew all about tactics. He had lived them his whole life as a Marine. How many times had he taught his riflemen this simple concept? If ambushed, it is imperative to charge through the ambush zone to kill the enemy. No trying to outflank the ambush. High diddle -diddle, right up the middle, make a hole, make it big and kill every fucking thing in the ambush zone. The worst thing that you could do was to freeze with fear when walking into an ambush. A violent attack through the zone was the only way to escape. In a way, it was an element of surprise. Most thought an enemy would fall back, disorganized and could easily be finished off. Except for Marines, that's when they attacked, hit hard and drove through an enemy. That was his plan and he hoped it worked.

He walked into Gentleman Jack's bar and looked around. He spotted two men guarding a door in the back and to the right of the bar just like the Schnoz said. He nodded to the group of Marines at the bar. One of them yelled out and punched a guy at the bar; the other Marines started a bigger ruckus. The two men at the door walked to the edge of the bar area. He slipped behind the guards and walked through the back door and ran into the guard on the inside. He stuck his .45 into his face.

"Be really quiet or daddy will have to put you to sleep," he said.

The guard stared back at him. "You must be awful tired of living."

Mac looked at him with a disappointed look on his face as he reached in and took the .38 from him and used the pistol to slap him across his ear.

"I told you to be quiet, didn't I?" Mac pushed him toward the closed door leading to another room.

"Where does that door lead to wise guy?"

"For me to know and you find out," he said.

Mac reached around the front of the guy's pants and unbuckled his belt.

"You a pervert?"

Mac slapped him hard across the back of his head.

"Take off your belt and hand it to me." He handed his belt to Mac.

"Lie on the floor on your stomach, hands behind your back. That's a mighty long belt fat boy."

Mac tied his hands behind his back. He reached into his pocket, took out a small bottle of chloroform and put fat boy to sleep. He took out the Schnoz's lock pick tools and opened the door slowly and peeked in. Tony had taught him well. Sliding into the darkened room, he heard noises in a room off to his left. Moving closer to the door, he listened carefully. He smiled; it looked like he was going to find Jack with his pants down again. He opened the door, flipped on the light and started to laugh. Jack blinked in surprise as the lights came on.

"Every time I see you, Jack, you are enjoying yourself. You are always in a compromising position and smiling. Instead of Gentleman Jack, I'm going to call you Smiling Jack."

Jack reached for his gun. "I'm going to call you a coroner, you son of a bitch."

"No, Jack, don't do that, or I'm going to shoot off your tiny dick. Put your hands where I can see them."

He reached over and pocketed Jack's gun.

The woman spoke up. "Can I put my clothes on while you two boys finish your squabble. I'm getting chilly."

Mac looked at her and said, "Yes, it is quite evident," and smiled. "Stay right where you are while Jack and I discuss a few things."

He looked at Jack. "Put some clothes on; you are embarrassing mankind."

Jack reached down and put his pants on and sat on the edge of the bed.

"I'll give it to you; you got balls!"

"More than I can say for you ole boy," Mac wisecracked.

"Yeah, but later on, I'll still have mine."

He walked over to Gentleman Jack and told him to stand up. When he did, Mac hit him as hard as he could in the stomach, followed by and an uppercut to the face.

Jack groaned, splayed across the bed. He slowly sat up and shook his head. He wiped some blood off his face with his hand and asked Mac for something to staunch the blood trickling out of his nose. Mac looked at him and poked him with the barrel of his .45.

"Use your sheet."

Mac pulled up a chair and sat down across from Jack.

"You sent your boy to hurt me, Jack. He put me in the hospital for three whole days, you pecker head. I came close to dying, all because you wanted to send a message to me. A simple phone call would have been much better than a beating. But no, Jack, you had to make a tough guy statement. Now, you are forcing me to be a tough guy, and here I am."

He heard the girl shivering. Her nipples stood so far out he could hang a wet towel on them.

"Put your shirt on, sister, and the rest of your clothes, and sit back on the bed. Jack is getting excited."

He turned and stared at Jack.

"All I did, Jack, was take a photo. I would have sent you a framed copy if you just asked me."

Jack reached into his shirt pocket and grabbed a cigarette and lit it, frowning as the smoke curled into his eyes.

"Gumshoe, I know you don't want to brag, but how about the homo? You sprung him when he was in the process of paying me off. You pissed on me twice and as a businessman, I can't allow that to happen. Now you've come in here and bothered me again, at a most inopportune time. So, gumshoe, that is three times, you have interfered with me. Three strikes, you are out."

He blew a cloud of smoke in Mac's direction and smiled. "The odds of you getting out of here in one piece are nil to none, and you know what gumshoe? I could really like you. You and I are alike in so many ways."

Mac started to pull out a cigar. Jack stopped him.

"Go over to my desk and pick out a Cuban. If a man is going to smoke his last cigar, it might as well be a decent one."

Mac walked over to the desk and lifted the lid on the humidor. He reached in and grabbed a handful.

"Thanks, Jack. What do these cost, twenty-five cents apiece?"

"Please, gumshoe, don't insult me: try a buck apiece. They come from a place called Cuba. Ever hear of it?"

Mac walked back to the bed.

"If this is my last cigar, a man ought to accompany that with a good bourbon, Jack ole boy; what do you say?"

Gentleman Jack stood up. "Can I grab you a bottle?"

Mac smiled at him, "Hell, this is one fine cigar. Where is your bourbon?"

Gentleman Jack pointed to the cabinet across from his desk.

"Let me go to the cabinet and get it. You must be sore from the punch I gave you."

Jack's smile disappeared.

Mac opened the door and saw the .38 sitting on the shelf next to the bourbon.

"Well, well, I thought we were becoming good friends, Jack. I'm very disappointed in you. It seems like you can't trust anybody nowadays. Now, because you are a bad boy, I'm going to take this beautiful bottle of bourbon with me and all of your Cuban cigars."

"Gumshoe, you are going to die as soon as you leave this room. You must be smarter than that."

Mac looked at Gentleman Jack as one would look at a very small boy making ridiculous statements. "Jack, let me tell you something you might find fascinating. I was the valedictorian of my Catholic high school and taught by Jesuits. I was offered a full scholarship to Notre Dame. My father was a priest and my mother was a nun. And I'm going to walk out of here as Jesus walked on water."

Gentleman Jack looked up at Mac, shaking his head. "That's quite a story. Maybe you can walk on water, but on the other hand, you shouldn't make up so much shit, gumshoe."

Mac stared at him. "How much money you got on you, Jack?"

"You robbing me, gumshoe?"

"I want to make a bet. All the money in your billfold that I get out of here alive to cause you more trouble. So, let's see your billfold."

Jack took out his billfold and handed it to Mac.

"What do I win if you lose, gumshoe?"

Mac looked like he was joking. "Of course, you get my scalp, buddy."

Mac counted out the bills, $347.00. "You sure you want to bet all this money."

Jack looked at him and said, "I'd bet more, but that's all the money on me at the moment."

Mac pulled out a whistle. He gave two loud, short whistle blasts. The sounds coming through the door sounded like a buffalo stampede. Twelve Marines barreled through the door. Staff Sergeant Jay White Feather spoke up. "You okay, Mac?"

Mac smiled and gestured towards Gentleman Jack.

"I'm fine, but the gentleman on the bed is not so fine. He keeps losing bets."

Mac pulled out the money and gave it to Jay White Feather. "Give the $300 to Gunny Jones at the hospital. He will know what to do with it. This $47.00 is for you boys." Mac turned back to Jack.

"You keep on with your foolishness, and your health is going to definitely suffer. Just remember the ole saying in the Corps. A Marine can be your best friend or your worst enemy!" He turned and started to leave the room.

Jack stood up and looked at Mac and threw him a kiss and uttered, "Bacio Della Morte."

Chapter 23

The Black Orchid bar

Burke sat at the bar in the Black Orchid. He was a happy man. He had talked to his father, who had talked to his congressman, who had then talked to the Navy and Marine Corps, and Gunny Wojo was then transferred to a returning heavy cruiser that needed immediate repairs back at Pearl Harbor. The gunny would soon be having a beer with him.

In the meantime, he placated Admiral Johnson on a daily basis filling his head with the minutiae that made up his week and followed Kincaid around like a puppy dog. He followed him so closely that one bad fart would give him away. The commander was drunk most of the time and never noticed him. The past few nights Kincaid left the Quonset hut and skedaddled to the Black Orchid, where he played Blackjack and seemed to lose his ass. The chips in front of him disappeared as quickly as his bourbon. Just before he left each evening, he visited an office to the right of the bar and disappeared for a few minutes, then left the casino and went to the Officers' Club and drank until closing.

He found out that Gentleman Jack owned the Black Orchid and was respected by everyone. Not the kind of respect most people desired, but a respect for a that man could get you killed. From what he could gather without asking a lot of questions that might not endear himself to Jack, he surmised Jack and Kincaid were somewhat joined at the hip. He noticed, for example, when Kincaid left the Black Orchid, someone followed him until he was ensconced behind the BOQ bar and then made a phone call and left.

Yesterday, he followed the fat man he encountered at the BOQ visiting Kincaid. Now the greasy fat man was visiting the Black Orchid. Things were beginning to fall into place. Kincaid, DeVito and Gentleman Jack might be working together, and he had just about figured out why. He didn't particularly like the conniving admiral or the drunken con man, but if he could relate to anybody, it would be Kincaid. Just a few months back, he might have acted like him. He didn't know if Kincaid might be the guy being set up for the fall, wanted to steal the money, or was simply being black-mailed. Why would Gentleman Jack's boys follow Kincaid? The only way to find out was to talk with the commander and just maybe help him take advantage of the fat man and Gentleman Jack. That is if he was not planning to steal the money. Of course, it was all conjecture at this point because he didn't know exactly what was on Kincaid's booze-soaked mind. He decided to go back to his BOQ. He had some phone calls to make to his dad.

Chapter 24

Admirals office, Pearl Harbor

Lieutenant Burke finally got an audience with the admiral. The admiral had brunch with some friends that consumed most of the morning. Burke knew somehow; he had to convince the magisterial one to help him with a problem. The admiral said that he would give him ten minutes. Burke patiently explained that Kincaid spent a lot of time with two men, Joe DeVito and a man who people called Gentleman Jack, who, without question, was the leader. All of them probably were conspiring to steal the money.

He could tell from the admiral's facial expression that he thought Burke was the stupidest person in the whole world.

"Lieutenant Burke, once again, I must remind you that your job, and your only job, is to follow Kincaid. You follow him. You gather intelligence on him, and you fucking give me your detailed report on the son of a bitch. I don't give a rat's ass about somebody named Gentleman Jack or anybody else. Your goal to watch is Lieutenant Commander Kincaid, a naval officer who I believe is conspiring to steal money from the U.S. government. When he is arrested, I'm sure the investigators will follow up on any other people involved. We are not a police force, and you are not a police officer. Your job is intelligence."

"Sir, with all due respect. I believe this Gentleman Jack is helping Kincaid steal the money. It would help to know what type of people we are dealing with. The best and quietest way, Sir, is to send his fingerprints to the Fingerprint Factory in Washington, D.C."

"Lieutenant Burke, the Fingerprint Factory is processing 35,000 fingerprints per day, and the only prints now being checked are those identified as potential saboteurs and enlistees. My damn message list is filled with code warning me not to burden them down with mundane requests. It takes a person four fucking hours per set of prints to check, mount, and file. That is not counting the number of fucking hours searching by hand through the filing system to find someone!"

He noticed that Johnson's face was rapidly turning from red to almost purple. "Concentrate on Kincaid, Burke. He's the one we really want!"

He walked out of Johnson's office, feeling naive and stupid. He should've known that Johnson was only interested in one thing. Getting Kincaid behind bars, preferably with a sadistic Marine Corps guard beating him daily without rhyme or reason. He lit a cigarette and walked slowly to his car. His problems were piling up like dog shit, and in the present moment, seemingly unsolvable. He had to get Gentleman Jack's prints, then somehow wire them to the Fingerprint Factory, then have one person spend hours comparing and finding possible matches and for what? It all centered around an idea that kept him up late at night. A warning, a stupid warning more instinct than reason, an idea that he thought Jack was more important than just a normal hustler. If Jack were part of a larger organization, it would put them all in extreme danger. Fat DeVito dripped convict. There was more than even money that Kincaid was in mortal danger. On top of that, he had to follow Kincaid 27 hours out of 24; a man who seemed more interested in drinking and gambling than stealing money. He threw the butt on the ground and got into his car and headed to his BOQ to think. His loyalties were with men who fought and died in the stinking jungle on Guadalcanal. Certainly not with an obsessed, crazy admiral.

* * *

Burke waited in his BOQ for the phone call from his father. While waiting, he drank two gin and tonics and chewed his nails down to the quick. When the phone finally rang, the harshness of the ring made him jump. He grabbed it before it rang a second time. He smiled as he recognized the softness of his father's voice.

"Just want to tell you, son, how proud we are. The Navy Department released the news that you were awarded the Silver Star and Purple Heart. Why didn't you tell us?"

He was silent. His thoughts went back to seeing Gunny Wojo fighting for his life. Best, he thought, if he made up a little white lie.

"Didn't know myself, Dad. Look, I hate to keep asking you, but I need your help more than ever."

"How are you feeling? Are your wounds healing?"

"Tell Mom to quit worrying; I'm feeling great!" He told his father the whole story, minus the facts he couldn't tell him.

"Look son; Senator Patrick is still mad at me about getting your friend transferred out to Pearl. It cost him some political capital that he had been saving. You say this is of the most urgent business?"

"Yes. It must be done in the next few days. I will get you the fingerprints; then, I will need special dispensation to walk prints through the system."

"I can't promise you this will work, son. As soon as we're off the phone, I will contact our beloved senator and let him be a patriot in this troubled time. But I can't promise you he will do it."

"This is important, Dad. Find some way to make the bastard do it. Blackmail him if you have too!"

His father laughed. "He probably is being blackmailed by half the Congress. Anyway, why can't you get a general or admiral to ask for this? He would love to help out someone he could curry favors in the future."

"Just a lieutenant by the name of Burke."

His father said. "Our senator is no saint. In fact, he is a downright snake in the grass. I have one more card to play. If I'm lucky, I won't end up in jail. Remember, it might not work. How will you get his prints, son?"

Burke sipped on his gin and tonic. "If I have too, I'll knock out the son of a bitch and print him myself!"

He heard his Dad laugh on the other end.

"That's a real Burke for you, son. Get that son of a bitch's prints any way you can!"

"And dad, get the senator's help any way you can."

Burke said goodbye to his father, made another gin and tonic, turned off the lights, and turned his thoughts to fingerprints. He was worried about what would happen if his dad could not help him. He still was going ahead and getting the prints. Sometimes you just didn't have enough time to do things the right way.

Chapter 25

Pearl Harbor, BOQ

Kincaid thought about what had happened in the last few days. What initially were some thoughts about taking the money turned quickly into when and how he was going to take the money. Gentleman Jack basically told him to either work with him or end up as fish bait. Jack reminded him about his friend Rose, who was working for him, and it would be a shame if something happened to her.

He heard the knock on the door and opened it. Big Joe DeVito walked in and had to move sideways to get his belly through the door. Kincaid spoke first. "You Joe DeVito?"

He spoke with the cigar still in his mouth. "Yeah. . . I was told you had some news to give me about our little deal. Something about our chemistry."

DeVito gave a large, cigar-stained smile.

Kincaid walked around the room feeling deep in his gut that he should call the whole thing off. Maybe it wasn't too late to get the hell away from Gentleman Jack and his business associates. Looking at his guest, he dismissed the thought with some regret.

"Yeah, I got to thinking about some of my chemistry classes at Annapolis while staring in my Jack Daniels last night and I remembered something. A class about alcohol and money. And then I remembered something my chemistry professor showed us. He made a bet with us."

DeVito pulled out his Zippo lighter with a picture of a naked woman on the side and relit his cigar, smoke filling the small BOQ room.

"While you are giving me a science lecture, professor, how getting me a drink."

Kincaid went to his cabinet and pulled out a bottle of Jack Daniels.

DeVito grabbed the bottle and poured himself a drink. "Go on, professor, continue your science lecture to the unwashed."

"As I was saying, I remembered this lecture, and I realized that I could show you how we are going to burn the money, but not burn the money! Show you what we need to do at the sugarcane factory before throwing the money into the furnaces."

Kincaid opened his briefcase and withdrew a pad of paper and started to write a formula on the pad. $C2H2OH+4)2>2CO2+3H2O=energy$.

DeVito stared at the formula, scratching his head,

"Hope you can make it so I can understand it. I never finished the eighth grade. But I could buy and sell you; remember that, professor."

Kincaid did not smile. "It is very simple, really. We will have ten 50-gallon drums filled with a ratio of 50% alcohol and 50% water. Here, let me show you. Give me a $20 bill."

DeVito pulled out his wallet and turned away from Kincaid, shielding his money, and pulled out a one-dollar bill, blowing on it to ensure none stuck together.

"You don't need a twenty-dollar bill, professor."

Kincaid took the one-dollar bill and soaked it in a glass of half alcohol and half water. "Joe, do me a favor and pull out your Zippo lighter and burn this bill."

DeVito looked at him like he was crazy.

"I can smell the alcohol from here. You're crazy!"

Kincaid grabbed the bill from DeVito and said, "Come on, Joe, we have to trust each other, don't we?"

Joe flipped open his Zippo, and the bill erupted in a small flame. The Zippo's flame engulfed the dollar bill.

Kincaid continued his lecture. "In simple terms, a combustion reaction occurs between the alcohol and oxygen, producing heat and light (energy) and carbon dioxide and water. The bills are soaked in an alcohol-water solution, and the alcohol has a very high vapor pressure, and pressure is mainly on the outside of the material; a dollar bill is more like fabric than paper, which is nice if you ever launder your money."

Kincaid tried to smile. "The temperature at which the alcohol burns is not high enough to evaporate the water, which has a high specific heat, so the bill remains wet and isn't able to catch fire on its own. After the alcohol burns, the flames go out, leaving a slightly damp dollar. Feel this damp dollar bill?"

DeVito finished listening to the lecture with his mouth wide open, the cigar clenched in his stubby fingers while watching the bill's flame disappear while he touched the currency.

Kincaid said, "So you see how this is going to help us?"

Joe DeVito pulled his sloppy, wet cigar out of his heavily muscled jowls and smiled.

"I get it, commander? It's simple. But how is it going to help us? I got lost about ten sentences back."

Kincaid's mouth opened in exasperation.

"All we do, Joe, is soak some money in this solution and then pull them out of the furnace after ten minutes. I visited the furnaces at the sugarcane factory. The furnace has a huge thick front door, and when you open it, you can pull on a huge grate that rolls out. The grate also rolls out from the other side, which also has a door. There are spaces between the burners where ashes can fall onto a conveyor belt that carries the ashes to a storage tank. No one in front of the furnace can see the back of the furnace because of the wall. Let's say I'm stationed at the sugarcane factory, with the beautiful money at the front of the furnace. My men throw in some mailbags of money doused with this formula. Let's say ten or twenty bags filled with money. The money is verified and signed off after getting thrown in the furnace and the doors are closed. It gets hot as hell in the room. The Treasury agents get bored. The room fills up with alcohol fumes. Pungent alcohol fumes make the guard's and agent's eyes water and they need to get fresh air. The flames are licking higher and higher. After five or ten minutes, my confidants on the other side open the fire door on their side of the wall and pull out the bags that are still burning and throw them on metal dollies. When they stop burning, we throw them in the back of the deuce and halve and cover them with ashes from the burned money and leave. My guards will be stationed one-hundred yards in all directions ensuring there are no prying eyes. We take the truck filled with the money covered with ashes and unload the money and load up the ashes onto the garbage boat. We take the garbage boat out to sea to dump the ashes and take our money and bury it We wait until the war is over and we are rich men!"

"What you must remember, Joe is we will have competition stealing the money. Bank presidents, administrators, military officers, and God knows who else will be stealing as much money as possible. . .good, reputable citizens of our country before we even start to bag the money. There is no way to ensure all the money is accounted for. All the government is interested in is getting rid of the two hundred million dollars, so the Japs don't get it. The law-abiding citizen is going to make us all rich. The average schmuckatelli has no idea they are going to be fleeced. We might as well get our share. I will make sure those greedy bastards are able to line their pockets and will be more interested in getting away with money than watching me!"

Kincaid smiled as he realized DeVito was starting to get it! He could see that he was imagining people stuffing money in their pockets. One dollar for the furnace and ten dollars for him! Now the plan had to be implemented. He asked Big Joe DeVito what would happen if someone found out about their plan.

Joe smiled and said. "Let's say they'll be going up in smoke!"

He looked into the gangster's eyes and swore he could see two smoking gun barrels pointed at him....

Chapter 26

Chinatown Police Station

Mac stood on the corner of Bethel and Hotel Streets and looked at the three-story police building. Two massive front doors were on the corners of the building. One door on each side ensconced into a gigantic stone facade going up two stories. He felt like he was walking into a castle never to be heard of again. Maybe it was the turrets above the windows. As he approached the entrance, he saw the words Chinatown Police Station carved into the stone above each door. Looking further up, he saw bars covering the third story of windows flanking each street side. "Must be the jail that I soon will be in," he thought.

He walked into a large foyer; a cool draft coming from one of the hallways to his right. He walked up the police sergeant who was manning a large desk with a sign indicating he was the Desk Sergeant.

"I'm looking for Detective Chin," he said. All eyes turned toward him. Everyone stopped talking. He felt as if he had a social disease, and one of the men in the room gave it to him.

"I'm looking for Detective Chin," he said again.

The desk sergeant nodded toward one of the police officers. The surly-looking detective told Mac to follow him. They walked down a long hallway and three doors down. He stood before a door marked Homicide Bureau. He thanked the sergeant and walked into a quiet, dimly lit space with only two men sitting at desks. He walked over to one of them. The detective ignored him. Mac tried to be noticed by him.

"Shamus, go sit down on the bench and keep out of my way until I want to talk to you, and right now, I don't want to talk to you."

Mac walked over to the bench and stood staring at the detective.

The detective looked into a paper bag and pulled out a can of sardines, opened up the contents, and forked some sardines onto a cracker while continuing to ignore his invited guest.

Mac watched as Chin stuffed another overloaded sardine cracker into his pie hole and asked, "How can you eat that shit? You're stinking up the whole building."

Chin's eyes narrowed as he drank from his coffee cup. He stared at Mac but continued to ignore him. He got up and told Mac he had to go to the bathroom and make a good Marine. Twenty minutes later, he came back to his office, buckling his belt.

"Nothing like taking a good shit, war hero."

Mac took a big draw on his cigar and blew smoke at the detective.

"Nothing like cigar smoke to hide the stink of shit!" said Mac.

"That may be so, war hero, but your ass is knee-deep in shit. You got more trouble than Custer had with Sitting

Bull. You get my drift? You killed one man and brutally beat another man senseless. You can't be doing that in my precinct unless I allow you to do that and you didn't have my permission. I'm God over the thirty-six acres of Chinatown. You are a pissant!"

Mac leaned over the desk and smelled the garlic, sardines, and bad dental hygiene of Detective Chin and stared.

"I'd appreciate it if you would stop beating your gums. Tell me why I had to report down here. I defended myself against two hoods who wanted something from me, which happened to be my hide and all I got out of it was three days in the hospital. I gave you my statement and the government lawyers talked to you. So, arrest me, book me, or let me get the hell out of this sardine smelling pigsty!"

Captain Chin smiled, showing gold-encrusted molars.

"You're a dangerous man and I can see nothing but bad coming to you. I will piss on your grave, war hero before it is all over. If I were you, I would watch my back very carefully; you have many enemies and very few friends. Also, I would advise you to stop asking questions that will only lead to your demise. You'll come back with more blood on your hands and I will deal with you the way I deal with the scum on the wharves."

Chin smiled and stroked his goatee as he watched the expression on Mac's face.

"I'll take your advice seriously, Chin, and if I'm being harassed, you'll be the first person I come to see, but it won't be in your office!"

"Get out of here, you insolent dog, before I change my mind!"

Mac stood up. "What about my license and automatic?"

"Enjoy the odor of my urine on your license and .45; I hope it amuses you."

Captain Chin laughed and yelled for someone to retrieve Mac's possessions.

Mac put his urine-soaked license and .45 in a bag and walked out of police headquarters, making a mental note that Chin was going to pay for what he did. Pissing on his license was one thing. Pissing on his .45 was a mistake Chin would live to regret.

* * *

When Mac arrived at the Bombay Alley, he went into the bar, sat down, and asked for bourbon. He let out a groan when he saw the Schnoz enter and go behind the bar. Ever since Momma Leone put him in charge of the bar, he had become a little dictator, fussing and mussing over all his duties and responsibilities. Schnoz wanted to work behind the bar because he didn't want to be a waiter or bounce soldiers, sailors, and Marines the size of Mt. Mauna Loa. He told Mac, a broken nose his size would make Sitting Bull's nose like a pimple on a boot's ass! Mac roared with laughter and said that would be too cruel for the world to behold. So, he had not only become the bartender; he ran the place like he owned it. In a very short time, he had learned that the Schnoz was a very talented and smart man.

The Schnoz looked like Humphrey Bogart in one of his movies. Spiffy in a white coat and black bow tie. He came up to Mac frowning and tried to grab the bourbon he was drinking.

"You know you're not supposed to be drinking with your gut recuperating!" he said. Mac bellowed back. "Leave my damn drink alone, you soon-to-be ex-bartender. If I wanted to be henpecked, I'd get married!"

"I'm going to tell Kathleen you aren't cooperating," yelled the Schnoz.

Mac shooed the him away and stared into his glass, inhaling the sweet caramel aroma. He took a swig and promptly grimaced. It seemed he was on everyone's shit list—Gentleman Jack's, Chin's and now even Kathleen Van Deer's, thanks to him getting hit in the gut.

Mac took a large swallow and grimaced. He probably was the only person on Gentleman Jack's shit list because everyone else was dead. Every time Chin heard his name, he reached for his blackjack. Momma Leone was depressed, and somewhere out there, Wojo was fighting for his life. Maybe it was time to go home to Cleveland, Ohio, and Father Gibbons. He yelled out to the Schnoz for another drink. He was on edge. Tomorrow, he would find out if Wojo was alive.

He finished his second drink and walked back up to his office. He burped up a bit of his breakfast and the two hotdogs he had for lunch.

He went up to his office and plopped in his chair and stared at the picture of him beating Wojo in the title fight. Maybe at this moment, they were wrapping his body in a canvas weighted bag and sliding him into Davy Jones' locker. He had heard nothing from Gunny Jones. Tomorrow Kathleen would be getting the list of new casualties coming in. He would find it hard to sleep tonight.

Chapter 27

Pearl Harbor

Gunny Wojo looked at the calendar behind the pharmacist mate's desk and realized that four months and one day had passed, since he left with Mac traveling to the exotic port of call that was Guadalcanal. At least that's what the author of the tourist book called it. Six weeks after he was wounded his left shoulder still made cracking noises and was still stiff as hell. Part of his right lung was missing; but all in all, he considered himself lucky. He had lost thirty pounds, but he had gained some of that back. He was not the same bruiser as before, maybe more like a light heavyweight. He still had that herculean right fist, and his fingers could still pull the trigger on his .45, and that made him a very dangerous man. When he hit Pearl, the doc would most likely put him on a thirty-day convalescent leave. If he needed more time, he could ask for it. He fingered the watch and swore the same oath he said a thousand times before.

* * *

Lt. Burke watched Gunnery Sergeant Wojo walk down the gangplank from the cruiser that was docked and scheduled for repairs. He looked thinner, but ready for action, and it took all of Burke's discipline not to run over and welcome him home.

While watching Wojo, he massaged the puckered wound on his leg. The small indentation in his skull caused him some headache pain, but the leg wound made him limp like an eighty-year-old man. His days of flashing his tennis skills at the country club were over. In fact, his sojourn away from his privileged and monied life made him realize what a fool he had been. He wanted to live a different life. Watching the gunny walk down that gangplank made him just want to live a clean purposeful life.

It was easy to keep track of Gunny Wojo because with a last name like Burke, privileges opened up whenever he needed them. He wasn't afraid of using his wealth or family name to help his cause. It also helped that he was a member of the Intelligence community. Burke told his driver to follow Wojo's cab. He wanted to find out where Wojo was staying and to find out if he was searching for someone, and if he was, decided to join forces and help kill the son of bitch.

Chapter 28

Mac's office, Bombay Ally

Mac smelled her presence before he actually saw her. Since Guadalcanal, his ability to detect the slightest floral odors matched that of Seadog's. When the door opened, he almost fell out of his chair. A magnificent woman entered his office with her head tilted slightly downwards, a wide brimmed black hat low over her face, a veil covering her facial features. Her navy-blue suit clung to her body like paint on a car. Her perfect legs were braced with nylons accentuated with a black seam going up the back of each leg. Her high heels accentuated the long, lanky, tapered shape of her legs. Mac could only stare without manners or grace.

"May I sit down?" she asked.

Mac stood straight up and guided her to the chair in front of his desk. He kept trying to peer into her face, but she kept moving her head slightly away.

"I have a problem, Mr. Mac. A man I care about is in trouble. At the rate he is drinking and the way he looks, I don't think he will live much longer. I'm afraid something bad will happen to him."

Mac tried to look into veiled her eyes. "What is your relationship with this man?" He was hoping she would mention her uncle, brother, or sister. Mac kept trying to pierce the veil without luck. He kept thinking about vibrant floral red lips framed by soft creamy skin.

"He's my uncle," she said. Mac leaned back in his chair and smiled.

"I'm sure you realize, miss. . .please, excuse me; I'm sorry, I didn't hear your name?"

She looked away from Mac wiped a tear away with a handkerchief.

"I'm afraid if you see my face, Mr. Mac, you might find trouble heading your way. I wouldn't want cause trouble because of me."

"Wouldn't it be better if you lifted your veil and I could talk to you face to face? Any trouble your face causes me would be well worth the effort. And besides, I'm a grown man. I can handle myself. You let me worry about any problems you might give me!"

She lifted her veil and Mac saw the face of trouble. Sitting right in front of him was a Virginia Mayo look-alike. A face that had launched a thousand ships and put a couple of hundred dollars in his pocket. And maybe bought him a grave.

"What took you so long to contact me?"

"I didn't know if I could trust you, Mr. Mac, but Uncle Tony told me you're an guy and I could trust you."

"The Schnoz, excuse me, Tony, told me that your brother knew me on the canal; who is your brother?"

"Sergeant Billy Kincaid was my brother; he was wounded on Guadalcanal and died at the naval hospital three weeks ago. Did you ever meet him, Gunny Mac, personally, I mean?"

Gunny Mac lowered his eyes said, "No, I'm sorry. I never met him."

"Anyway, he said you were an okay guy; no Marine was better except maybe Johnny Basilone."

"Nobody is better than Manila John. . . I mean nobody." said Mac. Thinking of Manila John made Mac want to weep. None of them would have survived Bloody Ridge if it wasn't for him. While in the hospital he had heard John had earned the Medal of Honor. He should have gotten two for what he did that last night.

"Are you ok, Mr. Mac? You look so sad.... "

"I'm fine; just thinking of a friend, that's all." Mac tried to soften the look on his face.

"Are you sure your uncle is in trouble?" he asked.

She lifted up her head and looked at Mac. "He's a navy officer stationed at Pearl Harbor, and he is indebted to someone I work for, and it is a large sum of money. I work for Gentleman Jack, who owns the Black Orchid."

Mac was getting so tired of hearing about this guy. Every time he turned around good ole Jack was standing in his way. "May I ask what you do for Jack?"

"I'm his bookkeeper, Mr. Mac. I handle Mr. Jack's filing, correspondence, answer the telephone, and some office accounting."

"How did you find out about your uncle's gambling debts?"

"His file was sitting on Jack's desk. I saw my uncle's name on it, so I opened it and read the staggering amount he owed Jack."

Mac was sure the file was put there for her to see it, but why?

"I believe Miss Kincaid; your uncle is safe for the moment. Jack has an investment to protect. Now, if he feels he is not going to get paid back, that's another story. We have been talking about your uncle; what about you? Tony told me you are being followed by someone; is that correct?"

"The past seven days." She looked down at the floor as if trying to remember something. "Sometimes one or two people have been following me, at least I think so."

"Have you seen these people hanging around where you live?" asked Mac.

She nodded her head up and down. "Yes, I have, but only on the weekends."

"When did you start working for Gentleman Jack?" asked Mac.

"About two weeks ago."

Mac got up and walked around the room and stared outside his window. He didn't want to scare Rose and tell her what he was thinking. Maybe, just maybe, she was an insurance policy ensuring that her uncle paid Jack off.

"What can you do to help us, Mr. Mac?"

"Call me Gunny Mac, Rose. Can't stand that word Mr."

She smiled. "Yes. Gunny Mac fits you much better."

"We will find out who is tailing you, how many, what their schedule is, and then we will decide on how to handle it. Do you feel scared by these men?'

"No, I see them at the Black Orchid all the time. One is short, and the other has tiny teeth."

Mac started to laugh. "Short shit and Big Gums!"

"Do you know them, gunny?"

"Unfortunately, we have met, and I'm sure we will meet again."

How much will this cost me, Gunny Mac?'

"Tony paid me to watch over you if you needed my help."

She handed Mac a card.

"My full name is Rose Kincaid and my information is on that card. Can I expect some news from you in a few days? I worry about my uncle and I worry about people following me."

"I'll call you in the next couple of days; don't come here because you're being followed…."

She slipped her veil down and walked out of Mac's office. For some reason, Mac thought he was being set up by Jack and that didn't make him feel good at all.

Chapter 29

Chinatown

Wojo had made some headway in the last three days. He knew which army unit had been on their flanks during the fight for Bloody Ridge before being wounded. Now he had to find some members of that unit. The original unit had been stationed at Schofield barracks before heading to the Canal. Talking to some of the ladies, they told him that the Schofield barracks dogface's favorite bar was the Black Orchid. The only way he was going to settle this was to find the guy who shot him. He inserted a clip in his .45 and put it in his waistband. His loose-fitting Hawaiian shirt concealed the weapon with ease. He walked down Pearl Street and watched the crowds of uniformed personnel standing in line to get into the bars. It was hard to believe that a war was happening at this very second. Men were dying alone and afraid in the rotten, stinking jungle, and people in Chinatown acted like they had no cares in the world. His anger flared just enough to make him feel the need for a drink. He looked up at the bright neon sign blinking above him, The Sea Turtle Lounge and Bar. He lit a cigar and decided this bar was as good as any. He pushed his way into the bar. A drunken sailor told him to watch it, but that was before he could see the hulking Marine.

Inside the bar, the air smelled like, stale cigarette smoke, perfume, body odor, and stale beer. That made a Marine smile. He drank in silence, watching for any soldier with the Twenty-Fifth Infantry Division patch on his left shoulder. By his second drink, he spotted what he was looking for and he moved next to the soldier. He bought a bottle of whiskey and pushed it toward the soldier. The soldier nodded thanks.

Wojo said, "Nothing to it. I figured any man who was on the Canal should have a drink coming his way!"

The soldier looked up at Wojo with watery blue eyes. Without the slightest waver, he threw down the whiskey. He wiped his mouth with the side of his hand.

Wojo poured two more drinks. He looked at the soldier. "How long since you left the lovely Canal?" Wojo watched the reaction of the soldier.

"Not very long. I still have jungle rot and nothing I do makes it go away. Even rubbed gasoline on it! Got it really bad in my bunghole. He laughed. I was afraid if I farted, I'd set myself on fire. The girls don't like it when you start scratching your ass while sitting at the bar."

It was hard for Wojo to keep from laughing his ass off. Mostly, he remembered the itching between his toes. It was so damn bad he'd drop to the ground no matter where he was and rip off his shoes and scratch until it hurt too much to scratch anymore. The smell was enough to make anyone gag. It was a worse than Limburger cheese. Wojo poured his new friend a couple more drinks and suggested they go to the Black Orchid.

"Used to be," the soldier drawled, "here and the Black Orchid was the place to go. Now, some dumb fat Hawaiian gangster owns this bar and overcharges for everything. Easier to get rolled in his bar than get laid."

Wojo fingered the watch. "What unit were you with?" Wojo continued to stare into his drink.

"I was with the 2nd platoon, A Company, Second Battalion, 25th Infantry Division. We went in with eight hundred men in the battalion and came home with three hundred men. And with that said, I need another drink!"

Wojo grabbed the soldier's arm and pulled him off the seat.

"This place is dead, let's close it down and visit another bar and have some fun."

The Hubba Bubba was across the street. When he walked in, he knew why it was so popular. Women were standing around looking for anybody that resembled a male. Wojo noticed three or four women with only one man. As soon as he and the drunken soldier walked in, several ladies surrounded them. As soon as they found out he was a Marine, they left the table as fast as they could. Wojo started ordering drinks as quickly as the B-girl could serve him. Drinks started to come fast and furious.

He waited until he thought the soldier wouldn't remember his questions the next morning.

"Did you know anybody by the name of J. Calamari?" The soldier didn't respond. He grabbed the soldier by his arm.

"Did you hear me?"

The soldier's alcohol pickled eyes tried to focus on him. He smiled. "Of course, everybody knows who Jack is."

Wojo asked, "Is that what the J. stands for. . . Jack?"

The wasted soldier's head crashed onto the table. Wojo got up and left him at the table. Let the whores have him.

A girl got up from a nearby table and hurried through a bamboo door leading to where Koholo Kaimaika was sitting, eating his heart out. He stopped shoveling the pasta in his mouth and spoke.

"What is it, my beautiful Pua Aloalo?"

"A big tall Marine came in and asked interesting questions! He was looking for a soldier by the name of J. Calamari." After listening to what she had to say, he grunted with satisfaction.

The Marine had been asking questions for two days. He would find out why he was asking questions. This type of information Gentleman Jack paid good money to get. He looked at her.

"Make sure you take what you can from the soldier and have him thrown in the alley with the sewer rats."

The fat man got on the phone and told Gentleman Jack he needed to talk to him. He had some exciting information with a few embellishments.

* * *

Burke followed the gunny at a safe distance and smiled. He was hunting and asking questions and that was good. He lit a cigarette and followed him until he went into his hotel across the street from the Hubba Bubba. Lieutenant Burke turned around, went across the street, and went back through the bar and out the door leading to the alley. He found the soldier sprawled out next to the garbage cans.

He got him to his feet and took him to his car, throwing him in the back seat. He'd find out what Wojo was asking him one way or the other.

Burke took the soldier to a coffee shop not far from the bar. He shook the soldier awake and filled him with coffee. The soldier mentioned that the big mother showed him a watch with the name of one of his fellow soldiers on it, a J. Calamari who had been on the Canal with him, and that's all he knew. Burke let the soldier sleep it off on the beach. He went back to his car and drove to his BOQ to see what Kincaid was up to. Then Burke figured he'd drive back and see what the hell Gunny Wojo's next move was going to be. He was onto something. . . a showdown he was not going to miss!

* * *

When Gentleman Jack had first arrived in Chinatown, he had been told about some possible competition from a fat man by the name of Koholo Kaimaika. The war had brought more opportunities for money and corruption to the islands. Sailors wanted what all sailors wanted, women and whiskey. When they exhausted women and whiskey, they wanted a tattoo. What made Koholo so interesting to a man like Jack was his vast legion of lowly paid informants. He knew what was going on where it mattered the most. His thoughts were interrupted by knocking on his door.

"Come in, Koholo." Jack was always amazed by the sight of him. He weighed about three-hundred-fifty pounds with curly black hair straddled by a brown fedora. Today he wore a Hawaiian shirt tucked into the most exquisite linen trousers. Topping off this ensemble were highly shined spats on ridiculously small feet.

"What information do you have for me?"

Koholo looked at the chair off to the side of Jack's desk but decided it would be too tight a fit.

He stood next to Jack's desk. "This information I have is interesting. Worth at least fifty dollars."

Jack offered him a cigar from the box on his desk. Koholo grabbed several.

"I'll be the judge of that."

"It is very interesting information," said Koholo.

Koholo's money-grubbing heart knew when he had Jack in the palm of his hand.

Koholo leaned on Gentleman Jack's desk. "Light my cigar and hand over fifty bucks," he said.

Gentleman Jack looked at him with a disquieting half-smile.

He reached over and lit the fat man's cigar. He reached into his wallet and pulled out fifty bucks and waved it at him.

Koholo licked his lips. "Haven't I always given you good information, Jack?"

Sometimes the fat man didn't get all the facts straight. He liked to feel more important to Jack than he was. But he had to admit he had helped him more than once.

He took the money from Jack.

"The last two days a big Marine has been going around Chinatown asking soldiers about a certain person. The way he asked about this person intrigued me. The name was J. Calamari."

Koholo handed him the slip of paper with an address on it. He saw Jack's face and decided he better leave quickly.

"Nice doing business with you, Jack."

He turned away and walked out the door.

Jack's face hardened and darkened as if chiseled from obsidian. He looked down at the address the fat man had written down. The No-Tell Motel hotel was not far from the Black Orchid across the street from the Hubba Bubba. His big payday was coming up soon, and nobody was going to mess with that. This Marine had to talk and die tonight. His boys would take care of this immediately. He dialed the phone and made his call.

Chapter 30

Mama Leone sat down next to Mac at her breakfast table and beamed at him. "You know, Mac, I never had children, and if I had a son, I would want him to be like you."

Mac looked up from his plate after shoveling in a large piece of fried spam with a dressing of scrambled eggs. "Momma Leone, you are the mother I never had."

Momma Leone smiled a sad, lonely smile. "Thank you, Mac. Since you've rented from me, I have never been less lonely and happier." She looked down at the table and was silent.

"What's wrong, Momma Leone?"

He lifted her chin with his hand.

"I have a business proposition for you Mac, and I hope you will consider it. I need your help."

He poked the last of the eggs into his mouth. "Is that all your problem is? You know Mac is your man."

She smiled. "No, Mac, I'm leaving Hawaii for a while. Maybe forever. My sister is ill back in California and needs my help. I don't know how this will turn out."

She placed her hand on Mac's arm.

"This is where I need your help. I want you to run this place while I'm gone. We will share 50/50 on the profits. You can send my check to my sister's address by the first of each month. If I don't come back, I will give you the deed to this bar and you send me forty percent of the profit's till I die."

Mac was stunned.

"Momma Leone, I don't know anything about running a bar. I can hardly do my job as a shamus. I possess no business sense. I was a good Marine and now I'm a lousy civilian. I think you need to find a better guy than me."

Momma Leone patted Mac's hand.

"I've been aware that I would be leaving for a while. You know what must be done. No different than taking care of a platoon of Marines. A while back, you asked me why I put Tony in charge of the bar. I'm fond of that funny man. He knows more about this bar than I do. He protects it with his heart and soul. Most of all, he would never let anything happen to you. He loves you like a brother. I confided in Tony that I would be leaving. He loves this place as much as I do. He will help you. I need you to protect me and my financial interests."

Mac felt his heart grow heavy. He touched Momma Leone's hand and couldn't believe what he heard himself saying.

"I'll do my best to help you, Momma. I'll do my best to protect your interests and I'll miss the hell out of you."

"One more thing I must ask of you to do for me."

"Anything Momma."

"Keep Lieutenant Van Deer happy. She cares about you deeply. Make sure you don't let her go. You have no idea what she has done for you."

Mac felt like a backpack had just been strapped to his heart.

"Momma, I know exactly what you mean."

Within a week, Momma was gone.

Chapter 31

Naval hospital, Pearl Harbor

Gunny Jones gathered them together. Two Marines helped the gunny into a wheelchair and pushed him through the endless corridors, through the swinging hatches into the bright sunlight. Gunny Jones put on his sunglasses and smiled as a soft breeze swept over him and caressed his face.

"Pecker heads, it's good to be alive," he said as he watched a navy ship slowly pass Punta Point.

They wheeled Gunny Jones around and pushed him to the benches that lined the point. He told his Marines to grab a seat. The gunny's grey, clear eyes surveyed the Marines in front of him. His eyes settled on Sergeant Peterson, a 22-year-old from Boonsboro, Kentucky, a Silver Star winner with two Purple Hearts and the best pistol shot in the 1st Marine Division. But now, shooting left-handed was his only option because of shrapnel still working its way out of his right eye and head. Gunny's eyes switched to Corporal Reynolds from Tupelo, Mississippi, a young 20-year-old Marine with a set of shoulders that matched Lou Gehrig's. Prior to his wound, one of the best wrestlers Gunny Jones had ever seen. Now, he was trying to rehabilitate from his head wound. His eyes traveled to Sergeant Thompson from Arlington, Texas, who won a Silver Star for rescuing seven wounded Marines, but shrapnel from a mortar round caused a head and eye wound, resulting in a loss of patience and anger issues.

Next to Sergeant Thompson was Corporal Alan McGee from Johnson, Maine. When you pictured a lumberjack, Corporal McGee was what you imagined. At 6'4", he looked like a giant oak tree. After being shot seven times, one careening off his hard head, he charged a Japanese machine gun nest and killed all the Japs, and he too was awarded the Silver Star. Last, but not least, Lieutenant Peter McCaffery, padre of the First Marine Battalion, Navy Cross winner, Silver Star winner, and two Purple Hearts. Gunny Jones smiled at Padre McCaffery, remembering how fearless in combat the padre had been. Never complaining, always smiling, sometimes crying over the dead and wounded. The padre was shot in the head while defending his wounded Marines, killing four Japs in hand to hand combat. Now, the padre was quite different and quite funny. He was still a great pious priest, but his language filter had been erased for the time being because of his head wound. He would say the weirdest things while conversing with people. Gunny Jones had laughed when he heard that the padre went to a bar in Chinatown and had blurted out, "Look at the tit's on that broad!"

Gunny Jones said to them all, "Look, gents, you have all done your duty to the Country and Corp. Each of you gave the highest form of love for your country; your sacred blood. Right now, we have another battle going on here in Chinatown and a couple of Marines need your help. I think this battle could be dangerous to your improving health…."

Sergeant Peterson moved closer to Gunny Jones. "Hell, Jonesy, we are Marines, and most of us won't be landing on any more beaches with our buddies. We know that we are pretty useless to anyone and everyone. But remember, we are Marines, and we will always be Marines. One fucked up Marine is worth any three men. We can still fight! Especially for our fellow Marines."

"We were crazy to begin with when we joined this outfit anyway," laughed Sergeant Thompson.

"Okay, boys, take one step forward if you want to be part of McCaffery's raiders."

All the Marines took one step forward and then mobbed the padre.

Gunny Jones never loved the Corp more than at this moment. He couldn't think of a person more loved by the Guadalcanal Marines than Padre McCaffery. A man who showed them it was for a man to love his God. His favorite saying 'Praise the Lord and pass the ammunition,' became a rallying cry for many a Marine.

The padre had recruited all these Marines out of the psych unit where he was a patient. If these Marines were all right and passed muster by the padre, they were the right Marines to ensure Mac's safety.

Gunny Jones gave them a pep talk, outlined their mission, and told them that the padre would brief them on the particulars.

Chapter 32

Mac had visited Gunny Jones last night and been given the excellent news that Gunny Wojo had arrived aboard a cruiser coming into Pearl for repairs. Jones had talked to Wojo briefly and said that he looked thinner, but in good shape. Wojo gave Jones the address where he was staying and said he better get a visit from Mac. Now Mac was going to relax because tomorrow night was going to be quite a celebration. He whistled a few bars to Moonlight Serenade as he unlocked the door to his office. Limping into his bathroom, he reached up on the shelf and grabbed a pan. He walked over to the sink, put some Epsom salts in the it, and let the hot tap water dissolve the crystals. Rolling up his pant legs, he took off his shoes and socks and stuck both feet in the steaming water. A slow smile spread across his face. His feet throbbed as bad as coming off a 20-mile hike with full combat gear. Eight hours of detective work earned him a big, fat zero, just two aching dogs. Mac almost leaped out of his chair when he realized his Seadog was not around. He spotted the note hanging off his lamp. "Seadog visiting with the boys in Ward D, he'll be back late tonight," signed Tony.

Mac smiled when he realized he was going to be alone for the rest of the evening. He poured himself a drink, pulled out a cigar, and swished his feet around in the pan. All was right with the world. His aching feet were immersed in five inches of steaming water, making them feel like a million bucks.

That's when he showed up. He walked in with an air of superiority, his cane striking the floor hard with each stride. He was a large man well over six feet, with about 230 pounds on his frame, his eyes brimming with a devilish light. His eyes roved around the room, appraising his surroundings. He smiled down at Mac who had his pants rolled up with red feet like a lobster. He peered at Mac with the curiosity born of a man of great patience and understanding while staring at the cigar hanging from Mac's lips. He let out a laugh short of a roar. He spoke first. "Are you the son of a bitch that works here?"

Mac grabbed his cigar before it fell out of his mouth. The padre hit the pan of steaming water with his cane.

"Are you deaf? Are you the private detective, Gunny Mac?"

Mac was speechless. The three rows of ribbons on the huge chest caught Mac's immediate attention. First was a Navy Cross, followed by a Silver Star and two purple hearts. His eyes got even bigger when he noticed the crosses on the officers' lapel.

"Yes, padre, I'm Gunny Mac," he said.

The padre extended a large hand toward the gunny and Mac's hand disappeared in its meaty grip.

"Glad to meet you, gunny. After you're done with that pan fill'er up with hot water. My jungle rot is killing me. While you're associated with me, gunny, you may drink and smoke as long as I am invited to smoke and drink with you. But no fornication! You are not a fornicator, are you?" he asked.

For the second time in over 20 years Gunny Mac was speechless. Padre McCaffrey mumbled to himself as he walked into Mac's bedroom area.

"There is room for bunk beds. My chief will construct them and bring in mattresses, sheets, and pillowcases. There seems to be enough room to bring in twelve dressers and still have a storage area for footlockers."

He tapped the wall to his right with his cane. "Of course, we will remove this wall."

A confused Mac followed the padre through the rooms leaving wet footprints on the floor.

"There's been some sort of mistake, padre," Mac stammered.

Padre McCaffrey whirled around quickly, almost running into Mac.

"No mistake, Gunny Mac. It's all been arranged. Your big-nosed bastard friend arranged it all. I've been praying, and God has answered. I'll be back tomorrow. I'll soak my feet then." He walked over to Mac and placed his hands-on Mac's head.

"Lord, bless this son of a bitch, and with your help, this poor bastard will have plenty of booze and cigars for both of us. If not, Lord, help him find them. Lord, please take care of this fine man."

With that, he limped out of the room.

Mac had been around priests and nuns his whole life and he knew that priests didn't act like this or swear like a drunken sailor. No priest has a Navy Cross, Silver Star, and two Purple Hearts.

The padre was right, though; he would find out more about what was going on when the big-nosed bastard came in. Mac added more hot water and Epsom salts to the pan. Then he poured another drink and mumbled to himself. Mac was just a bit perplexed at the appearance of the padre. Something was going on, and he was going to get to the bottom of it. Mac relit his cigar and waited for the big-nosed bastard to come back. He fumed and waited. Forty minutes later, his office door creeped up. A nose appeared like it had a life of its own through the crack.

"Mac, I didn't know if you were up or not?" he said.

"Come here, Tony. Tell daddy all about the padre."

Tony looked like a deer caught in the headlights of a car.

"Don't know anything about no padre, Mac," he said. He abruptly left before Mac could ask him a follow-up question.

Mac called Kathleen and told her about the padre.

She started to laugh. "We all decided you wouldn't mind helping some Marines who need a place to live for a while. Isn't that true? Would you Mac? Just while they recuperate and can be discharged to go home."

Mac said, "It would have been nice if someone talked to me instead of hearing it from a lunatic."

Kathleen put her hand over her mouth to stifle another laugh.

"You mean to tell me you don't want to help your Marines out?"

Mac knew this battle was lost.

"Of course, I do. When is this all supposed to take place? And how many Marines are going to be living with me?"

"These Marines are badly wounded like you were. Most with head wounds. They are learning to overcome their

193

injuries and they need you now more than ever. Anyway, Seadog will have plenty of playmates."

"You mean crazy playmates."

Mac was silent for a moment.

Kathleen smiled and took a deep breath. All was going to plan. He had no idea that they were moving in to take care of him.

"I think the padre is meeting with the Navy Seabees at this moment to rearrange your upstairs."

Mac let out a sigh. "Rearrange who's upstairs? What are you talking about? No one changes anything without Momma Leone's permission. I need Momma Leone's permission to make any changes to her building!"

Kathleen heard the irritation in Mac's voice and did her best not to break out in laughter.

"Don't worry about that, Mac She gave her permission before she left."

Mac shook his head and realized that his life was going to change once more, especially with a certified clerical lunatic telling him what to do daily.

"What about the lunatic with the cane?"

"He'll be good for you!" Don't forget, Mac, one of the Marines can work in your office, filing papers, cleaning, answering your phone."

"All of them drinking my booze!"

Kathleen let out a laugh.

"Well, Mac, you will have to find a good hiding place!"

"Easy for you to say, but a Marine can smell liquor and root it out like a hog roots out an acorn."

"Will I see you tomorrow night, Mac? New casualties are coming in, and I won't get off for at least the next two weeks. How about some drinks together and a walk on the beach?"

"Yes, if the lunatic of a padre allows me to go out with you!"

Chapter 33

Bombay Alley

Mac stood over Tony's shoulder and looked at his accounting figures.

"What is our profit?"

Tony pointed to the figure at the bottom of the page.

Mac let out a low whistle and then a wow.

"You sure we made all that money this week?" asked Mac.

"The books don't lie, Mac. Since the Marines learned that you were an owner, this is the only bar they go to!"

"Where did you learn to do this type of work?" asked Mac.

"It's simple, Mac. On this side is all our expenses and on this side all our receipts. You subtract one from the other, and the rest is our profit."

"What about taxes?"

He looked at Mac as if he didn't expect the question.

"A bar is an all-cash business, Mac. Do you get my drift?"

"We don't want to drift into jail," said Mac.

"Mac, the figure you are looking at is pure profit." His face became serious. "I'll cheat within reason."

Mac looked at Tony with new respect. Mac still couldn't believe the figures.

"Cut a check immediately and send it to Momma Leone with her 50% and ask her if she needs anything. If she needs more money, give her everything. Cut a check for yourself for 25% of what's left."

"Boss, I have been paid my salary."

"That 25% is your profit for your half stake of mine in the bar."

Tony fainted right out of his chair.

Mac ran to his side with a glass of water and poured it on the Schnoz's beak. His eyes opened up and a smile came on his face. Before Mac could stop him, Tony planted a kiss at the top of his forehead and said, "Thanks, boss."

"You are earning your money. With part ownership, you are responsible for the bar and the building and everything that goes along with that. We need to make sure Momma Leone gets the money she needs. If we don't make enough, she gets most of the profit."

"Boss, if we continue to make this much money each week, in a year, we won't need no more money for the rest of our lives."

Mac was glad they were making money. Taking care of twelve of Uncle Sam's Misguided Children (USMC) was costing him.

"Make sure that if you need to hire more Marines, you do it, and take it out of my share."

"No boss, it will come out of my share."

"I told you to stop calling me boss, partner."

Tony grinned. "Okay, Mac."

"Make sure no one is stealing from us. Make sure we are not giving free booze to no one except if he is a Marine from the hospital."

Tony smiled and shook his head in agreement. "Been doing that, Mac."

Chapter 34

Gunny Wojo's hotel, Honolulu

Burke pulled in across the street from Wojo's hotel and waited. His patience paid off. He watched as a guy got out of a cab and entered the building. He took out a pen and wrote down the cab number. Something didn't seem right. He was as big as Wojo with a black crew cut and was all business. He wrote down the time.

Mac slowly walked up the stairs and stood outside Wojo's door. It was slightly ajar. He placed his .45 along the seam of his trousers, waited a few minutes, and walked into the room. The room looked like King Kong had been looking for his stash of banana's or his girlfriend. Mac's eyes drifted over the carnage and stopped when he noticed the two crumbled forms on the floor. He called out to Wojo and heard nothing. He walked around the room and tried to figure out what to do. Times like this, he needed a cigar. He bit off the end of a cigar and lit it. It helped him think clearer. It looked like the two palookas were dead. He bent down and checked their pulses. They were alive and breathing like babies. He searched them and pulled out their colts and placed the ammo in his pocket. He walked over to the toilet and threw both pistols in and then took a leak. He pulled out the nearest palooka's wallet and smiled at all the money. He stuffed the bills in his pocket. He grabbed a glass off a table, filled it with water, and dumped it on the two disfigured faces. He'd eventually make these boys talk, and it might even be fun.

They rolled over and tried to sit, groaning from the beating they had taken.

Mac sat on the edge of an overturned chair and marveled that the two guys could even move. He relit his cigar, throwing the still-burning match at the nearest one.

"Stop whining like eight-year-old girls and tell me what happened?"

The bigger one stood up, swaying on his feet.

"That son of a bitch hit like Joe Louis!" he looked down at Mac.

"Who in the hell are you?"

"Just a guy like you, after the same guy as you, except my face is not going to need reconstructive surgery."

The second guy got up and screamed when he looked in the mirror.

"Oh my God, look at my nose. It ain't supposed to be where it is!"

Mac looked at him and smiled. "Why are you boys after this guy. What did he do to you?"

The bigger one spoke. "You got a name?"

Mac pulled out his pistol and pointed it at him.

"Now, I know you don't have a rod because yours is sitting in a bowl of piss. I figure that puts me at an advantage. So, dummy, I'll ask the questions. If I don't get the right answers, well, you don't want me to explain all that."

They looked at each other and back to Mac. Their silence told him they were not going to talk.

"Tough guys, are we?" said Mac.

He picked up an end table leg that lay on the floor. In one quick motion, he broke it across the misshapen face in front of him. The man went down as if he had been shot. He held on to the last ten inches of the leg and advanced upon the man with the broken nose.

"Just maybe the doctors can fix your nose. Maybe they can't, but if I break this furniture leg on it, well, if I were a betting man, I would say highly improbable. What do you say? Because I have somebody to kill today and I could easily make it three. Your buddy didn't get a chance like I'm giving you."

He began shaking. "We were paid to find this guy."

"Why? Don't lie to me, or I'll pound on your nose till you go insane with the pain."

"We were to ask him about a guy he was asking about on Guadalcanal and then kill him."

"Who is this guy, the one who sent you. . . tell me more."

"He owns the Black Orchid and is meaner than a rattlesnake."

Mac figured out exactly who paid them.

"How much he pay you to take care of this guy?"

The guy looked away from Mac with eyes looking at the floor.

"Two hundred bucks."

Mac waved his pistol in the air as if he lost control over what direction the barrel was going. His voice dripping with disdain, he said. "Is that all a man's life is worth to you. A measly two hundred bucks? Give me both your wallets asshole and be quick about it."

He handed Mac the wallets. He pulled out the first driver's ID card. "Are you Antonio Percelli?"

Hacking and spitting out blood, he nodded yes. Mac looked into the empty wallet. Mac acted innocent. "Where's all the money?"

"The big guy must have taken our money. I had over two hundred dollars in there."

He then threw the empty wallet at Percelli's head.

He knew he had to impress upon these two guys that their lives hung in the balance. That he was the meanest son of a bitch in the whole world, so they would never forget he existed and would come back and kill them if need be. Holding onto the two licenses, he spoke.

"Take your buddies clothes off. Strip him buck naked and throw the clothes in that sink. Take off your clothes and throw them in the sink."

The man stood swaying on his feet. "What for?"

Mac couldn't believe what he just heard.

"What did I just tell you, pecker head?"

He took the end of the furniture leg and smacked the guy in his balls.

He slowly sunk to his knees and threw up on the floor.

"The next time you give me a what for. I'm going to set your balls on fire. You are not having a good day, my man. I would listen carefully to what I tell you."

The palooka struggled to his feet and took off his clothes. Naked as a jaybird, he took the clothes off his partner. He grabbed both of their clothes and slowly waddled to the sink and threw the clothes in.

Mac said, "You boys have been very bad."

He set fire to the clothes with his zippo. He walked back to the two men. He pushed the standing guy in the face, and his fat ass landed on his buddy's face. Mac started laughing and couldn't stop. He wondered if his brains were scrambled. Sometimes he got the weirdest thoughts!

"Get off his face; you look like you're enjoying it too much!"

The humiliated gangster stood up, shaking like a leaf his face as red as a raw beet.

He stated, "I'm going to find you and kill you."

Mac put his pistol to the head of Percelli and cocked back the hammer.

Mac laughed. "Leave the big Polack to me. . . don't bother him, forget me, or I'll tell broken nose how you sat on his face, you pervert and if he doesn't kill you, I will kill you deader than a doornail. You got way more problems with me than ole Jack or him. If I were you, I'd run and hide, stay in the shadows, go underground. See a good plastic surgeon. That's if you want to live!" Mac took what was left of the furniture leg and broke it over his head.

The slob with the broken nose started to stir. He stared up and saw Mac.

Mac lightly tweaked the guy's beak, he screamed and passed out right next to his buddy.

"Real tough guys, aren't we," Mac said out loud. Mac smelled his fingers and wiped them on Percelli's face. He washed his hands in the sink and sprayed water on the burning clothes.

Turning around, he grabbed the full bottle of bourbon and smiled. Wojo must have been in a real big hurry to forget his bourbon. He had to find more information about what he was up too. He knew his buddy of 18 years needed help. Like times in his past, Wojo was in trouble and running out of time. He was going to have to rely on the crazy Padre and his band of crazy boys. He might not be as smart as Charlie Chan or Michael Shayne, the next best private detective next to Chan, but he was learning quickly.

* * *

Burke wrote down the number of the cab and waited for the big guy to get back into his cab and leave. He pulled out his pistol and went up the stairs and saw two doors to his right and one of them was slightly open. He peered in. The room was torn apart, and two naked guys lay on the floor. He walked into the bathroom and saw the smoldering clothes and the pistols in a sea of piss. Somebody was not fooling around. The two naked guys were in terrible shape.

He walked back down to his car and drove to a phone booth. He called the yellow cab company. The dispatcher gave him the address of the guy they dropped off at Wojo's.

Ten minutes later, he pulled in front of the address. He parked his car across the street and watched the building for several minutes. A pale red neon sign glowed on the building, The Bombay Alley. Above the sign was a large window shaped in a half-moon. He read the lettering on the window, Gunny Mac, Private Detective. He got out of his car and stood before the entrance to the bar. Looking up toward the window, he could see the big guy smoking a cigar and staring out toward the street. Visiting the detective would be his first step. He walked in the crowded bar and on the wall was a sign showing him the way. *Upstairs Office of Gunny Mac Private Investigations.* Burke walked into a bustling office filled with men going in and out.

Sitting at the desk was a young man, and just above him was a picture of Wojo battered, and Gunny Mac smiling with his arm in the air, showing victory. He looked down at the young man who looked sixteen years old, except for the fresh pink scars around his eye and head.

"I'm looking for Gunny Mac."

The young man looked at him.

"Do you have an appointment with him, Sir. He is a very busy detective."

Burke looked down and smiled.

"It is very imperative that I see him now."

"No, Sir, you first need to have an appointment."

Burke decided he had enough of the small talk and started toward Mac's office door. Just as he put his hand on the door, he heard a familiar click. He turned around to find the young man pointing a .45 at him.

"Please come around to the front of the desk, or I'll blow you to kingdom come."

Burke put his hands up and walked around to the front of the desk. The young man pushed a buzzer, and four guys came running out of the side room, all brandishing .45's.

Following the four men came a navy officer resplendent in his uniform. He walked up to Burke.

"Who are you, and how can the Gunny Mac Detective Agency help you?"

"First of all, you can put your guns away. I just want to see Gunny Mac without getting shot."

"Are you heeled? And if you are, keep your hands up, but nod your head yes or no."

Burke staring at four weapons, nodded yes. The Padre unbuttoned Burke's coat jacket and pulled out the .45.

"I hope you have a good reason for this weapon, Sir, or my boys will ensure your days of crime are over."

For the first time, he noticed the crosses on the lieutenant's uniform.

"Are you really a padre?"

"The question is not who I am, but who you are and why you walk into this office armed like a thug."

The door to Mac's office opened and he walked out.

"Is this one of Jack's boys?" Mac asked.

Burke immediately knew that Mac was his guy.

"May I put my arms down. I can explain everything. You seem to think I'm someone who I'm not," said Burke.

The padre nodded yes, and he lowered his arms. He put down his arms.

"If it is okay, may I reach into my coat pocket without being drilled by your detectives," he said.

"Slowly," said the padre.

Burke reached in and took out his badge and handed it to Mac.

He looked at it and said, "How do we know it's real?" asked Mac.

Burke looked at him and smiled. "A real detective, aren't we?"

He pointed to the picture and said to Mac. "That's Wojohowitz and you must be Gunny Mac."

Surprised, Mac said, "Follow me."

He went to his cabinet, retrieved two glasses, and poured each of them a drink. He handed one to Burke and sat down behind his desk.

"So, you're the famous Gunny Mac. Hero of Bloody Ridge. Hero to Gunny Wojo."

Mac smiled. "Hero to Gunny Wojo, really?" said a surprised Mac.

"You are the best friend of the gunny, I, on the other hand, have no best buddies."

He took a sip of his bourbon.

"What does Naval Intelligence want with Gunny Wojo?"

Burke rolled the glass of bourbon between the palms of his hands and quizzically looked at Mac.

"What's with the picture on the wall above that maniac who wanted to blow off my head?"

Mac ignored Burke as he took a sip of bourbon, picked up his cigar from the ashtray, and relit it. Mac smiled with the cigar clenched between his teeth.

"That maniac Mr. Intelligence Agent is Sergeant Peterson, who is recuperating from head and eye wounds. And I am not you, but if I were you, I would never, never not listen to him. That picture is my favorite picture of me beating the gunny's ass in front of ten thousand soldiers, sailors, and Marines. Again, why are you asking about Gunny Wojo?"

Burke downed his drink and thrust his hand out for more.

"Damn, son, you are worse than Wojo; you got to sip it and enjoy it, not down it like it's free."

Burke waited until Mac filled up his glass again.

He raised his glass high in a toast. "To Sergeant Peterson, God bless him." He downed the drink and thrust out his hand again for a refill.

Mac looked at him with reverence. He shoved the bottle across the desk toward Burke.

"Hell, son, my arm is getting tired of filling your glass every five seconds."

Burke filled his glass with more bourbon and sat back down, his face sorrowful and downcast. "Before the war gunny, I'd drink a bottle of bourbon before I went out. I had an expense account. My father owns a business that stretches from the Atlantic to the Pacific. I almost took the company to the brink of bankruptcy. I was a drunkard, a womanizer who had no respect for man, woman, child, and to be quite frank, no self-respect. The only reason I got into Harvard was because of my father and grandfather. I never earned anything in my life. Everything was given to me and I took it. I expected it."

Mac filled up his glass and looked at Burke like a priest hearing a confession.

"The only reason I got into the navy was because of my father and grandfather. I barely passed Intelligence School by the skin of my scrotum. I had no moral compass. If I didn't know where I was going; certainly, the navy didn't have any clue where I was heading. I was human debris, like flotsam that sucks up to the sides of ships and leaves a stain."

Burke finished the last of his drink and filled his glass almost to the brim.

Mac said, "Go on; this is getting interesting."

The first effects of the bourbon hit him. He squeezed his eyes tight to keep the tears locked in place. His words started to slur slightly.

"The navy knew they had a first-class idiot on their hands. A man-child who never earned any of the life he was living. So, God bless the navy; they did the only thing they could do. They shipped my lazy ass to an organization that would make me or break me. I remember the navy captain smiling as he handed me my orders." Burke rubbed his hand over his eyes. "Lieutenant," he said. "We are sending your worthless ass to work with Uncle Sam's Misguided Children." And then he laughed at me. He made me feel like shit. Do you know what happened to me next, gunny? They sent me to Forward observer school and attached me to the 1st Marine Division." Burke broke out in strangled laughter. "I said I wasn't going to do it. Three gunnery sergeants told me I was going to do it and do it well. I laughed at them and told them to kiss my ass. They smiled and then they pummeled my ass. They fractured a rib and my nose, needless to say I graduated at the top of my class. At the end of the class, they asked to speak to me. They saluted me, shook my hand, and said they were proud of me. Can you fucking believe that!"

Mac topped off Burke's glass to the brim.

"Anyway, I went with all of them to Guadalcanal just like you, gunny, and that is where I met Gunny Wojo. He told me something I'll never forget."

Burke started to giggle and then let out a small sob. "It's hard to be a man when you never had to be one before. I grew to respect my Marine comrades and Gunny Wojo."

He drank half his glass of bourbon and stared at Mac. "If I were to be honest, I grew to love them all. Those three gunny's, two died, and the other is still recuperating from his injuries."

He downed the rest of his drink, stared at Mac glassy-eyed, and passed out in the chair. Mac turned off the sconces in his office, watching the lights from the bars across the street dance across the walls in his office. For some reason, at this moment, the neon lights reminded him of the votive candles people lit for their loved ones in church, flickering red lights of mercy for all the tormented souls. He heard of people's hearts breaking brought on by pain. But what about the soul. When does it absorb too much agony and pain and crack open like an egg? How much human suffering could his soul and the soul of the young man passed out in front of him take before they wither like grapes on a vine and lose contact with God? He sighed, finished his drink, and looked down at Burke. He looked so young and innocent.

He threw him over his shoulder and carried him to a bedroom and put him onto a bunk bed next to the padre.

The padre looked over at Mac putting Burke to bed and smiled. He patted Mac on the arm and said, "Good night Mac, we will take care of him."

Mac nodded and went back to his office. He needed to talk with God.

Chapter 35

BOQ, Naval base, Pearl Harbor

The next morning Burke drove to his BOQ with a hangover from hell. His head hurt something awful. His mouth was dry as a cotton ball, and what was left of his stomach, heaved like a destroyer plowing through a tropical storm. Last night he drank a minimum of half a bottle of bourbon in a very short time. No thanks to Gunny Mac. The trouble was he didn't remember much. At the moment, everything was as fuzzy as some mold on a piece of bread. He could kick himself for getting drunk. Today was an important day and his brain felt detached from his body.

He had gone over his thought process involving Kincaid, DeVito, and Gentleman Jack and knew he had slim proof of wrongdoing, and time was running out. All he had at this point was conjecture and that Kincaid was burning the money sooner than later. Making a mistake at this point would blow his entire undercover investigation. He then would replace Kincaid on the admiral's shit list and that

211

would be worse than a hangover in hell. But he trusted his instincts concerning Kincaid.

He had a little of Kincaid in his own make-up, at least just a short time ago. Kincaid was nothing but a soup sandwich and was near the breaking point. The commander had a terrible gambling problem, a drinking problem, and on top of that debts, which led him right into Gentleman Jack's hands.

For eight days he had followed Kincaid and the two shadows that followed the commander, sniffing for his scent like a blue tick hound dog. It almost looked like a comic scene out of a Chaplin movie. A long train of people following each other and everyone oblivious.

How the commander could work all day, kiss the admiral's ass, drink and gamble all night and still wake up early the next morning, made Burke think Kincaid was not human. He had to end this game of charades soon and confront Kincaid, then use his charm on the commander and get what he needed. He decided it was now or never.

He lit a cigarette, walked over to Kincaid's door, and found it difficult to raise his hand and knock. What would he do if Kincaid told him to kiss his ass on the public square? No crime was committed, and he had no evidence showing the commander was going to do anything. It wasn't a crime to think of robbing the government. Burke began relying on his newfound instincts, which was a bad sign. But he remembered the Marines on the Canal and knew he wanted to be like them no matter what the cost.

Adrenaline surged through his body. Now or never, he thought. He knocked forcibly. The door opened quickly and Burke lost everything. His professionalism and his speech he was going to give. He just started laughing. Kincaid looked like a fucking raccoon. He looked more like a raccoon than a real raccoon.

"What the hell are you laughing at?" asked Kincaid.

Burke shoved him into the room as his laughter turned into a friendly smile.

"Doesn't matter, commander."

Kincaid stared at him with suspicion and then some recognition formed in his rheumy blue eyes.

"You have been following me. One of Jack's boys, making sure I keep my end of the bargain. Before you know it, you son of a bitch, you'll want to drink my liquor. Get the fuck out of here."

Burke decided to play along with the idea that he was one of Jack's men.

"Look, Kincaid, be nice to me, or I'll tell Jack you are not playing ball with him."

"I've done everything he has asked and more, but you make sure you tell him to leave my niece alone, or a letter will tell the navy what the hell he is doing."

Burke now understood that his instincts were on target and that he needed to get the whole truth from the commander. He sat down on the davenport and said," Get me a drink ole man and let's chat, shall we?"

Kincaid looked at him and said, "You aren't one of Jack's men, are you?"

Burke smiled and said, "No, I'm one of Uncle Sam's boys."

The color drained from Kincaid's face as he half stumbled to where the bourbon bottle sat on his dresser. He looked like a defeated man on his way to death row. He poured the booze into a glass and held it out to Burke with a trembling hand.

Burke's stomach gave a churn as he smelled the bourbon.

Kincaid sat in the chair next to him and sipped his drink and watched Burke. "You don't look so hot yourself."

Burke moved his jacket to the side, showing his holstered .45 as he reached for his wallet. Commander Kincaid stared at the .45, his face turning bright pink.

He opened his wallet to show him his badge.

Kincaid was silent while reading the lettering on the badge.

"Naval Intelligence. . .fuck me to tears."

Burke snapped the wallet closed and sat back and just watched Kincaid's reactions. The next few moments were crucial. Especially, what Kincaid was going to say about Jack and the scheme to steal money. He just wondered if he could trust the son of a bitch. Despite all he knew about Kincaid, he thought he could like the man. Burke took a sip, hoping the hair of the dog would help his stomach. He though it uncouth to puke all over Kincaid's floor.

"My assumption, commander, is that the admiral doesn't particularly care for you. Am I wrong? If I'm right, I need to know why. Why does this admiral hate you so much?"

Kincaid got up, rubbed the back of his neck, and took a long sip of bourbon. He filled up his glass and walked around the room.

"Sit down, commander, you are making me dizzy. Believe me, you don't want to make me dizzy."

Kincaid stopped and sat down next to Burke.

"Let's say I took advantage of a certain wife who was lonely and trying to get back at a certain husband. I didn't know the pompous ass knew. I guess he had you follow me around, and you told the admiral that I screwed his wife."

Burke's face took on a look of amazement.

"Don't tell me you didn't know?" he said.

"You mean to tell me you fucked the admiral's wife?"

"Yes, more than once."

Burke smiled and started to laugh. "Unbelievable, no wonder he wants you rotting in prison."

Burke wondered how much he should tell him. He decided to throw the Hail Mary pass. "Commander, I have been following you long enough to figure out some pieces of the puzzle."

Kincaid leaned back in his chair and let out a long sigh.

Burke hoped that he had guessed right. "I decided to confront you because I need to understand what the hell is going on, so I don't end up as your cellmate. If you don't agree to help me, I will let Gentleman Jack fuck you till your ass bleeds and then turn you over to the nice sweet honorable admiral who will have his way with you. A scenario that I would not want to entertain, but then again, I'm not you. The bottom line is if you help me, I'll help you, and by that, I mean, no charges, and you can shove this investigation up the admiral's big soft white pimpled ass. If you don't cooperate fully and truthfully with me, you'll be at Quantico with Marine guards kicking your skinny ass around and shitting splinters from all the billy clubs shoved up your ass for the next twenty years. I know about you, DeVito, and Jack. You'll have to do everything that I ask of you or no deal. The admiral will never get his revenge on you and you won't get your revenge on the navy - a total wash for you. Just remember, I can't help our country or you unless I know everything. You cannot leave anything out or you could get both of us killed. Do you understand?"

Kincaid looked at Burke with eyes that were red primed and tired. Kincaid looked like a beaten puppy.

"They are in a position to hurt my niece. If you promise to protect her, I'll play ball, but if you don't, no dice, and you can do whatever you want with me."

Burke finished his drink and smiled. "Just one question Kincaid, are you thinking of stealing the money?"

His eyes couldn't hide the turmoil swirling around behind them. His eyes seemed to glow red. "Well, let's just say I entertained the idea, Burke."

Burke said to him. "Glad you didn't lie to me, commander, that would have been unfortunate on your part." He continued. "Now let's get some hot coffee and get down to business. Are you expecting anyone tonight?"

Kincaid shook his head no.

"Then we have a lot of work to do. We need to devise a plan that will keep both of us out of the hoosegow. I need to know everything you discussed with the bastards."

Kincaid had a worried look on his face." How many people are involved in this, and who will be protecting my niece?"

"I'm asking the questions, Kincaid. You just keep yourself concerned about the instructions that I give you! Let's get to my room and pound out the details."

* * *

One hour later, Commander Kincaid returned to his room. His plans so far were coming up roses. He played Burke like a fucking Stradivarius. This last piece of the puzzle was somewhat of a surprise. He was amazed at how it was all falling into place, events lining up like a constellation. All because one man wanted to fuck him. He smiled and wrote what had transpired tonight, so he would not get all mixed up on who was fucking whom.

Chapter 36

Black Orchid bar

Gunny Wojo walked to the payphone inside the Black Orchid and made a call to Mac. Somebody answered the phone with a voice that irritated the hell out of him.

"Gunny Mac Detective Agency; how may I help you?" Wojo could not believe it.

"Is Mac there?"

There was a pause, "You mean, Detective Mac, don't you?"

Wojo said, "Look, he's just Mac to me. Is he there?"

"Please refer to the esteemed detective Mac with a proper title and more respect, Sir."

Wojo demanded, "Who in the hell is this?"

A clipped voice answered back. "You called here, Sir. I didn't call you. Don't you know who you are calling?"

Wojo felt pressure building behind his eyeballs which was undoubtedly going to cause him a retinal detachment.

"Can you leave a message for Mac from me."

"You mean Detective Mac, don't you?"

"Yes, tell Charlie Chan junior that Wojo's in trouble and people are after him. Tell him to get over to the Black Orchid now. I'll wait for him." Wojo hung up.

Sgt Peterson yelled out to Mac that Wojo was in trouble and was waiting for him at the Black Orchid.

Mac slipped his .45 into his holster and ran out the door. In less than five minutes, he walked into the dimly lit bar and saw Wojo standing by the back door. Wojo waved to him and pointed at two rough-looking guys. Mac nodded and sat down at a table, facing the two men leaning against the bar and ordered himself a bourbon. They had a look about them that smelled like rotten cops-a smell like kimchee. A third man joined them, then a fourth. While taking a sip he watched one of them tap his buddy on the shoulder and look at him. They started toward him but one of them said something and they went back to the bar. They ordered drinks and watched him, like vultures waiting to descend upon a still moving carcass. Mac looked back over his shoulder searching for Wojo and didn't see him. Turning his attention back to the bar he noticed only one man staring back at him. Something was wrong and he decided what was going to happen next, needed no plan. He downed the last of his drink, got up and walked through the crowd and out the back door to find Wojo. By the smell and sight, he was in garbage can alley.

His breath exploded outward as his body slammed into the brick side of the building. He hunched his shoulders and turned slightly, as another punch landed more or less across the meatiest part of his back. His instincts as a fighter served him well as he rolled into several garbage cans. Lifting the lid off one of the garbage cans, he used it as a shield protecting his brain housing group. He struggled to breathe as his lungs gasped for air. He was acutely aware of three figures surrounding him, methodically kicking him in all his tender areas. He desperately searched his waistband for his .45 warding off clanging blows with the garbage lid. His hands soon found the familiar butt of his .45 as a hard kick to his head bounced his noggin off the cement. He knew he only had seconds to respond, or he would die with the stink of garbage in his nose.

With his last spurt of adrenalin, he pulled his .45, from his waistband and fired up at his attackers, backing them off. He struggled to a position with his back resting against a garbage can smelling of rotting fish. A streetlight was flickering off and on, bathing the ally in light one minute and darkness the next. A glint of light from the streetlight flashed off a knife blade. He saw movement in his right peripheral vision; turning he saw Wojo grab an arm and pull a man to the ground. In the next second, Wojo had twisted the knife out of his hand, stabbing the assailant through the arm. As Mac looked down, he saw a pair of shoes. He looked up at a knife blade held above his head. In the next second, the man was bowled over by Wojo's body slam. The knife clinked on the ground. Mac grabbed it and rammed the knife through the man's shoe and into the foot. Mac never heard such howling in all of his life.

With one of the men down, the rest scrambled down the alley. Mac tried to stand up but fell back to the ground. He rolled to his knees and pushed himself to his feet. He stuck the .45 in his waistband and looked at his hand. It was covered with blood.

Wojo smiled and looked down at a puddle of blood, in the middle was a police badge.

Wojo smiled, "Just like old times Mac."

He picked it up and looked at the number on the badge. He tossed it to Mac. They heard the whining of sirens in the distance. Mac took his foot and pinned the man's head down and pinned the cop's badge through the guy's cheek. "He ought to have his police badge back, don't you think Wojo?" asked Mac.

"Let's get the hell out of here Mac, before his friends show up."

Mac grabbed Wojo's arm to steady himself. "Thanks for saving my ass. My place is up ahead. The cops will be all over me. See me tomorrow. If you follow Hotel Street to our right, and then left at the Police station and follow the Sununu Stream, which is North of Chinatown you will be on South Hotel Street. I'm upstairs above the Bombay Ally. I have to get back to my place." Wojo nodded and soon disappeared in the shadows of the ally. Mac turned in the opposite direction. He was desperate to get lost among the teeming masses of service members and get his senses right.

* * *

Mac heard footsteps coming up the stairs toward his office, sounding like a bull in a china store. He quickly put the letter he was writing into his top drawer. He could tell who it was by how much noise Callahan made. Like a moose climbing the stairs. The door soon opened. "Callahan here," came a voice with a slight accent. He was a big, broad-shouldered

Chinatown police detective with a twenty-two-inch neck and Mac guessed he tipped the scales at 275. Callahan was the result of the union between a 6'7' Irishman and a very tall Chinese woman. He towered over a tall Gunny Mac. Next to him was a skinny cop with crooked teeth.

"What you looking at?" Callahan said. You keep looking at me like that and I'll think you have a thing for me." Mac smirked at him and blew him a kiss.

He made a beeline for Mac's desk and swiped the bottle from the drawer.

"Where you keep your clean glasses?" His ruddy complexion showed that he had a couple of belts before coming over.

Mac, acknowledging his bourbon was not long for this world, shook his head and pointed to his cabinet. "You can use the one with my toothbrush in it."

Without comment, Callahan snagged a paper cup from the water cooler's dispenser, then dropped into Mac's chair which groaned in protest. He poured generously and tossed back the lot. "Always a pleasure to drink your bourbon, Mac. Now, time to spill your guts. Two cops were stabbed, and the description of the shooter fits you - big and ugly."

"Sounds to me like a description of you, Moose, aside from the absence of the word stupid, that is."

Callahan sneered and poured himself another, again draining the contents of his cup.

Callahan had met Mac at the hospital weeks ago. He dropped by to pay his respects after reading about Mac's exploit's on Bloody ridge. He had left his flask of bourbon after having a toast with Mac.

The cop next to Callahan snickered.

"Things have changed since we last talked." Mac moved into a dingy secondhand chair on the other side of the desk. "I have a good number of clients now. Perhaps one of them hired me to find out what you can't."

The tendons in Callahan's neck tensed, and he came forward. "I know you've got a forty-five, so let's have it."

Mac began to sweat. "Sure," he said, "When I see a warrant."

"What the hell?"

While Callahan stared at him, red-faced and fuming, Mac realized he had one more card to play.

"Say, aren't you out of your jurisdiction?" he asked. "This isn't Chin's domain; it's under the control of Admiral Johnson's provost marshal." His confidence invigorated; Mac got to his feet. "Now, why don't you get the hell out of my office and go do your job. Find the guy who assaulted your coppers."

Callahan grabbed Mac's bottle of bourbon and said, "Something doesn't pass the smell test, Mac."

"I told you before, Callahan. Chin wants my ass because I shot one of his benefactor's boys in my office when they tried to kill me. He doesn't like me, and I don't like him, so go roust someone else."

Mac grimaced as Moose poured another cupful of his quickly vanishing bourbon.

"I'll have your investigators license as fast as that damn dog of yours is ugly," he growled. The other flatfoot spoke. "Let's run his jarhead ass in and visit Captain Chin. He laughed and said, "We'll take that damn ugly dog and let Chin have him for dinner."

Mac got up and walked over to the standing detective.

Mac stared at the detective until he blinked. "Look, wise guy. I got a right to protect myself and any paying clients, and I'm going to do just that, and I don't care if you like it or not! Don't fuck with my dog."

Callahan stood up.

Gunny Mac growled back at the two cops. "As I said, you two are several hundred feet out of your jurisdiction and I'm under military control. Now beat it before I make an official complaint to the US government," said Mac.

"All right, you two, stop the jostling," said Callahan. "Look, just tell me where you were late last night?"

"What time last night," Mac asked.

"I'm asking the questions, Mac," Callahan shot back.

Mac smiled and walked over and grabbed a cigar from Callahan's pocket. He lit it slowly and puffed till the end was hot. He looked at Callahan. "I was sleeping like a baby. If you want a witness, talk to Seadog. He's more honest and upfront than Chin."

The standing detective spoke. "What time was that?"

He looked at Callahan and said, "What you got there Moose; is a 4F cop."

"Oh, leave him alone, he's got flat feet," said Callahan.

Mac stood next to the standing detective.

"Look, I got a dozen witnesses that will say I was here from 1800 hours till you mugs showed up here bothering the hell out of me," answered Mac.

"Why should we believe you sleuth," wisecracked the standing detective.

"Go on," said Callahan.

Mac stuck out his glass to Callahan and smiled a please through clenched teeth. Callahan poured a smidgen of bourbon into Mac's glass.

Mac walked up to Callahan sitting in his chair, put his hands on his desk, and leaned forward.

"Look, Callahan, my wounds haven't healed yet. Why would I stab two cops…?"

Mac moved closer to Callahan's partner, looking directly into his eyes.

"Why should I want to stab two of Chin's crooked cops? If they got stabbed, they probably were committing a crime." He walked back to Callahan and said. "That's all there is, Callahan."

The skinny detective chimed up.

"Why should we believe you? Your face is all bruised?" Gunny Mac turned around to face the voice.

"Why? Because half the coppers on the force are as crooked as your front teeth."

The skinny detective started to reach for his blackjack.

Seadog let out a growl that sounded like a grizzly bear in heat.

Mac turned away and walked over to Callahan.

"The more I think about it," said Mac, "the more I believe I'm being set up by Chin's badge - wearing thugs!"

Callahan got into Mac's face and half-shouted. "We are not all crooked. Quit telling me we're all crooked! What your forgetting is that when you set foot in Chinatown proper, you'll wish you had a copper friend, so don't push me too far or you might end up where the sidewalk ends!" Callahan walked back to the door, turned around, and looked at Mac. "We are not all crooked. You can bank on that!"

* * *

Wojo stood in an alley deep in the shadows and watched the Bombay Alley. Two police officers were leaning against their patrol car smoking and joking, watching the comings and goings on Hotel Street. He needed Mac's help in more ways than one. He was broke, tired, and sore from stem to stern. He felt his ribs and hoped they were not cracked. With only one lung healthy, his breathing was difficult. He had no choice, but to stay hidden until the cops left and somehow sneak in to see Mac. The realization came to him that just maybe, they found out who he was and putting the screws to Mac. He smiled through a spasm of pain, engulfing his chest, as he thought of Mac getting the third degree. Usually, it was him getting the third degree, most of the time from Mac. He leaned against the building and stifled a spasm, praying that the cops would leave soon.

Chapter 37

Bombay Ally

Mac had spent most of the night searching for a 16-year-old girl and was famished.

Momma Leone had taught the Schnoz how to prepare his morning breakfast and it was waiting for him. He sat down, drooling over his favorite breakfast of crisp Hawaiian bacon, eggs over easy on top of a fried piece of Spam. On the side some fresh pineapple and strong Hawaiian coffee. His ecstasy was interrupted by the arrival of Lieutenant Burke. Mac was not happy after Burke grabbed a plate and started helping himself to his breakfast. The pesky naval officer was driving Sgt. Peterson crazy asking for Mac for the last two days.

"Look, Mac, I have some problems here, and I'm all alone. I could use your help. Wojo is in trouble, a certain bastard of an admiral's on my ass waiting to throw me in jail, a Commander Kincaid is being blackmailed, and guys by the name of DeVito and Jack and Chin are trying to steal money that a crazy president is trying to burn. Most of all, I need your help getting the fingerprints of Gentleman Jack."

Mac pointed to the uneaten Spam on Burke's plate. "You going to eat that?"

Burke made a face. "You are going to eat two pieces of that shit?"

Mac forked the Spam over to his plate. "This is the caviar of the islands."

"Have you been listening to me?"

"I'm a talented guy; I can eat and listen at the same time. You forgot a few things. Captain Chin of the Chinatown police wants me dead. Gentleman Jack wants me dead, and I shot at two crooked cops working for Chin. I got a lot on my plate, like trying to stay alive. By the way, that name Kincaid rings a bell. A Rose Kincaid would not be involved in all this, would she?"

Burke watched in disgust as Mac stabbed another large piece of Spam, sprinkled it with liberal amounts of hot sauce, and put it between slices of buttered toast.

"Yes," said Burke.

"We have a person who is of interest to both of us," Mac said between bites of Hawaiian caviar. "Tell me more about this Rose girl."

Burke grabbed the last piece of bacon before Mac could devour it. "I don't know much about her except Kincaid is always fussing over her safety. It seems she is working for the man who wants to kill you."

"Charlie Chan would say that there is no such thing as a coincidence, and we have a big one here. Look, Lieutenant Burke, I'm meeting with somebody that I know who can help us. As soon as I discuss these things with him, you'll feel much better. We need some planning and a little bit of luck."

Burke looked at his watch. "Thanks for breakfast. Time to see what Kincaid is doing today. Call me when you have some answers."

If he had hoped his life would turn into a Charlie Chan movie, Mac's hope was coming true.

He hoped Wojo was going to get in touch with him soon. He'd appreciate it if the big lug was watching his own back and Mac's because trouble was following them both. In the last few days, two men watched his every move unafraid to be seen.

He'd have to do something about them at some point, but now he had to figure out how he was going to get the fingerprints of Gentleman Jack so that Burke could wire them to the Fingerprint Factory. His instructions were to ensure that he got each thumb and finger, from both hands and they had to be good clear prints. He reminded himself he needed the prints ASAP. Burke told Mac not to worry; he would be handling the operation's intelligence, keeping the group safe from interference from Jack and Captain Chin.

Mac went upstairs to his office and spent the next four hours napping and thinking about how he was going to get Gentleman Jack's prints.

Mac opened his eyes when the padre walked in. He sat in the chair across from Mac and tapped his cane on the floor, clearing his throat several times. Mac stared at him, knowing what that meant. Reluctantly, Mac opened his drawer and pulled out the bottle. He poured both of them a drink.

"Thank you, Mac, my dear boy. How about one of your tasty cigars to smoke while enjoying this libation?"

He looked at his cigar box and noticed that four cigars out of twenty were left and then looked up at the padre.

Smiling sheepishly, he looked at Mac, grabbed the cigar, smelled it, and ran it underneath his nose.

"You better order some more cigars, Mac. You don't want to run out of them."

Pushing the cigar box on the desk toward the padre, Mac blurted out, "Here, you might as well have the rest of them."

The padre smiled and puffed on his cigar.

"You know what Kipling said, don't you, Mac? *A woman is just a woman, but a cigar is a good smoke.*" He burst out in uncontrolled laughter while pounding the desktop.

Mac knew his office, and living area was now an insane asylum.

He stared at the lunatic priest and thought about all the different people that war brought into his life. Mac, knowing the padre would chastise him if he used the King's language the wrong way, tried to enunciate each word.

"What I learned just a few hours ago has enlightened me about your presence here. You're an educated man, padre, taught by the Jesuits about logic and such and I need your help in figuring out a problem. It's a complicated problem that must be done subtly but done quickly. Will you help me?"

The padre stuck out his broad chest. "I'm ready to use my great intellect to help solve your problem, my dear Mac."

"I need the fingerprints of a local gangster. A print of each hand's fingers on fingerprint forms without him knowing what happened."

The padre got up and walked around the room for several minutes in deep thought. He turned around to Mac and said,

"I got it. The logical strategy of establishing claim by showing that it's opposite leads to absurd consequences is known as reductio ad absurd um. My dear detective, this will solve our problem. When must we have the prints?"

Mac's mouth fell open, and his cigar crashed and burned on the table. He quickly put it back in his mouth.

"Yesterday."

"My dear gunnery sergeant, you will have your prints in less than two days. I will need several copies of the fingerprint cards." With that, he got up, grabbed the remaining cigars, and limped out of the room.

* * *

The padre gathered his small tribe in the bunk room next to Mac's office. He blessed the group as he did every day. His multitude of Marines had grown to over twelve, after he recruited six more Marines from the psych unit. Each Marine was highly decorated and brave. He would need all his men and resources to procure those fingerprints. He informed all of them what needed to be done and they helped him devise a strategy for the upcoming mission.

Chapter 38

Padre McCaffery's office, Bombay Ally

Padre McCaffery realized that he needed to recruit more Marines from the psych unit at the naval hospital. His duties and responsibilities seemed to be growing faster than Mac could finish off a bottle of lousy bourbon. Last night his band of merry Marines had completed the mission to get Jack's prints. He was surprised by how easy it was. He was in high spirits because he had helped the illustrious Gunny Mac and the young Burke when they had needed him the most. Now he was analyzing his growing list of jobs, making him puff furiously on his cigar. He had to ensure Mac's safety, but the Polack was his problem. They couldn't find him. Their only saving grace was how Mac had described him. He said he was so big that he stuck out like a Triple D cup.

He was concentrating so hard that he flinched when the tip of his cigar reached his lips.

He walked into Mac's office, hoping to find where Mac hid his good cigars. He reminded himself to tell Mac to buy better cigars. This last cigar tasted and smelled like Jap tobacco and left a bad taste in his mouth. He ignored the new box of cigars on Mac's desk and started searching for the delicious cigars. The last cigars he had from Mac's private stash were intoxicating, smooth, and elegant with a slight finish of cedar and vanilla. He hoped the gunny was not getting cheap on him. Opening the last cabinet, he smiled as he found where Mac stashed his favorite cigars. The cigars were hidden behind a bible. He looked up to the heavens and smiled, surely this was a sign from above. He asked God to forgive him as he grabbed a handful and walked back to his office. Twenty minutes later, he solved his scheduling problem. He knelt at his desk and bowed his head. The pain started fissuring through his back, up his neck and then creeped across the back of his head, like the spidering cracks of a broken window. Small intense bursts of pain, accumulating in a dull roar right where the bullet took a chuck of his skull, a small price to pay in the service of his Lord and country.

"Dear Lord in heaven, bless my country, my Marines, and the mission we are on today. Thank you for including me to help Gunny Mac and his mission. Dear Lord, I will not let you or my Marines down. My wounds and pain are nothing compared to the pain of the cross. I know my mind is not the same, dear Lord. Forgive any transgressions I commit, and remember my heart is yours with no reservations. Amen."

Mac walked into the office, looking for the padre. Sgt Peterson pointed to the padre's room.

"You did it, padre. In God's name, you did it. Open up, so I can see your lunatic face so that I can kiss it."

Padre McCaffrey said an "Our Father" and opened the door.

"Yes, my dear Mac, you said the Lord's name in vain, and you mustn't do that."

Mac stared at the padre, started laughing, and walked in the room, closing the door.

The padre stood staring at Mac, his jaws working the cigar up and down, grinding his teeth. Mac went right up to the padre and kissed him on the forehead.

"Tell me how you did it? Why was there colored paint or something on the envelope?"

Padre McCaffery took a puff on his cigar, waving his hands around.

"Well, Mac, I had to devise a plan to hide the ink on his fingertips, and if I dare say, my plan was brilliant, and my Marines perfect in their implementation of my bold, outrageous plan."

Mac walked over to his desk and sat down. "Let me get comfortable while you tell me about your brave and courageous exploit." He leaned back in his chair and put his feet up on the desk. "Go on, padre."

"After some reconnaissance over two days, we knew where to take Gentleman Jack and his bodyguards. A six-foot-tall Hibiscus hedge grew along both sides of a path leading from his back door to his car. We knew what time he would be leaving his office. Our reconnaissance indicated he would have three guards with him. We waited for him. We chloroformed them all and took his prints."

"The great thinking of a Jesuit mind, padre," said Mac, smiling

"Ah, but my brilliance hasn't been fully relayed to you yet, my dear Mac."

The padre took a puff on his cigar, enjoying every moment explaining his audacious plan with his overdeveloped cranium. A haughty look came over his face. "I figured that Gentleman Jack would notice his finger covered with blue ink and surmise someone took his prints. Then I remembered an RKO movie I saw onboard the troopship taking us to the island paradise of Guadalcanal."

Gunny Mac got up and poured both a cup of coffee. He handed one to the padre and then settled back behind his desk to enjoy the heroic exploits of the padre. "It was a movie about some South Seas cannibals painted in bright colors dancing around their boiling pots as they prepared their evening meal. My dear Mac, the colors got my keen attention in completing my diabolical plan. I did some reading about these native cultures and found out certain colors had significant meanings."

Gunny Mac started to get a feeling this was going in the wrong direction.

"So, I brought some additional colors with me. Red signifying violence and the color of war-making, black paint was worn on the face for war preparation. Yellow; the most inauspicious color, portraying the wearer ready for death and meaning a man who has lived his life well and will fight to the death. I also brought some other colors along for fun."

Now Gunny Mac knew something was going terribly wrong.

"Now, my dear Mac, the stage was set. We took three neat sets of prints. Then genius took hold. We painted each finger a different color, red, orange, green, and so on. We covered the blue areas with dark black paint. I have to admit, Mac; I was having fun. So, I say to myself and the boys, let's paint their faces."

235

Gunny Mac let a small groan escape his lips.

"Oh, no, Mac, you might be thinking that was the end of my genius."

Mac started to hyperventilate.

"I hung a sign around their necks. 'We no like white men. Leave our women alone'. For some realism, I left several rows of shark teeth on his chest."

Mac felt himself getting dizzy. He held on tight to the armrests so that he wouldn't slide out of his chair.

"Of course, we did this to Jack and all his henchmen. We left them lying on the pathway and got out of the vicinity quickly." The Padre started laughing. "They are going to have a major problem."

Mac weakly said, "What problem?"

"The paint, actually it was some sort of dye mixed with water. I couldn't wash it off my fingers."

Mac opened his desk drawer to grab his bottle of bourbon. He couldn't remember when he needed a drink so bad, but it was gone. "Where in the hell is my bourbon?"

Padre McCaffery looked down at the floor with shame written across his face. He left the office and returned with the bottle and handed it to Mac. "I took a drink in celebration of our success."

Mac grabbed the bottle and then grabbed the Padre's hand and saw the stains. At first, it was just a giggle, then it morphed into a crazy, out of control laughter. He pounded the desk in fits of uncontrolled frenzy. The Padre began to laugh. Mac got up and walked to the Padre and hugged him. He managed to get some words out between the laughs. "We are dead men. Dead men."

Chapter 39

Gentleman Jack's office at the Black Orchid

Gentleman Jack awakened from his chloroform-induced slumber after being carried into his office. Smelling salts were placed underneath his nose, and his eyes slowly opened. He was looking into a hideous face of a cannibal, and he let out a scream.

"It's us, boss. Somebody painted our hands and faces."

As his hands came into his field of vision, he started to gag, tremble, and shake with rage. His hands were painted similarly to the faces before him. He shouted out, "What the hell happened to us?" he asked.

"We was attacked by some Hawaiian tribe."

"How in the hell do you know that?"

"Because of this here note that's on your desk, along with those beads, feathers and shark teeth."

Gentleman Jack read the note. "We no like white men! Leave our women alone." Gentleman Jack dropped the note with a sudden realization. He ran to the mirror and shrieked.

"Look at my face! What the hell have they done to me! Bring me some soap and water I gotta wash this shit off my face."

The men around him put their heads down. One of them spoke up.

"The paint don't come off so easy, boss. I scrubbed my face, and only a smidgen came off, it's some sort of dye."

Jack scrunched up his face and gave a screech that emanated from the bottom of an empty soul. He looked in the mirror and punched it, scattering broken glass over the room. "No one does this to Gentleman Jack; someone is going to die and die-hard. You boys were supposed to be watching over me and look what happened. Someone took you all out as easy as 1,2,3 and used me as a coloring book. I don't give a shit what you have to do. You better find out how to strip this shit off my hands and face, or I'll use you three as target practice. Find some chemist or doctor, somebody who can figure out what this shit is and get it off. While you are at it, find that fat Hawaiian bastard and bring him to me."

Gentleman Jack's next plan of action was to invite Chin over to his office and earn every last cent Jack gave him each month. Somewhere in the inner recesses of his instincts, Jack knew things were spiraling out of control, and he would have to use all of his networks to figure out what was happening and crush it like a bedbug. He looked into a shard of the mirror and his eyes burned with hatred. Someone was going to die for this.

* * *

Mac met with Burke later that afternoon in the Bombay Alley bar and asked Burke what he wanted to drink. "How about an Old Fashioned, shaken, up."

The Schnoz spoke up. "I've been studying up on how to make drinks. The boys say I'm one of the best." He poured two fingers of rye whiskey, mixed the drink, and handed it to Burke. "This is a New York Old Fashioned; let me know what you think?"

Burke took a sip and then took another sip and coughed. "Like everything in New York, a rather loud, rude drink. I will teach you how to make a Charleston or Savannah Old Fashioned. You will thank me."

The Schnoz's smile disappeared and a look of disappointment replaced it.

Burke turned around to face Mac and said, "Let me see those beautiful prints."

Mac handed the envelope to him.

"What's with all the colors smeared over the envelope?"

"Well," said Mac. "That's a story for another time."

A smile spread across Burke's face. "The prints are clear and fully developed. I could not have done a better job myself. I'll send one set of prints to my father, and you and I will keep a copy. As soon as I return to the base, I will wire photo the prints to our crook of a senator. He has promised us a quick turnaround. In just a few days, we will know the history of Gentleman Jack and possibly get him out of our hair and into jail. I will remind my father to keep in contact with the Senator to ensure those prints are a priority and the results sent to us. I'm just worried someone will misplace his prints with the thousands that come into the FBI daily. We both know that Gentleman Jack is more than a local gangster. No one grows an organization like his in a couple of months without outside resources and becomes the most powerful crime boss in Chinatown."

Burke slapped him on the back and left to go to the Pearl Harbor Base Communication's Center.

Mac ordered another drink from the Schnoz. A lot had happened in the last few days. Mac was worried about the missing Gunny Wojo and wondering about Lieutenant Commander Kincaid and his niece. He thought it would be nice if Charlie Chan would help him decide what he should do next. Something wasn't right. He just prayed nobody else decided to enter into this unfolding chaos.

The padre walked in and sat down in front of Mac. "Have you heard anything about Gentleman Jack?" he asked.

He poured the padre a cup of coffee. "So far, I don't think he has figured out who did it. That is damn good, but I have a feeling before it is over Gentleman Jack will be hunting us down. Right now, Wojo is in trouble. I'm in trouble. You are in trouble and so is Lieutenant Burke. We all are knee-deep in crapola. I will need your lunatic brain more than ever."

Padre McCaffery looked at Mac and toasted him with a coffee cup.

"My exceptional brain is at your service, Gunny Mac, and we will prevail or die in the process."

That did not make Mac happy. Looking closely at the cigar in the padre's mouth, he let out a grunt. "You found my good cigars. I see nothing is sacred, padre."

The padre winked at him. "Do you chastise a man of the cloth for such a small earthly delight, my dear gunny?"

He slapped the padre on the shoulder and said. "Let's sit down, smoke a great cigar, and develop our plan."

The padre put his arm around Mac's shoulder and said, "And don't forget the bourbon, my dear Mac."

Chapter 40

Admiral Johnson's office, Pearl Harbor

Burke was on his way to visit the admiral. He knew that he was going to be in trouble, but it just had to be that way. He was worried that Johnson would take him off the case unless he gave him some red meat. The problem was that he had no red meat, just a bunch of nothing. Especially since he was working on everything except what the admiral wanted him to do. At this point, he didn't know what the hell was going to happen.

Admiral Johnson sat daydreaming at his desk, almost dozing happily. He was dreaming of Kincaid and in his mind's eye, saw him in the brig, a Marine with bulging muscles slowly tapping his billy club along the blood strip on his dress blue trousers. "Listen up, swabbie, and I'm only going to tell you once, you miserable deck ape. When I tell you to step on the yellow footprints, you better step on them or I'll smack your teeth down your throat. All the yellow on those painted footprints will be covered by your dainty little foot. When

I tell you to stop and you don't stop immediately, I'll shove this billy club so far up your ass you will be farting splinters for a month." Admiral Johnson smiled, almost giggling at the thought. His thoughts were interrupted by his intercom on his desk. "Sir, Lieutenant Burke is waiting for you."

He didn't like this Burke, and as soon as he gave him what he wanted, he would write him a fitness report that would torpedo any chances of a career in the Navy.

"Send him in."

Burke stood at attention before Admiral Johnson and reported.

"I haven't heard from you in three days, Burke. I thought I told you no more than two days should pass before we talk. The next time you do this to me, your fitness report will indicate a lack of attention to detail, loyalty, and I'll add a lack of probity to round it out." His voice rising, he pointed his stubby finger at Burke. "I'm an admiral and you are a lieutenant. I've told you repeatedly to get your head out of your ass and communicate with me every other day, in person!"

Burke stared at the admiral and dreamed of putting his hands around his fat neck and slowly squeezing until the admiral begged for mercy. Better yet, when this business was all done and wrapped up, the admiral's fitness report would be shoved down his goitered throat.

Burke tried to hold back a contemptuous smile as he told the admiral what he wanted to know.

"Kincaid has not been out of my sight and that is the truth, Sir. If he takes any money he will be nabbed with definite proof of guilt. And you, Sir, will be the only admiral in the fleet who understood the possibilities of a naval officer stealing with such a flagrant disrespect of the law."

"So, our little investigation is going as planned, and it is going to make me a happy admiral, right lieutenant?"

"Yes, Sir, it just might put another star on your shoulder boards, Sir!"

The admiral stood up. He grabbed his white gloves and cover. "Very well, lieutenant, make sure you see me tomorrow and give me a complete update. Right now, I have to go to the Officer's Club for a Hail and Farewell."

Burke did an about-face and almost ran out of the room.

Chapter 41

Gentleman Jack's office, The Black Orchid

Gentleman Jack had contacted almost all the dermatologists in Hawaii to rid his hands and face of the ridiculously colored pigments. One doctor gave him some white cream that was supposed to suck the colors out of his skin's pores. At the moment, his hands and face were covered with the white perfumed cream. He could see with extreme satisfaction that the white facial cream was turning the color of the pigments.

A voice outside his door said Chin and the Hawaiian had arrived and were waiting for him. He looked up from the mirror he was peering into and said, "Come in." To his satisfaction, the fat Hawaiian and Captain Chin came in together. He stared at them, waiting to decipher a smile or a smirk that he would beat off their faces.

He pointed to the fat Hawaiian. "I pay you way more money than you're worth and what do you do for me? Some of your Hawaiian friends paint me up like a fucking cannibal and threaten me. I ought to kill you now, you son of a bitch. Explain to me how this happened?"

The Hawaiian started to shake in terror, his rolls of fat jiggle through his linen shirt.

"Jack, it wasn't any Hawaiians who done that to you. Somebody did this to hide the real reason they did this to you."

"Be serious. What could anybody want with me? They didn't even take my money."

Jack rolled his eyes and almost snorted.

"Give me a few days, and I'll try to find out who did this to you. Many people are working for me around the clock, searching for an answer." He looked at Jack with his round brown eyes.

Jack stared at him with a cold unforgiving stare. "What about the note, the feathers, and the stupid shark teeth? And the colors. I read that the colors represent Hawaiian tribes or some shit like that. The pigments are pigments that the Hawaiian's use all the time. How would you like it if I painted your fat ass with those pigments? Then you would understand how I feel." Jack stood at his desk and jabbed his finger at Koloho, his face contorted in anger, covered in white cream, making him look insane. "You better find out who did this to me and let me deal with them. You understand, fat boy?"

Kolohlo shook his head and spoke up. "Chloroform is not easy to find, Jack. My people didn't do this. I have a feel about the Hawaiians around the island. My informants are saying they were not Hawaiian."

Gentleman Jack walked up to Koholo and poked him in his ample belly. "I don't give a shit at this moment who did it. Find out who did! Now get out of my sight before I kill you!"

Koholo turned around quickly, getting out of the room as fast as he could waddle.

Jack looked at Chin with the same disgust.

"Chin, I give you a one hundred dollars a month to help me navigate the corridors of Hawaiian politics and give me police support when I need it, and right now, I need it. Get off your sardine cracker eating ass and find out what the hell is happening around here. In just a few days, we are going to hit pay dirt, and I don't want somebody to fuck it up. Do I have to work your Chinese ass over?"

Chin stood with an impassive face betraying no emotions or thoughts about Gentleman Jack. He paused before he spoke.

"Have you considered that it might have been that shamus at the Mac Detective Agency? He has ball's the size of grapefruit and from what I hear, he has bested you several times."

Jack understood how much he needed Chin and Chin knew that. The insult would be paid back at a later date. Too much was at stake.

"How right you are, Captain Chin. I paid greenbacks to have him taken care of and he is still walking upright like a fucking Neanderthal. Your shiny badge did not take care of the problem. If I remember correctly, he stabbed the shit out of two worthless police officers. Remember Chin, and never forget, Kincaid and the money come first."

Chin's face looked down. He had been told to take care of the shamus and he hadn't done it.

Captain Chin gave a half bow. "The shamus has made fools of both us. It will not happen again."

"Again, Chin, if it was this Mac guy, why would he go through all that trouble to paint me up, it doesn't make sense to me. Not his style. More of an in your face guy."

"Maybe he got somebody else to do it for him?" said Chin.

"Why? Chin, you are barking up the wrong tree. He's a stupid jarhead, take my word for it."

Chin stood up and quickly said, "I'll put several men on it right away. I think I know where to start, and I think I know where it will end."

Jack half stood and pounded his desk with both hands.

"Then get your ass out and there and find out who did this to me!" Chin got up and exited the room. He knew Jack was not fooling around this time.

* * *

Chin was so mad he threw his open can of sardines across the room, hitting one of his detectives. He pointed to the sardine - dripping detective. "Come here."

The other detectives in the captain's area held their noses as he passed by them.

"Take a couple of your boys and follow this Gunny Mac. I want information on what he does all day and report back to me. Tell me everything about this guy. Who he visits, who visits him, and what he eats for lunch. I want you to follow the Hawaiian bastard, and I want to know what he does every second of the day and report back to me. Now get out!"

* * *

Mac spent the morning searching for Gunny Wojo. He tried to think like his friend and that was a mistake. He started getting dizzy. He visited every spot the pecker head would go to and nothing. He had just vanished.

He caught a cab back to his office. He did not see the two men tailing him or the two Marines tailing the two that were following him. As soon as he entered the Bombay Alley, the Schnoz yelled at him to come over to the bar.

"The boys caught some guy sneaking in through the back door and have him in your office hogtied to a chair."

Mac slapped him on the back and ran up the stairs to his office. He opened the door to see two of his Marines pointing a .45 at a very livid gunny.

Mac started to laugh when Wojo exploded. "Get these damn ropes off me, Mac, so I can beat the shit out of these idiots. Especially the tall idiot who cold-cocked me with his .45. Everywhere I go, somebody is trying to kill me."

Mac nodded toward Corporal Reynolds. "Go downstairs and grab a drink until the gunny calms down. Sergeant Peterson, untie Gunny Wojo."

Mac put some ice cubes in a towel and handed them to him. "You have a small cut, but you'll live. It seems some people in Chinatown want us both out of action. I'm getting to know them all."

Wojo pointed to his head. "Yeah, some of them work for you." He got up, went over to Mac's desk, opened the drawer, and pulled out a bottle. He found the glasses and poured a drink for both of them.

Mac shook his head. "How come you always know where my bourbon is?"

Wojo shrugged his shoulders. "Years of experience working with you. I've developed a homing ability to sniff it out, especially your bourbon."

He raised his glass. "To Guadalcanal and to our boys that didn't make it home."

Mac made the next toast. "To us and those like us, damn few left."

Mac couldn't believe Wojo was with him again and he didn't want anything happening to him. "Wojo, you will be staying here. We have plenty of room."

They continued small talk about friends and their experiences until half the bottle of bourbon was gone.

Gunny Mac spoke. "Before we get drunk, I need to find out what happened to you on the Canal."

Wojo took a sip of his bourbon, silent, searching for the right words. He looked up at Mac with a rage on his face Mac had never seen before.

"It's all pretty simple, Mac. It was a patrol you and I could do in our sleep. Check out a cave, see if we could get some Jap prisoners, collect any intelligence we could come up with, and blow the cave. I had a navy lieutenant up in the tree line, watching us in an overwatch position.

"That would be Lieutenant Burke?"

"How in the hell did you know that?"

"I'll tell you later on."

"He was to keep communications with the battalion if something happened and get us help if we needed it. My translator and I went into the cave and found some Japs still alive. We tried to get them to surrender. The S-2 told me he wanted a prisoner. There were eight Japs inside that cave. Five were dead, and three still alive. One of the Japs turned to shoot me. I nailed him. I heard a noise further back in the cave and shot another Jap trying to get his rifle sights on me. I called out for our corpsman to check the Jap that was still breathing. He told me maggots were feasting on the guy like he was a Thanksgiving dinner, and that he didn't have much time left. We gave him some water and a cigarette. We interrogated the poor kid and found out there was a high-ranking Jap in the back of the cave, deader than a doornail. I went back and found a pouch next to him. As we were getting ready to leave, the Jap died, and we exited the cave. I opened the pouch and I'll be damned. The bag was filled with jewels."

Mac looked at Wojo, surprised. "Jewels?"

"Later on, I would find out they were off the swords of Jap officers killed on the Canal and the jewels were going back to the families in Japan. After that, things went haywire. Lieutenant Burke began jumping up and down and yelling Japs were to our right. All hell broke loose. Then he started yelling more Japs to our left. He started firing toward my left. I started firing to my right. We killed the Japs, and then I turned toward my left. I was hit in the back and went down hard. Someone stood over me and I couldn't make out his face. Everything was going dark. His hand went searching through my dungarees and pack." Wojo stopped for a second and took a deep breath. "I remember exactly what happened next. As I lay there barely alive, I heard the son of a bitch say something."

Mac filled his glass up, watched Wojo, and waited.

He looked into Mac's eyes.

"Go on, Wojo," he said.

"I heard him say, 'Where are the jewels?' I reached out and grabbed his wrist and somehow tore off his watch which landed on my chest. When they found me, they put the watch with my personal effects."

Mac said, "You sure it was an American who shot you?"

Wojo nodded and pointed to the watch on his wrist. "That is the watch I tore off his wrist. On the back is an engraved name. I'm going to find the bastard and kill him."

Mac got up and walked around the room. "How do you know the soldiers were not firing at the Japs and hit you by mistake?"

Wojo extended his hand out for a refill. "You know about the navy lieutenant who was with me. While in the hospital, I wrote him up for a Silver Star, which, thank God, was awarded to him. He wrote to me to say thanks and to report his wounds were on the mend. His letter filled me in on what I might have missed and explained his actions. At least two American soldiers were firing at my Marines, and they hit at least two. He also saw the bastard who shot me point-blank in the back. One of my Marines died and I'm going to make sure he dies as quickly as possible."

Mac looked at his friend and let out a big sigh. "That is one hell of a job, Wojo. He could have been KIA. Or shipped out to the states. There are over six million men under arms." Wojo smiled. "Mac, I got his watch with his name and high school. I'll find him. He doesn't know it yet, but he is a dead man."

Chapter 42

Hotel Street

Mac watched from the recessed door as Wojo walked down the street in his direction and approached the alley. Two men were following Wojo. Mac waited until they passed him, and then he stuck his .45 in the back of one of them.

"I think you boys need to raise your hands or I'll blow a hole through you the size of a bowling ball," said Mac. He took their weapons and his Marines tied their hands behind their back. Two cars pulled up and each man pushed into a separate waiting car. Mac got in one and Wojo the other.

They drove down to a deserted beach and all boarded a boat. The sun was just about to descend below the horizon.

"Well, well, it's still light enough to go swimming," laughed the Marine next to the outboard motor. Two Marines sat in the middle holding .45s on the two prisoners. Wojo and Mac sat at the front of the boat and watched.

"What do you mean, go swimming?" asked the younger of the two Hawaiians.

"Right off those shoals over there is where the sharks hang out and they're hungry, don't you think?" He took some rope and tied it firmly around each man. He then smeared them with chicken blood.

"What are you doing?" one of them gasped as his mind began to realize what was happening.

"Well," drawled one of the Marines, "I know that sharks can smell blood in the water which makes them go crazy. Isn't that what you heard? We are going to ask you some questions and if I were you, I would answer those questions truthfully and quickly. Now for the first question, why did you follow the big guy?"

They both looked at each other and answered at the same time.

"We were not following anybody. That's the truth!"

The Marines in the boat started laughing and passed around a bottle of whiskey. One Marine leaned close to them and laughed.

"Liar, liar, pants on fire." He pulled up on the rope and threw one of the men into the ocean.

"Don't forget to pull up on that rope, Ken; his arms are tied. We can drown him later if he doesn't talk."

He pulled up on the rope and the man bobbed to the surface.

"Are you ready to talk cause if you aren't going to talk, a shark is heading your way."

Before he could say a word, a shark took hold of him and tore him apart in the water.

"Damn, did you see that? Where in the hell did he come from?"

They looked over to the Hawaiian sitting in the boat; a big stain was spreading around his crotch.

"Please don't put me in the water. I'll answer any question you want. I won't lie. Please!"

"Well, I guess we have some cooperation now," said Ken. "All right, the same question again." He pointed to Wojo. "Why were you following that man?"

He looked down at the billowing clouds of blood just off the starboard side of the boat. "We were to sap him and take him to see our boss, and our boss was to interrogate him."

"Who is your boss, dummy?"

"Please; he'll kill me."

"Well, pecker head, would you rather get eaten by a shark?"

"Will you let me go if I tell you?"

Wojo sipped his whiskey and said, "Boys, where did you get this fine top-shelf whiskey?"

"Gunny Mac makes sure we get the best whiskey."

Wojo looked at Mac. "Ah, the benefits of friendship," he said.

Mac looked at the terrified man. "What we got here is a shit house lawyer, he wants to make a deal. No deal you worthless piece of shit. Throw him in the damn ocean."

The Marines smiled. "Ok, gunny."

Ken lifted the rope and pushed him in the ocean. The scream that came out of his throat sounded like a wild animal.

"Pull the ass wipe up before he gets eaten and we don't get our name," said Wojo.

Two of the Marines got the man back into the boat. He was babbling incoherently. The Marines looked down at him with disgust. They poured some bourbon in a cup and gave it to him.

"Now that was us having a little bit of fun. Who sent your fat ass to follow the gunny?"

Spittle formed at the corners of the man's lips. "Koholo. He is the owner of several bars on Hotel Street."

"What was he going to do to me after the interrogation?" asked Wojo, slurping down the last of his whiskey.

"I don't know. He never told me."

"The son of a bitch is lying; I can see it in his eyes," said one of the young Marines.

Another Marine filled up Wojo's glass. "Put him in the water for good this time," Wojo said as he slurped down a slug of whiskey.

"Please, I lied! He was going to kill you."

A Marine reached out and punched him square in the face.

"We are going to keep you under wraps in an out of the way place. If you are lying to us, we will drag your ass back out here and feed us some sharks."

* * *

Mac knew that he was next but didn't realize it was going to be so soon. Chin's men followed Gunny Mac to the door of the Bombay Alley. One of them pulled out his .45 and jammed it in Mac's back.

"Don't make a fuss or we'll put one in you right here," he said. Mac froze.

He had suspected someone was following him and so had taken some precautions. Mac exhaled when he heard some wonderful words.

"Keep your fingers off the trigger, boys, and raise your hands. It's ok, Mac, we got the sons of bitches."

Mac turned around and watched.

One Marine handcuffed them while the other watched them with his .45.

"Let's take them where we planned."

Mac nodded, yes. "I'm going with you, boys. I gotta see this."

They walked around the corner and got into a car.

In five minutes, they arrived at a warehouse. They pushed the two men inside.

Mac stood off to the side.

One of them spoke up, confidence dripping from his voice. "You boys are in trouble. You just kidnapped two cops."

The kidnappers sat at the table and laughed. Corporal Reynolds spoke first. He pointed to Mac. "Why did you want to kill that man?"

The surly one spoke up first. "We don't know what the hell you are talking about."

Corporal Reynolds leaned over, grabbed the man's finger, and smashed it with the butt of his .45. A groan erupted from the cop's mouth. Reynolds looked at the finger carefully as if he cared.

"That must hurt," thought Mac.

"Not broken but smashed really good. You have many fingers, idiot, and each one could end up looking like that one if you don't squeal and squeal good. Now I'm going to ask you another question and you better answer it. We caught you as you were about to shoot Gunny Mac in the back. We wanna know why and who gave you the orders."

Silence filled the room.

"I guess we gotta do it the hard way." He grabbed the cop's thumb and smashed it with the butt of his .45. Blood oozed from the crushed nail.

"Ah, fuck," yelled the cop.

Reynolds swung from his feet, flat-footed and connected with the cop's jaw. The chair skidded back about two feet and the cop fell to the concrete. Reynolds looked at the other sitting cop and smiled.

"You look like a reasonable crooked cop. Will you answer my question?" asked Corporal Reynolds.

The cop looked down at his partner lying unconscious on the floor, swallowed hard and said, "You boys are going to be hunted down like dogs. This is not going to end well for you guys. I'd stop now and get the hell out of Chinatown."

Corporal Reynold's grabbed the cop by his lapels. "You think you can go around killing Marines like we are cockroaches, you bastard? We spent the last year killing Japs. And right now, we hate you way more than the fucking Japs."

The Marines surrounded the cop. Each cuffed him around the face, hand and shoulders until he shouted out for them to stop.

Mac couldn't remember when he had so much fun. "Boys, you got some popcorn?"

The Marines snickered.

Corporal Reynolds sat on the table facing the cop.

"All right, start talking, you bastard, and you better not lie or so help me, you'll wish you were dead. You tried to kill a friend of ours and that is a killing offense."

"Captain Chin ordered us to plug that guy you call Gunny Mac."

"Why, you piece of shit?"

The cop looked all - around at the hardened faces surrounding him.

"You ain't gonna kill me, are you?"

"If you lie to us, you'll beg for us to kill you."

The crooked cop started spilling his guts.

A voice came out of the darkness. "He interfered with Chin's plans."

"Are Chin and Gentleman Jack working together?" The cop looked around, trying to locate the voice.

"Who are you?"

"Just answer the question you piece of shit."

"Everybody in this town is involved somehow with Gentleman Jack. He has half of Chinatown on his payroll."

The man in the shadow moved into the light. Alongside him were four armed Marines with shore patrol armbands.

"Gentlemen, these nice Marines are going escort you to our fine brig, run by United States Marines who can't wait to meet your acquaintance." Burke looked over at Mac and smiled at that prospect.

Chapter 43

Pearl Harbor, Base Communications Center

Burke drove the government sedan to Admiral Johnson's office, feeling unsettled and apprehensive about what he was doing behind the admiral's back. Even though he had the Pacific Fleet Intelligence Operations blessings, he felt like he was walking into a trap set by the admiral. He exited the sedan and looked out over the ocean, sparkling like a sea of diamonds. The air was laden with the smell of the tropics, molting things, along with the humidity that covered everything with a sheen of salt.

He wondered again if Johnson was running an intelligence operation on him. He quickly pushed that thought out of his mind. If he was, it was too late to change his plans now. He was wearing his uniform today because the admiral did not like to see him in civilian clothes. He was sure it was because he wanted him to stand at attention and understand how powerful and mighty he was, sitting behind his, "I love me" wall of plaques and commendations.

He entered the building and heard someone calling his name. He turned around toward the communications center. A young sailor walked toward him.

"Sorry, Sir, for yelling at you, but your message from Washington D.C. just arrived." He handed the file to Burke. He opened the file. It was a short-encrypted message; it read, "Fingerprints are of deceased soldier PFC Jack Calamari. (killed in action on Guadalcanal). Message attached to a copy of the fingerprint card. Any questions, please refer to file number 216-541954; deceased had known affiliation with California Cosa Nostra, arrest record included. Agent-In-Charge, Dan Forry."

Burke was right about his instincts. This changed everything. He took a deep breath. How in the hell could he be dead? Either the fingerprint factory made a mistake or Gentleman Jack was an impostor. Admiral Johnson's visit would take place at another time. Gentleman Jack was dead, and he didn't even know it.

* * *

Lieutenant Burke parked his car in front of the Bombay Alley, overrunning the curb with his front right tire sitting on the sidewalk. He pushed his way through the crowd of people and ran into the Bombay Alley as if his ass was on fire. If he were one - minute late, Mac's self-appointed secretary would read him the riot act. He looked at the young Marine and almost pointed to the clock but stopped.

"What the hell happened ˜o you," he said.

"You mean the bandages, lieutenant? I got shrapnel working itself out of my eye and head. What about it?"

Burke looked at Sergeant Peterson with sympathy. "You ok?" he asked.

The Marine looked up at Burke and replied. "Lieutenant. I got shrapnel leaking out of my brain, and one poking out of my eye. You are one minute late for your appointment with the gunny."

"I apologize, sergeant, but Admiral Johnson took more time than I thought."

The sergeant gave Burke a rake over with his good eye and let him into Mac's office.

Mac was talking to Padre McCaffrey and Wojohowitz.

Burke waved around a Navy Confidential file. "We got problems, boys. Wait till you see what's in this file."

He handed the file to Mac. "Take a look, Mac. Tell me what you think."

Mac opened the file and went through the fingerprint card and message. After several seconds he looked up, startled. "It says in this message that Gentleman Jack is deader than the Mahi Mahi I had for lunch."

Burke spoke up. "We need to check our copy of Jack's fingerprints with the copy of his fingerprints attached to the message from Washington DC."

Padre McCaffery went to Mac's filing cabinet and pulled out his copy of the fingerprint card. He walked into his office and returned with a magnifying glass.

"Let's make a comparison, shall we?" The padre took Burke's copy of the prints and started to compare.

Wojo took a puff on his cigar and said, "Does this fellow have a name?"

Mac looked down at Wojo. "It seems that our guy who is alive, but supposed to be dead, is a PFC Jack Calamari, United States Army."

Wojo immediately got up from his chair and pushed Burke out of the way. He grabbed the message from Mac's hand and read it. "Well, I'll be a son of a bitch." He took off his wristwatch and handed it to Mac. "Read the inscription on the back."

Mac walked into the sunlight streaming through the window and read the inscription. "Jack Calamari, George Washington High School. This is the watch you tore off the guy's wrist?"

Wojo said. "That's the bastard that killed my Marine, wounded Burke, and shot me. After he shot me, he searched me for the jewels. I tore the watch off his arm. After I kill the bastard, he is going to be deader than dead."

Burke spoke to Wojo. "The message says he is a member of the California mob with arrests for deadly assault, robbery, and fraud. Known associates are all members of the Cosa Nostra. This guy is the real deal, which means his support network is larger than we originally thought."

"No wonder that grease ball DeVito is working for him. They named DeVito as part of the California mob. So, we can expect that the mob wants to take over operations in Hawaii, especially in Chinatown and Oahu where the money is, where our military boys can be sheared like sheep," said Burke.

"If the dead guy is alive, nothing less than a stake through the heart will kill him," said Mac.

"I'll drive a .30-06 round right through his black heart," quipped Wojo.

Bending over the prints, the padre spoke. "My dear Mac, these indeed are the prints of the fornicator Calamari, alias Gentleman Jack."

Wojo lit a new cigar. "What I'd like to find out; who is the soldier killed in action, and how did he become Calamari?"

"May I make a bold suggestion?" asked the padre. Everybody turned toward the smartest and the craziest man in the room.

"Padre, we need you more than ever," said Mac.

"Using my rather logical mind, it is apparent that there is only one alternative. Gentleman Jack took the identity of a soldier killed during your fight and changed dog tags with him."

"Why didn't they identify Jack when he enlisted and arrest him?" Mac asked. "They took his prints. And why didn't they confirm the identity of the real dead guy by his prints?"

"I can answer that, Mac; the Fingerprint Factory wasn't up and running yet, when Jack enlisted," said Burke. " I'm sure at that point; his fingerprints were only going to be checked if he was killed in action and had to be identified. Millions of guys were enlisting. Why the KIA was not identified as who he was is pure speculation on our part. We are talking about a new system and millions upon millions of new prints. Burke shrugged his shoulders. "Maybe he was unidentifiable, who knows."

"May I please see the message, Mac?" asked the padre.

He glanced through it.

"Now, as I see it, my dear boys, we have a new set of problems to solve." The padre handed the message back to Burke. "It is imperative that we assume this is Jack Calamari, alias Gentleman Jack. He is, for a fact, tied in with the West

Coast crime family. His list of hideous crimes sent to us by the FBI tells us he is quite dangerous."

Burke interrupted the padre. "Don't you think he has the financial backing of this group, their intelligence capability, and manpower?"

The padre nodded in affirmation and spoke. "Another question we must answer is how many men are working with him, and is he sharing the money he plans on stealing. I would also assume some insider within the government is helping him. If that is the case, we are compromised."

Mac asked, "That means people who are supposed to be on our side might be working with him?"

"Exactly, my dear Mac, we must not trust anyone except the few in this room. We might all be dummies working for the man behind the curtain, the proverbial Wizard of Oz."

"One ace is up our sleeve," said Mac. "They don't know what we know about Jack. I'm beginning to smell a rat."

Burke spoke up. "We're at a grave disadvantage. I hope Kincaid is not working both sides. He'll do anything for his niece. Because of this new information, certain pieces of the puzzle just clicked into place. I'm afraid Jack knows an awful lot about all of us. In the last few days, Calamari's gangsters tried to kill Gunny Wojo and Mac. Now we know why Wojo needs killing."

"Yeah," said Wojo. "But does he know I have his watch with his name carved on it?"

Burke said, "Good question, gunny, but I don't think so. I think someone heard you asking questions."

Mac asked, " No one has tried to kill you, lieutenant. Do you think they know about you?"

"Don't know," said Burke. "I may be protected because I'm supposed to be setting up Kincaid. If they find out I got Jack's prints, I will be dead an hour later. They may or may not put two and two together and figure out we are working together. Calamari is not seeing the whole picture. Our problems are just beginning. Like how to stay alive. We all need to see the big picture, so let's quickly go over everything we know."

Burke walked over to the coffee pot and poured everyone a cup.

He continued. "Admiral Johnson ordered me to follow Kincaid. He told me no official orders would be authorized for this situation. I thought this was very strange, but then again, the man wants no responsibility if I fail, written orders would link me to him. He needs Kincaid to either steal the money or look like he stole it and then spend the next twenty years pacing in a ten by fifteen-foot cell."

"Why would the admiral want Kincaid in jail?" asked the padre.

"Kincaid told me that he screwed Johnson's wife up, down, and sideways."

"A fornicator of the worst kind," fumed Padre McCaffery.

Burke smiled. "So, Johnson wants Kincaid bad. I followed Kincaid around for eight days. Most of the time, he was drunk and trying hard to get drunker. I found out Jack has the commander by the balls. Sorry, padre."

"That's ok, Lieutenant Burke; we have balls. Perfectly natural."

"I put two and two together and figured out that Kincaid either wanted to steal the money, thought about stealing the money or was blackmailed into helping Jack steal the money."

Mac got up and poured some coffee into Burke's cup and stopped in front of him.

"How did Gentleman Jack find out about 'Operation Torch,' and that Kincaid was in charge of the operation?"

"It's no secret that Roosevelt wants the money burned and people are getting funny money to replace real dollars," said Burke. "It would be relatively easy to find out about Kincaid." Burke continued, "Gentleman Jack blackmailed Kincaid into helping him because Kincaid has huge gambling debts, close to five thousand dollars. He told Kincaid that his niece was close by ready to be snatched at Jack's leisure. Kincaid told me what a fantasy about had been stealing the money became a reality."

Burke paced the floor, half thinking to himself, while explaining his story to the group.

"One night I saw DeVito visit Kincaid in his BOQ and figured something was up. We know Kincaid, DeVito, and Gentleman Jack alias Calamari are pals and working together to take the money. The commander decided to work with us, but I feel he might screw us over in a heartbeat to save his ass. I'm meeting him tonight and getting the chronological order of events on burn day concerning, 'Operation Torch.' At the present moment, I'm so confused. I feel like Moe in a Three Stooges comedy, I seem to have lost my bearings, so I'm going to need all your help in putting all the facts together, in a manner that even a stooge understands. Mac, I'm going to need your planning ability to keep us alive. They know we are putting 'Operation Torch,' in play tomorrow morning and our plans are incomplete."

The padre pointed to Wojo and Mac. "Just keep in mind that Gentleman Jack and Chin are trying to kill you both."

Wojo looked at Mac, who shrugged as if to say, " what else is new."

The padre continued. "The following men want you dead. They are Captain Chin, supervisor of the Chinatown Homicide Division, Koholo, a wealthy bar owner and collector of intelligence, Gentleman Jack, the most notorious gangster in Hawaii, and Joe DeVito, a cold-blooded killer. Since we know that Gentleman Jack is forcing Kincaid to work with him to steal the money, we must assume our identities are not secret."

Lieutenant Burke chimed in. "As you know, we apprehended several of the men sent after you in the last week. He cleared his throat and looked at Padre McCaffery and some are now missing."

Padre McCaffery avoided Burke's eyes.

Burke continued. "By now, they know that we know more than they thought we knew. The men mentioned by the padre and the others certainly are out to make this war a personal means of consolidating power and money. We have broken more laws than I dare to mention. What will help us is martial law. Captain Chin's authority is next to none. I contacted General Jones and he stated that Habeas Corpus doesn't exist on this island during martial law. We can move civilians through military tribunals. We have full authority over anything or anybody that interferes with the destruction of the money. We all are still members of the Navy Department, and I have been permitted by the Navy Department to use you in any way I see fit. Of course, that is with your consent. If you agree, all of you involved in 'Operation Torch' will be Naval Intelligence agents under the same authority, the Department of the Navy." Burke reached into a bag and gave each of them a badge encased in leather. "The key is to stay alive and complete our mission by burning the currency and issuing new currency and in the process stop Gentleman Jack and his boys or Calamari whatever the hell his name is."

Mac spoke up. "We all know something is going to happen in the next eighteen hours."

Mac stood up and looked around the room. "We are now officially government law enforcement half of us crazy as loony tunes."

The office erupted in more laughter.

Burke walked to the front of the room next to Mac. "Kincaid has told me that we have less money than originally thought and are only going to burn the money at the sugar cane factory. That is tomorrow morning. If we can burn the money in one day, we will do it. Kincaid said the gangster Calamari wants and expects twenty bags of money. Remember why we are going through all this trouble. Admiral Johnson wants Kincaid's scalp at any price. He's blinded by pure hatred of the commander. Kincaid is helping us take down the Cosa Nostra and his only request is for us to protect his niece from Calamari. We must keep this information about the twenty bags of money we are giving to Jack, from the Treasury Agents because they work for Johnson. We will track the money and arrest Jack."

Mac shook his head. "We still have not figured out how we are going to track Jack. We know he's not stupid."

"We still have a few hours to figure that out. I'll leave that up to you, Mac. Just remember burning is to commence tomorrow morning at 0700 hours," said Burke. Wojo spoke up, "My Polack stomach is screaming for food. Let's get a bite to eat and come back and finish."

Chapter 44

Bombay Alley

They returned from a quick dinner and they got back to work. Mac said, "Let me get this straight. Kincaid will burn the collected money at the sugar cane factory. The money will be brought into the factory and stacked along the southern wall on the main floor of the sugar cane factory, where one huge furnace is located. The Treasury agents haven't given us a final count of how many bags of money." Burke stopped him. "Kincaid is at the sugar cane factory, ensuring the inventory sheets are final."

"Ok," said Mac.

Burke went on. "Each bag will be identified by a lead seal with a number initialed by the Treasury Department and tied to the mailbag clasp and a numbered tag. The front row of bags will start with identification number one and end at one hundred and fifty. The next row will begin with 151 to 300 and so on so on. The money's secured in the sugar cane factory by armed Marines."

"Go over what happens once we start burning the money," asked Mac.

"There are huge doors on Kincaid's side that open up to our side, so we can pass the money through. Inside the furnace are rollers on which the bags will rest. The inside surface of the furnace is approximately 150 square feet, enough to hold 20 bags of money. At a minimum, that is approximately 1 million to 1.8 million dollars on those rollers burning at one time."

"Where will I, Wojo, and the padre be located?" asked Mac.

"On the other side of the furnace, waiting to pull out Jack's 20 bags of money. We will let you know when we put them in. The first 20 bags of money will be soaked in alcohol. After Kincaid turns on the furnace and the bags are cooking, you will wait ten minutes and pull them out. Kincaid tells me the money will be slightly damp inside the bags and not burned. You will put the magnesium torches in each bag and set the timer for 24 hours. The magnesium torches are there in case we lose them and is our insurance policy. Then you will throw them in the bottom of the truck. We will drive this truck to the garbage barge and transfer the money to the barge. I assume the money will then be taken to vehicles that belong to Gentleman Jack. Then we will start tracking the bastards. Tracking these palooka's is going to be the tricky part; how do we track them? At this moment we don't know how they are going to transport the money. As you all know, we discussed various ways they could do that, one, by truck. They could stop the truck and load the bags onto smaller cars or trucks and head in different directions. They could take the money to a boat, load it up and leave. A PT boat is ready to follow at a distance. What we are not anticipating is a plane flying them and the money somewhere."

Mac looked at Burke and nodded his understanding.

Burke continued. "The plan is far from perfect, but we're covered on two fronts. If we lose them, the money will explode in flames like a Roman candle, and if we can track them, we will have them on ice and in Leavenworth for the next hundred years."

Burke walked over to the door. "Mac, I have to leave and see Kincaid, I'll call you tonight."

Mac took a puff on his cigar. "Before you leave, can we trust Kincaid to do what he says he will do? What if he doesn't do what he is supposed to do? We might all end up in Leavenworth. That crazy admiral you work for might not take kindly to what we are doing."

"If our plan goes wrong and millions of dollars get lost, along with the people who took it is an idea I don't want to entertain," said Burke.

"Just remember, no matter what happens, Calamari is mine," said Wojo

Mac put his hand on Wojo's shoulder. "I wouldn't have it any other way, Wojo. But this calls for more planning than we have done. Taking on the mob is not going to be a picnic."

Burke shook his head in agreement. "We now know all about this guy. Let's get him!" Burke gave a wave and left the room.

Padre McCaffery let out a howl. "One for all, and all for one." They all looked at the padre and grinned. How could they lose with a Jesuit priest as their partner?

Chapter 45

Bombay Alley, Mac's office

Mac leaned over and answered the phone by the second ring. He heard the panic in Tony's voice.

"Rose just called me. She said Jack is holding her hostage. Jack wants his money."

"She say anything else?"

"Just said money for her life."

"Okay, Schnoz." Mac hung up. Now he had to worry about another person's life. Lives were getting cheaper by the dozen.

Mac walked over to Padre McCaffery. "Tony the Schnoz has confirmed that Rose Kincaid is officially a hostage. Now we don't know if Kincaid will assist us with our plans and we don't know if he made a deal with Gentleman Jack or if he told Jack what our plans are. I wouldn't be surprised if he has done both."

Mac went to his desk and picked up a piece of paper.

"Wojo, run over to the arms depot and pick up this list of items."

Wojo whistled. " Do you expect a war? Three BARs, four Thompsons, ten 03s, ten forty-fives, and all this ammo?"

"Let's rationally look at this. I took pictures of Jack fornicating."

Padre McCaffery rubbed his jaw and said, "The bastard fornicator."

Mac continued. "I shot one of his men and beat another senseless. Then we knocked him out and painted him up like a cannibal. With, by the way, paint that took two weeks to wear off. After that, I went over to his den of debauchery and stopped him from fornicating a second time."

"You are doing God's work, Mac," said the padre as he crossed himself.

"Then I punched him in the gut, stole his bourbon and Cuban cigars, and embarrassed him. He gave me the kiss of death as I left. He is going to try to kill me before tomorrow morning, which is fine with me. Let's pour ourselves a nice big bourbon and smoke a fine Cuban cigar compliments of Gentleman Jack, and let's talk about our plans for tonight and tomorrow."

Mac looked more confident than he was. He had a sneaking suspicion that Jack was more in control than he was. He would never forgive himself if one of his boys died. He looked at the two men he would count on to make the mission a success.

Padre McCaffery smacked his lips and gave Mac a look of pure affection. "We are quite the team Mac, quite the team!"

Chapter 46

The Sugar Cane Factory

Burke drove over to the sugar cane factory to meet with Kincaid. Within hours, Roosevelt's plan would be carried out. Even though Guadalcanal seemed to be holding its own and a Japanese invasion might not happen, the money was going to be burned. One week ago, he could not have figured himself to be running a bootleg operation against an admiral, in cahoots with a drunken womanizing gambler, two crazy gunnery sergeants, a mad padre, and a slew of mentally deranged Marines. He was sure he was going to jail before this was said and done. People who messed with the Cosa Nostra usually ended dead. Yet so far, they had beat the odds to get this far. Kincaid was the weak link that could destroy them all. On top of all that, he had an admiral with deep government connections that wanted to ruin his life. What would happen when he gave the admiral nothing to incriminate Kincaid? Maybe a firing squad? He knew one thing; Mac would save him. He had to believe it. He parked his car and knocked on the door leading into the factory floor. A very pissed off Kincaid opened the door and started screaming at him.

"My niece just called me, you incompetent bastard! Jack has her. He made her call me to rub it in my face. One fuck up between us, and he cuts her damn throat. You could fuck up a wet dream, lieutenant!"

Burke walked over to where the rows of money were stacked. He leaned against the first row of bags and took a deep breath. "Look, Kincaid, let's look at the facts. Gentleman Jack doesn't know about me; he doesn't know about the men working on this case. I have purposely kept you in the dark for reasons that you can figure out. So, calm down, take a deep breath, and pour us some coffee; it's going to be a long day. I have to ask you a few questions, and I want your undivided attention."

"Let me tell you something, Burke. Jack seems to know a whole lot about everything. So, I wouldn't be so damn confident that he's as stupid as you think he is."

"Have you told Jack anything about me or what we are planning?" asked Burke.

"Now, why would I do anything like that, Burke?"

"You just said he might know about me?"

"I don't know where you got all your training, but you got short-sheeted somewhere. You are about the most naïve military officer I have ever seen. How in the hell are we going to ensure my niece is safe?"

"Kincaid, one question at a time. Does Jack know about me?"

"Look, Burke, I'm not a great gambler, but if I were a betting man, I would say he knows all about you."

"I find that hard to believe," said Burke.

"Look, you damn dummy. He found out I had a niece. He knew I oversaw the burning and collecting of the money. He knew when and where the money was going to be burned. He devised a plan to get away with the money. Jack seems to know everything about us without directly being informed by me. Don't you get it? He doesn't care about us. He will get his hands on many bags of money worth between 1.5 and 2.5 million dollars and he is going to get away with it. Odds are he will kill us all before he leaves."

"I'm just asking, Kincaid, just asking. I guess we'll see about that, won't we, commander. Especially since I'm a dummy and naïve, and so are the rest of us. Let's go over what we are going to do in less than twelve hours. Explain it to me again."

Kincaid took a big gulp of coffee, got up, and walked around the room. He gave Burke a petulant stare.

"We were right about a few things. The final count of the money collected is far less than the 200 million that we surmised would be turned in to us. Instead of the 1,280 bags projected, there are 846 bags, holding between $120 and $150 million. Each mailbag will have a numbered tag looped through the clasp where it is attached to a metal loop. As we load each group of twenty bags into the furnace, a Treasury agent will record it in a logbook. The bags we are concerned about are numbered 1-20. Tonight, I will soak them in my solution of 50% alcohol and 50 % water. These bags will be put in the furnace at 0700 hours. I will lower the BTU output of the furnace for the first 20 bags. They will be pulled out ten minutes later by you on your side, around at 0710 or 0715, and stacked on rollers until the flames burn out. Then they will be thrown in the back of the truck and be allowed to cool. At 0730 hours, I will put the next 20 bags in the furnace. I figure it will take around 20 to 30 minutes for each round of bags to burn completely at the maximum BTU output of the furnace. It may take more time; it may take less time, I don't know. We will have to experiment. I will do this for each round of 20 bags.

You will park the truck inside the building on your side close to the wall. The bags going to Gentleman Jack will be put in back of the truck to cool off. Once cooled off, you will place the magnesium flares halfway into each bag and set the timer for 24 hours. After that, you will cover the bags with the ashes from the furnace. One of your men will drive the truck to the barge and park it as indicated on the map Jack gave us. Your agent will leave in another car. Jack's men will unload the ashes onto the barge and transfer the money to whatever vehicles they use. I will stay, continuing the burning operations at the sugar cane refinery, lock the doors, and give orders to the Marines not to allow anyone in the building." Kincaid stopped talking and lit a cigarette. He offered one to Burke, he muttered a "thank you" and walked over to the factory overhead door and opened it. He took a drag on his cigarette and stared out at the rusty landscape. In a few hours, many lives would change forever. Hell, if Gunny Mac could save Bloody Ridge, he surely could save this operation. His thoughts turned to Admiral Johnson.

Tomorrow the admiral would be asking some critical questions that he couldn't answer. He'd be asked to hand over the proof that Kincaid was a thief. Burke knew his gonads were soon to be roasted chestnuts when the admiral found out that Kincaid was an innocent man. Admirals win - mere lieutenants lose.

He also hoped Mac had come up with a surveillance plan to track the money and Gentleman Jack, or all of them would be at his mercy. Sleep was going evade them all this very lonely night.

Chapter 47

Gunny Mac's office

The more and more Mac thought about Rose Kincaid, the more something did not add up. A nagging suspicion, like a thought hemorrhoid, kept pushing its way out of his unconscious id. It was getting late and he had to figure this out before tomorrow morning. He walked over to his filing cabinet and pulled out the two photos of Rose Kincaid. One given to him by the Schnoz and the one given to him by Big Gums. He sat down behind his desk and studied the photos. He placed them side by side. Something about the two photos bothered him. Something didn't add up. Then he thought he saw it. Maybe it wasn't important. He'd find out quickly.

He yelled out for the padre.

The padre walked into his office. "Yes, my dear Mac, what is it you need?"

"I hope I didn't bother you, padre."

"It is ok, Mac. I was just saying my devotionals. I can complete them later."

"Padre, I need your wonderful brain."

Padre McCaffery beamed. "It is always available to you, Mac."

"Look at these two photos and tell me what you see."

Mac sat back in his chair, closed his eyes, and waited to hear the padres soft but strong voice.

The padre studied the pictures for a few moments before giving Mac his summation.

"Both photographs are of the same beautiful woman."

He tapped the Schnoz's picture with his forefinger. "In this photo, she appears slightly younger, rather plain, with a cheap dress with no jewelry. Her facial lines, especially her eyes, indicate to me an unhappy, unsophisticated girl."

He picked up the photo Big Gums gave Mac and studied it carefully.

"This photo is much different. Hard to believe she is the same girl. Her facial expression is one of confidence and sophistication, but her eyes are more hardened. The dress she is wearing is much more expensive, and she has a costly bracelet on her wrist and some sort of ring on her finger. She is wearing diamond earrings that are quite large. She looks like an unhappy, sophisticated woman. The man in the photo is Gentleman Jack. He is touching her lower back as if he is guiding her to a door or chair, in an intimate way. They are both dressed up and look like they are going out on the town."

Mac went to the filing cabinet again and pulled out his magnifying glass. He hovered over the picture with Gentleman Jack. He stared at the image and grunted.

"My dear Padre McCaffery, we have been shanghaied, and I'm feeling very dumb."

"What do you mean, shanghaied?"

"This picture with Gentleman Jack was taken in his private room. I remember because I have been in it before. Which means Miss Kincaid must have been in Jack's room. What do you think of that, padre?"

The padre shook his head back and forth. "Which means, what is a nice girl doing in his bedroom?"

"Exactly what I was thinking, padre."

"Two fornicators, Mac. You catch them like flies."

Mac walked to the phone and called downstairs to the bar. "Schnoz, I need you ASAP."

Mac hung up, and before he could sit back down, Tony the Schnoz gasped for air at his door. "You ok, Mac?"

Mac smiled and showed Tony the picture of Rose Kincaid.

"Please sit down, Tony. Tell me more about this little woman- all the details. I don't want to miss one joyful birthday party you spent with this girl. Somehow, Schnoz, I got the impression from you, she was this sweet, charming little girl."

"I'm confused boss, what do you mean?"

"Do you want to tell me your part in this charade?"

"What's a charade, Mac?"

"I'll tell you later, said Mac.

"She has always been a little mixed up," said the Schnoz.

"Schnoz, this is very important. Tell me everything you know about this woman."

"I never had no family Mac, and over the years, I got to know her. I tried to protect her. She led a tough life for a little girl."

The Schnoz's face contorted with anguish. "I didn't lie to you, Mac."

"I hope you didn't my friend. I need more information about this girl, and I don't have much time."

He looked at Mac with thankfulness.

"She was constantly getting into trouble, and I kind of took the place of a daddy, just trying to help her."

Mac nodded. "Why did you come to my office and hire me to watch over her?"

"She came up to me and said she had a favor to ask of me. That I was supposed to contact you and tell you people were watching her. She gave me the hundred dollars to give to you. I gave you the hundred dollars. I gave you a picture I had of her. That's all there was to it, Mac."

"Did she have a brother who died on the Canal?'

"She said she did, but I never knew him."

"Does she have any relatives in the area?"

"No, Mac, honestly, I don't think so. I never saw anyone, ever."

"Is her real name Kincaid?"

"I always called her Rose, don't know her last name until she said it was Kincaid."

"What kind of trouble did she get into," Mac asked again.

He put his head down and stammered.

"She was stealing… money. It's hard for me to talk about the rest."

"What rest?" asked Mac.

He looked at Mac with pain in his eyes. "Prostitution."

"So, you don't know her very well, do you?"

"I met her when she was fifteen and maybe saw her three or four times a year. Whenever she was in trouble, she would find me. She'd ask for a few bucks. If I had any, I would give what I could afford. I had friends check on her and let me know if she was in trouble or doing bad things. I felt sorry for her. She was just a little girl who needed someone to help her."

Padre McCaffery went up to the Schnoz and put an arm around him.

"May God bless you for helping the fornicators of the world. Truly you are a man of God."

"Thanks, padre, for the prayer."

Tony walked up to Mac and said, "Are we still friends, Mac?"

"You did nothing wrong, Schnoz. It was me interpreting what you said in the wrong way. We are still partners and buddies. Don't tell anyone about what we discussed here. No one."

"I'd never do nothing to hurt you, Mac, never."

The padre spoke first. "I'm beginning to think she is in cahoots with Gentleman Jack or Commander Kincaid, and we are the dummies working to assist them in their thievery."

"That about sums it up, padre. We don't know if she's working for Jack, or Kincaid, or maybe all three are working together. But with your fertile brain assisting my gunnery sergeant peanut brain and Wojo's pea brain, we are going to pull off a Charlie Chan miracle."

Chapter 48

Wojo walked into the room with six Marines carrying heavy boxes. He pulled out the requisition form and read it off.

"One BAR, ten .03 Springfield's, ten Colt .45s, two Thompsons, one .03 Springfield with a scope and enough ammo to start a war."

Mac bent down and opened one of the ammo crates. "How many magazines do you think we need, Wojo?"

"Two bandoliers should be enough with ten magazines for the BAR, two drums each for the Thompsons, and five magazines for each .45. Also, twenty-five rounds per .03. If we need more than that, we are in big trouble."

Mac looked at the clock; it was nearly 2000 hours. He grabbed Tony the Schnoz by the arm.

"Close down the bar in one hour till tomorrow at 2000 hours tomorrow. Make something up. The shitters are clogged, a water leak, or we need to do spring cleaning. I want this bar empty until tomorrow night. Make sure everyone in Chinatown knows about our closing. We are going to have some visitors."

He nodded and went downstairs.

"You think that son of a bitch Calamari will visit us tonight?" asked Wojo.

"His boys may visit us tonight," Mac said. " Or early tomorrow morning to kill one or both of us. Maybe use it as a diversionary tactic. Take three of our Marines and organize a welcoming party for them. The padre and a squad of our Marines will go with me later to visit the sugarcane factory. We have a lot of work to do."

"Should we let Burke know what's going on?"

Mac thought for a second before he shook his head no. "He is supposed to be with Kincaid tonight going over tomorrow's plans. We need Kincaid and Burke out of the way."

Sergeant Peterson came into his office. "Gunny, Lieutenant Van Deer is on the phone. She said it's important she talk to you right now."

Mac picked up the phone and said, "Hello."

"Hello Mac, you need to come to the hospital now. Jonesy is not doing well. He seems to be giving up. His infections are winning. Tonight, we are trying a new antibiotic. There is hope we can beat this if he doesn't give up," she said.

Mac felt the blood rush to his face. His throat constricted; he sucked in some air trying to breathe. He threw down the phone, grabbed Seadog, and ran out of the room.

Wojo picked up the phone and listened to Van Deer and slowly put the phone down. His head dropped to his chest and one tiny tear rolled down his cheek.

* * *

Lieutenant Van Deer met Mac and Seadog at the entrance to the naval hospital and hugged him.

"Tonight, we are starting a promising treatment for him, but his body seems to be giving up. You need to be there for him. He loves you and Seadog."

Mac walked through the double doors of Ward D and stood before Jonesy's bed. He placed his hand over Jonesy's hand.

His eyes opened, and a smile crossed his face.

"Mac, what are you doing here?'

Seadog put his paws on the bed and nosed Jonesy's hand. "Seadog too?"

"I know one thing; Seadog and I are not here to say goodbye."

"Things are closing down. Don't know, Mac."

"That depends on you Jonesy. If it is goodbye, Seadog won't understand, and I don't know how I could explain it to him. You are his only uncle."

"I'm too tired to fight any more," he said.

"My brain housing group understands, Gunny, but my heart doesn't understand."

Jonesy turned his head away from Mac.

Mac spoke up. "Remember years ago, when we were at Parris Island Jonesy . . . and they were putting our dicks in the dirt. We looked at each other and wondered out loud if we were going to make it. Our DI asked us if we were queer because we were always together and helping each other out. When you were punished for an infraction and had to run with that damn .03 above your head, I volunteered to run with you, and when I was punished, you ran with me. Sgt. Cranston could never figure it out, and when we graduated, he pulled us out of the platoon. Do you remember what he said? That sergeant said that it was his pleasure seeing two numbnuts, exemplify what Semper Fidelis is all about. He left us with some wisdom. Do you remember Jonesy?"

Jonesy turned his head toward Mac. "Yes, I remember. The body will never quit on you, but you can quit on your body."

"Now there are some pretty tough Marines in this Ward with serious wounds who look up to you for strength to fight against terrible odds. Seadog and I are in that group. Marines never surrender to anything or anybody."

Jonesy looked at Mac. "It feels like you're running next to me and holding my damn heavy heart above your head."

"You carried me when my butt was in that bed next to you. I remember you saying to me that I was going to be ok. I remember drowning in my sweat and you hopping out of bed with that bad leg and hip wiping the sweat off me and putting ice chips on my lips and mouth when the thirst became unbearable, praying over me, and taking care of Seadog when I went into my surgeries. Every Marine is looking for inspiration and leadership from you. You may die, Jonesy, but never give up. All of us lost Marines need you. You can beat this just like we beat the Japs on the Canal."

"Message heard loud and clear, Mac."

"Lieutenant Van Deer told me your new treatment starts this evening to fight your infection. So, fight and fight hard. Seadog and I will see you tomorrow night. Wojo and I have a problem that needs settling in just a few hours or we would stay with you."

"Thanks, Mac. Thanks for squaring me away."

"By the way, there is a rumor going around that your promotion to first sergeant is approved," Mac said, smiling.

He offered his hand to him. He felt Jonesy squeeze his hand hard. Mac walked away, knowing he was going to make it.

Gunnery Sergeant Herbert Jones smiled. First sergeant; well, I'll be damned.

* * *

Mac made it back to his office within the hour. He saw the Western Union telegram on his desk. His heart skipped a beat. Telegrams were not good news. He hesitated and then tore it open.

> *Dear Mac,*
> *I couldn't reach you by phone. Just got word from a pilot friend that G Jack/DeVito with cargo by Pan Am Clipper to land 200 miles off California to waiting boat. Plane leaves 8:00- 10:00 PM tomorrow. Price $30,000.*
>
> *Caroline.*

He put the telegram on his desk. Good ole Caroline came through. He would thank her after this mess was done but Jack would get the money over his dead body.

Mac handed the telegram to Wojo.

"Looks like we have a couple of problems, Mac," Wojo said. "If he loads the money onto that plane, we'll be responsible for bringing down a Pan Am Clipper. The magnesium flares will burn them out of the sky. And it looks like he's going directly to the Clipper to load up."

Mac agreed with Wojo's assessment. "We have to drop the idea of the flares in each bag. I didn't think a plane would be involved. We will have to rethink what the hell we are going to do. That makes it certain he will pay us a visit. What's your plan for tonight?" asked Mac.

"Tony made sure everyone in Chinatown knows we are closed. Sewer backup. Sergeant Peterson will be upstairs with two other Marines watching for any entry into the building. He will call us if there is trouble at the number you give him."

"What do you mean, we? You are staying here," said Mac.

"No, that one-eyed, hard-nosed, crazy pecker head of a sergeant can handle things here. Where you go, I go."

Mac looked at his best friend and saw the look in his eyes, no use arguing with him.

"Let's hope they leave us alone tonight because we are going to be busy. The padre, you and me, will go to the sugar cane factory and get settled into a hiding place while Burke is entertaining Kincaid at his BOQ. But we have to leave ASAP. Are Sergeant Peterson and his men in place?"

Wojo gave a thumbs up. "I'm following you guys in the truck. Our Marines from the wacko squad should have replaced the guards by now, securing the area around the factory. They are under strict orders from me to relieve the present security, let us in and watch for anyone attempting to enter the area or building."

Mac clapped Wojo on the back. "We need to get in that building and do what we are going to do. We need to do it quickly without mistakes. If anyone shows up, make sure the NCOIC warns us. Ten of our Marines will come with us."

Wojo grabbed his .03 Springfield, "I'm ready, Mac."

"We leave in thirty minutes," said Mac.

Chapter 49

Bombay Alley 2330 hours

The Marines at the Bombay Alley were ready. They had checked and rechecked all doors and windows, making sure only the back door and upper windows were unlocked. Sergeant Peterson wanted to funnel any marauders into his kill zones. He looked at his watch for the hundredth time. It was now 1130 hours in the evening and nothing but quiet. It was then he heard the creaking floorboards beneath him and someone walking into a bar chair. He signaled to the Marine watching him from Mac's office to call Mac that intruders had entered the Bombay Alley. He gripped his Thompson machine gun and pointed it down toward the noise. He left one small light on in the stairwell as instructed by Mac. From his spot, with his good eye, he could see the stairs going down which were in dappled shadows descending into darkness.

A clanking sound came in the direction from one of the bedrooms. He signaled Corporal Reynolds to move toward the noise. He nodded and moved silently to the open door of the room and looked in. It was empty. The second-floor window had been left open on purpose. The room was mostly dark except for the neon lights from the bar across the street shining in. He walked closer to the window; his body was hugging the wall. A grappling hook hung from the window. He peered through the opening, watching two guys climbing up the rope. They were within four feet of the open window.

"You bastards have made a huge mistake."

They looked up at him and saw the knife. He spat a honker of tobacco juice onto the man's face and laughed. They started to climb down the rope.

He cut the rope and watched them drop to the alley. "Thanks for dropping in, boys."

When they hit the ground, it sounded like two watermelons dropped from twenty feet onto the cement. Their groans sounded like a cow mooing. He turned around as a third guy came into the hallway from the room across the hall firing at Reynolds. The shot went wide, going through the open window and ricocheting off the brick side of a building. Reynolds fired and his target went down. He kicked the intruders revolver away.

"Looky here, another cockroach. We seem to be infested. You are a very lucky cockroach, I missed your head and hit you in the hand. Any more of your type of infestation coming up from windows or attic?"

"I don't know. Get me a doctor."

"How did you come up here?"

"The fire escape."

"You know how you are leaving?"

The man's eyes widened with horror.

He hoisted the man to his feet and dragged him to the window. He could hear the two men moaning below the window. "Your choice; window or fire escape."

He nodded quickly. "The fire escape."

"Who sent you?"

"Joe DeVito"

"Thank you, Mr. Cockroach."

Corporal Reynolds bent down and slammed the .45 hard into the left foot of the gangster. He let out a scream. He slammed the .45 hard into the right foot, hearing bones crackle.

"Now, I will help you to the fire escape. Please be careful, going down. Having one bad left hand and two broken feet is so dangerous, going down steep stairs."

Corporal Reynolds punched him in the face knocking him through the window and onto the fire escape landing. He locked the window.

He walked back down the hallway and stopped next to Sergeant Peterson.

"What the hell went on back there?"

"Three cockroaches down, sarge. What's going on here?"

Sergeant Peterson looked down the stairs.

"We have some cockroaches that are scurrying downstairs, around the bar area."

"How many?"

"Don't know, but sounds like three or four," whispered Peterson.

A voice boomed out from below.

"This is the Chinatown police. Shamus, just walk down the stairs with your hands in plain sight or we will set fire to your building and cook your ass."

Sergeant Peterson yelled out. "We are Federal agents. Throw your weapons down and walk up the stairs with your hands held high."

"Fuck you! This isn't a western asshole and you ain't John Wayne."

Peterson heard bolts slamming home.

Peterson pushed and dragged Reynolds away from their spot. A flurry of gunshots erupted through the floorboards. Bullets smacked all around the two Marines.

"They don't like us very much, Sarge."

"All we want is the Shamus, and we will leave the rest of you alone. We won't burn down the building. You have three minutes."

Sergeant Peterson whispered into the Corporal's ear, "I think the sons of bitches are right below us. Cover your ears."

He pointed the Thompson's barrel where he thought he heard the voice and pressed the trigger. The burst from the Thompson shattered the silence. He sent a line of slugs across the wood floor down into the bar. Both Marines ran down the stairs firing at anything that moved. Three men went down bleeding on the floor. A fourth man stood with his hands up, holding a Molotov cocktail burning in his right hand.

Sergeant Peterson waved the barrel of the Thompson at the man.

"Blow out that flame, ass wipe, or you will end up like your friends."

He blew out the flame.

Corporal Reynolds grabbed the bottle from his hand and punched him in the head.

"It is a sin to waste good booze, you worthless bastard!"

Peterson searched the wounded men and disarmed them. "Who is the son of a bitch that did all the talking?"

One of them pointed to a cop wounded in the leg.

"I didn't find a badge on any of you. You really cops?"

"I'm bleeding to death here, get me a doctor."

He slapped the guy across the face.

"Concentrate on what I'm asking you? You cops or some wharf scum?"

He sat and stared off in the distance.

Corporal Reynolds walked over and stepped on the bleeding leg.

The man screamed.

"When did you start being so nice, sarge?"

"I didn't want to get blood all over my shoes."

Corporal Reynolds raised his leg again as the man blurted out. " No, DeVito sent us."

Peterson shrugged his shoulders at Reynolds, and he stepped on the leg again. "Any more of you?"

He screamed, "No, damn it, just seven of us. Get off my damn leg."

Peterson started up the stairs. "Keep these guys covered while I call the number Lieutenant Burke gave me and get some MP's and an ambulance here."

Chapter 50

Pearl Harbor Naval Base

Burke paced back and forth across the hallway from the admiral's office like an expectant father. The phone call from the beast himself told him to get his ass double quick to his office, or the shore patrol would pick him up. Whatever the admiral wanted; it was not good news. He kept looking at his watch, wondering if Kincaid would wait for him and their meeting. Burke turned around and looked down the hallway and saw two members of the shore patrol, making their way toward him.

One of them was an ensign who spoke to him. "Are you Lieutenant Burke?"

Burke took a drag on his cigarette, burning a quarter inch into ash and answered, "Yes."

"Sir, we have orders to escort you back to your BOQ room where you will be under house arrest until the admiral can see you, Sir."

"Under whose orders and why, ensign?"

"Admiral Johnson's, Sir, and I don't have privy to the reason why."

"Admiral Johnson is not my commanding officer and is not in my chain of command. I am not under orders to him, by him, or under him."

He flashed his Naval Intelligence badge at him and said, "I'm working undercover at this moment ensign, and if you get in my way, your next assignment will be in the outer fringes of Alaska chewing blubber with the Eskimos. After I leave you, check with Base Intelligence, and they will back me up. Get the hell out of my way."

"What am I to say to the admiral?"

Burke frowned. "If I were you, I would get the hell out of here and disappear."

"Sir, my orders are to escort you to your BOQ and to let you go if the admiral has not called me."

"I'm not going to my BOQ, you bastard. I'll wait here."

The ensign pulled out his .45 and told Burke to sit and wait.

Burke looked at the admiral's door and threw his half-finished cigarette against the nameplate on the door. It was late, and he wasted the last three hours in the admiral's charade.

* * *

Mac and his boys arrived at the sugar cane factory and were relieved their Marines were on patrol around the factory and guarding the entrance. They were met by one of Mac's NCO's who opened the gate leading into the sugarcane factory. "Nobody has been in and out, Mac. Three of my Marines are down the road to stop anyone from coming in."

"Don't let anyone in until you see our truck leave. Make up any excuse. Pretend you are calling Lieutenant Burke. Call me instead. After our truck leaves, you can't let anybody in here without proper identification."

They unlocked the front door and walked in, quickly searching the factory floor and office. Wojo saw the phone and pointed to it.

"You better call Sergeant numbnuts and see if he is ok"

"Why do you keep calling our fine Sergeant Peterson numbnuts?" asked Mac, smiling.

"Because he's a looney bird."

While Mac was reaching for the phone, it rang. He picked it up. "Mac here."

"Seven men attempted to kill us and burn down the Bombay Alley. All seven of them are casualties. One of the idiots told us that a Joe DeVito and Captain Chin sent them. They were not cops. Hired men. The Provost Marshall showed up and is investigating."

Mac gave the ok sign to Wojo. "Make sure you tell them this is an intelligence operation and to keep silent about this until tomorrow. Make sure you find Lieutenant Burke and tell him what happened at the Bombay Alley and not to worry about us."

Mac looked around and said, "Sergeant numbnuts just saved the Bombay Alley. Something is going to happen soon. We need to complete our job and get a nice spot to watch what the hell happens."

Wojo backed the truck into the service area where the mail bags were standing upright as if at attention in rows of 150 ready to be burned. Mac went over to the first row of 846 bags of collected money. He took a deep breath to calm himself down. Millions of dollars stacked and packed in mailbags, all with round identification tags hanging from their clasps. It was enough to get the larceny flowing through his veins. Wojo and the padre joined him.

"We better start doing what the hell we talked about before someone comes and visits us," said Wojo.

Mac nodded without saying a word. They walked to the truck and unloaded 20 bags filled with paper scraps. They stacked the mail bags filled with paper in a row.

Padre McCaffery walked over to the rows of money and stopped at the first 20. He took a pair of scissors and cut the identification numbers off the mailbag clasps. He unwired the lead time-stamped tags. He handed the lead tags to Wojo and the identification numbers. Padre McCaffery helped him restring them with identical string and laid them off to the side. Wojo got into the back of the truck. Mac walked to the first row of stacked money, now without tags, grabbed a bag, and handed it to Wojo. Inside of five minutes, they loaded all 20 bags worth between $1.5 million and $2.5 million in the truck. They looked at each other and smiled. Padre McCaffery put the identification numbers and lead tags onto the new bags. They stacked them back where they stood before. It took the three of them less than 30 minutes and the job was complete.

Wojo got into the panel truck adorned with Wonder Bread on its sides and drove to the back of the Bombay Alley. The indispensable Sergeant Peterson and the unflappable Corporal Reynolds waited for Wojo to unload and stack the mail bags in the Bombay Alley's storage room.

* * *

Mac and the padre climbed the factory's back stairs and picked a spot to survey the furnace floor area where they could keep the money in full view.

"My dear Mac, somebody is in for a real surprise!"

Mac smiled from ear to ear. "Wish I could be there when the son of a bitches open those mailbags. If we are right about Kincaid, he has a little over three hours to make his move."

Thirty minutes later, the garage door opened. Commander Kincaid strode into the floor area. He closed the garage door and went to an area left of the furnace in the shadows. Hinges screeched as he lifted the steel doors off the floor. He pressed a button on a steel beam adjacent to the steel doors. A light came on and shone onto him from the bottom of the elevator shaft.

The elevator screeched as it rose to floor level.

Mac and the padre stared at each other in disbelief.

"What the hell is he doing?" Mac whispered to the padre.

"Don't know Mac, but something is up, the fornicator looks like a man on a mission."

He stood on the elevator, leaned over and pressed the button again and disappeared. Mac told the padre he was going down to have a look-see. Mac walked over near the elevator and peered down and saw Kincaid piling on mailbags. He hurriedly went back and joined the padre.

"Wait till you see this, padre. Kincaid is up to something interesting. Let's see what the maniac is up too!"

The elevator rose to the surface and Kincaid pulled off 20 mailbags and put them in rows of 10 on the floor. Mac and the padre looked at each other and shrugged. He went to the mail bags going to Gentleman Jack that Mac had replaced with scrap paper. He cut off the ID tags, and the lead stamped tags and put them on the bags he brought in. The bags which now had no tags, he placed on the elevator and took them down. Fifteen minutes later, the elevator came up. He sent it down and closed the steel doors. He put the tags back on the bags and put them in order as before. He opened the garage door and drove out the gate. One of Mac's Marines came in.

"Everything okay, Mac?"

Mac walked down the stairs and approached the young Marine. "Good job, Sergeant Whitaker, everything is great. Close the garage door and make sure no one is allowed in. We will be out of here in fifteen minutes."

Mac turned around to the padre and said, "What the hell was that all about?"

"My dear Mac, let us go investigate this arousing and astonishing event!"

Mac lifted the doors and pressed the power button and they descended underneath the factory floor. They turned on the light illuminating stacks and stacks of sugarcane. Railroad tracks went in both directions. They walked back until they reached a large overhead door. A truck was parked just before the garage door. Mac pulled the tarp up and saw wooden pallet's filling the bed.

"The bags have to be in this truck somewhere." He walked around to the back and lowered the tailgate.

"Well, well, look what we have here, padre."

The padre investigated the back of the truck.

"How ingenious, Mac."

The pallets were lying on a metal floor, two feet above the truck bed. Inside the crawl space were the bags of scrap paper.

"Padre, there are going to be many surprised people."

"Only one problem, padre. When he learns what is in these bags, then he will figure out that the money is missing." Mac put the tailgate back up and got the tarp tightly around the pallets as before.

They both got back on the elevator and walked out the door to a waiting jeep and laughed all the way to the Bombay Alley.

* * *

Come evening, a pile of butts lay at the foot of the admiral's door. Burke, nervously tapped his foot against the chair leg, glanced at the clock on the wall for the umpteenth time.

After 2300 hours, enough was enough.

He stood up and approached the ensign. "You can just shoot me, you son of a bitch, because I'm leaving."

The ensign stared him down. "Is that right?"

"Damn right, that's right. Something stinks about this, and so help me, I'm going to see that your little self-serving ass is barbecued charcoal black."

The ensign set his hand on his forty-five.

"Please, we both know you don't have the guts to use that." Burke poked the guy's chest hard enough to send him stumbling back. "And you can tell that fat prick of an admiral that I'm going to piss all over him the next time I see him."

He stormed out of the building and headed directly for the Bombay Alley.

* * *

"For God's sake," Burke said, striding into Mac's office, someone give me a drink; I'm about to go out of my mind."

"Now, now, youngster," Padre McCaffery said dropping into the ancient floral-print sofa, sending up a plume of dust. "We mustn't use the good Lord's name in vain."

Mac, relieved to see the lieutenant, pushed a half-full glass to the edge of the desk. Burke lifted it, took only a small sip, and set it down.

"Careful there, kid," Wojo said, jamming his massive frame into one of the client chairs. "Wouldn't want folks going 'round thinking you are a hooch hound."

Mac stifled a chuckle, knowing well Wojo's bewilderment for any man that sipped bourbon. Where was the Burke who busted in here the first time, Mac wondered? The one that downed several shots in one go and promptly passed out?

Guess he learned to pace himself.

"Where in the hell have you been, lieutenant?" he asked. "We've been trying to reach you all day."

Burke lowered his head, shooting a glance toward Wojo.

"I was apprehended by the shore patrol under the orders of the admiral. After nearly four hours of waiting on that fat prick, I scrammed. Almost four hours waiting on him, and he never showed."

Padre McCaffery's brow shot up.

"What time was that, lieutenant?" Wojo asked.

"Just before 2000 hours until now."

Mac got up and poured them all some bourbon. "Weren't you supposed to meet Kincaid right after you left us?"

"Yeah, but I missed the meeting." Burke paced the worn mahogany floor. "I tried calling his BOQ room, but no answer." He stopped, running a shaky hand over his standard-issue buzz-cut. "I'll have to try again later. We got to get this schedule down pat, so we know what the hell we're doing."

Padre McCaffrey rose from the sofa and put an arm around Burke's shoulder. "You're pretty keyed up, lad. Take it easy. If you don't reach him tonight, we know we have to be at the burning site at oh-seven hundred. Your job is to monitor Kincaid, make sure he burns each bag according to the manifest. We'll be on the other side, taking care of business. It's too difficult to track where the money is going, so we'll be tracking the whereabouts of Chin, Gentleman Jack, and DeVito after they take the money. They'll eventually lead us to it. And when they do"—he patted Burke's shoulder and drew away—"we'll be ready."

Burke crossed his arms and chewed on this for a while, seeming less than convinced.

Mac, eager to pacify the kid, for all their sakes, gestured to the abandoned tumbler on the desk. "For someone who needed a drink, you don't seem too thirsty. Go on; you look like you could use it."

Burke hesitated, then shook his head.

"Suit yourself," Mac said, transferring the contents to his glass. "So, when we couldn't get hold of you, we were forced to take care of a few things ourselves."

The alarm on Burke's face was palpable. "Such as?"

"Such as, we replaced the guards with our own Marines, so we'll have more control over who comes on the premises. We checked the bags to ensure they had the proper sequence of numbers and confirmed the total number of bags as indicated on the manifest. Everything's good to go. We've got four Marines each, assigned to Gentleman Jack, DeVito, and Chin."

Mac exchanged glances with McCaffrey and Wojo as, slowly, a slight, crooked smile broke the tension on Burke's face, and his shoulders relaxed.

"No wonder you guys are so calm," he exclaimed. "You got it all figured out."

Wojo laughed, drained his drink, and slammed the glass down on the desk. "All we have to do early this morning is to make sure everything goes according to plan."

"Now," Mac said, getting to his feet, "you go and find Kincaid, have a talk with him." He moved around the desk and escorted Burke to the door. "We'll see you in a few hours—oh-seven hundred. Anything changes between now and then, with Kincaid, give me a call." Mac gave him a friendly shove through the door and closed it.

"Why didn't you tell the lieutenant about the Boeing Clipper?" asked the padre.

"Because it doesn't matter. Jack is not getting near any of the money. Why have the lieutenant worry?" said Mac.

He settled down behind his desk. "Now, we need to try to figure out what the hell is going to happen tomorrow and get ready for it!"

"We can come up with some guesses," Wojo said.

"We now know Kincaid did plan on stealing the money. He stole the money that was going to Jack. But stealing the money doesn't make sense because Jack is going to be very pissed off." He looked around the room for help. Padre McCaffery puffed furiously on his cigar.

Mac spoke up after a few seconds of silence.

"We figured out that Kincaid's niece is not his niece. She is the girlfriend of Gentleman Jack. We surmised Kincaid and Jack, used her to make us believe that Kincaid had a reason to help Burke and sanctify his resolve to help Kincaid."

"Maybe Kincaid is going to feign innocence and blame Burke for stealing the money?"

"That's a possibility, Wojo," said Mac.

"Maybe Gentleman Jack is going to have an accident? If I was a betting man. I'd say Jack was going to be dead as a mackerel very soon because you would be stupid to cross Jack without an ironclad plan," said Wojo.

That statement from Wojo made Mac think hard.

He shook his head as if confused. "This is incredible. We give Jack worthless bags filled with scrap paper. Kincaid thinks it's Jack's money and steals those bags of paper. Kincaid takes bags of what he thinks is money and replaces them with bags of paper. Is this incredible or what? This coming morning all the evidence gets burned. We have two thieves with bags filled with paper products, how funny is that? Now we just need a little luck on our side! Let's get to work. We have a shitload of work to do."

Chapter 51

Gentleman Jack at the Black Orchid

Gentleman Jack sipped his dirty vodka martini stirred not shaken, sat back in his chair, and pontificated on his next step. That stupid private detective Mac and his merry band of idiots seemed to know every move he made. As of yesterday, he had lost four men and didn't know what happened to them. Tonight, Chin and the Hawaiian were going to take care of the shamus. Chin bungled the operation yesterday, losing two cops and four other men, while the Shamus was still alive. Chin was going to be dead very soon.

He never wanted to kill a man more than this Mac. He closed his eyes for a second and imagined a million dollars on one side of a scale and then saw a picture of the Shamus on the other side. It might be worth a million dollars to put a slug into him. He thought about it back and forth, a million dollars, or kill the Shamus. He could kill him after the money was safe in California. Jimmy the "Weasel" could help him kill the Shamus wherever he might be hiding.

They had grown up together in the streets of Los Angeles stealing food and whacking people over the head for money until they whacked in the head a guy named Stefano "Fingers" Valentina who happened to be walking his wiener dog, Big Sam. They took all the money in his wallet and left him lying on the sidewalk. Fingers woke up because Big Sam was licking his eyebrows off his face. It took Fingers exactly two hours to find them. He grabbed both thirteen-year old's by the ear and told them they were going with him. Fingers told them to get their asses out of the car and into the house. He made them sit at a table while he put on an apron. "You boys look a little skinny, I'll make us a pasta dinner and then you are going to tell me what you did with my money that you whacked me over the head for and stole. Got it?"

Jack remembered how scared they were and how good that pasta dinner tasted. Fingers made a double recipe, and nothing was left except the painted flowers on the sides of the bowl. He told them to wash the dishes while he sat in the living room, smoking a cigarette. When they finished, he ordered them to sit on the couch in front of him.

"Where is my money, boys?"

Jack, the bigger of the two, spoke up. "We took your money and then we was robbed by some neighborhood gang."

Fingers rubbed his jaw and spoke. "I had $52.00 in that wallet and got whacked in the head by you two assholes. What do you think I should do about this situation?"

The boys shrugged their shoulders.

"Anybody does that to me normally would be buried in a ton of cement under one of those fancy apartments going up. I might still do that. But I think I figured out what to do with both of you. If you screw me, I'll throw you in the ocean and let the sharks have a nice Italian dinner. You boys will work for me until you pay me off triple. You work for only me. After you pay me off, we might consider more employment. If I like the work, you do."

Jack smiled when he remembered how Fingers got them into the family. Nothing too small to do for the only family he knew and that included, extortion, racketeering, fraud, and murder. He did it all before the age of twenty. Jack's luck ran out when Uncle Sam drafted him into the army. The family was a patriotic organization, and happy one of them was fighting the Japs.

He called the Weasel about three weeks ago and told him how much money "Operation Torch" could net them. His good friend came up with some great suggestions, and both agreed on one of them-a plan which would enable him to focus on the next series of moves. In less than twelve hours, Kincaid would have the money ready to be picked up. He had to concentrate on the next twenty-four hours, which were crucial.

The surprises he had in store for all the fools believing they would get any money delighted him, and he let out a guffaw. But his plans were on a timetable and had to be implemented in sequence. Taking care of all possible contingencies was the hard part. He could only try to figure out what strategies his enemies might use to thwart his plans. He not only had to worry about Kincaid, the private detective Mac, but the other idiots, Capt. Chin, and Koholo the insufferable fat Hawaiian. His plan was quite simple. Captain Chin and Koholo would kill the private detective tonight and he would have Chin and the fat Hawaiian think he was leaving them money without telling them he was leaving the island. They would be left with nothing and he would be long gone. Kincaid's archenemy, Admiral Johnson was going to ensure the commander spent years in jail. It was all planned out thanks to the Weasel. For the first time since he got to Hawaii, he felt reassured that victory was in his sights.

Chapter 52

The Bombay Alley

Mac took some aspirin and swallowed them down with some stale cold coffee. The padre stuck out his hand. Mac threw the bottle to him. It was 0300 hours in the morning. No sleep tonight. Too much going on. He lit his third cigar and walked to the chalkboard.

"All right, guys, let's look at this again."

"Caroline's telegram informed us that Gentleman Jack plans to take the money via the Clipper."

The padre walked over to Mac's window and looked out. "What time is his flight, Mac?"

"Tonight," said Mac. "Kincaid said that the money will be burned by 2100 hours and Jack's flight is scheduled right after that. Caroline told us that the plane will be waiting for Jack between 2000 and 2200 hours. My best guess is that he will fly out sometime between those hours. He paid the pilot $30,000 to take him two hundred miles off the coast of California to rendezvous with a boat with his mafia friends. If he escapes, we are all dead. Any ideas?"

"We can't let him get on that plane," said Wojo.

"Give me one of your tasty cigars, Mac, while I exercise my synapses to ponder this predicament," asked Padre McCaffery.

Mac reached behind him and grabbed the last of Gentleman Jack's Cuban cigars. He shook his head as he handed it over to the Padre who grinned as he lit the cigar. Mac watched him as he walked around the room billows of cigar smoke filling the room.

The padre suddenly stopped, snapped his fingers, and said, "I got it, dear Mac. This will work better than our original plan. We get to the sugarcane factory and take Kincaid's bags out of his truck and bring them to the floor. We wait for Kincaid. We tell him we know he tried to steal the money. We must not go through with soaking the bags in alcohol because they are paper scraps." He yelled out loud in frustration. "Help me, Lord, think like a damn good Jesuit."

He raised his arms to heaven in supplication. "Sorry about that, my dear Lord." He ran his hand across his face and became silent. "I have to stop thinking like a protestant."

He turned and walked to Mac and grinned. "I've got it. I've got it. We must take Kincaid's bags out of his truck and burn them in front of him. We then tell him that he will be going to jail if he doesn't cooperate with us."

He slapped his hands together and walked to the chalkboard and faced Wojo and Mac. "We tell Kincaid there is only one way out of this mess. He must call Jack and tell him that there has been a change in plans because of Lieutenant Burke. He tells Jack he must meet with him so that he can get the money to him. That place will be the best place to end this plot."

"Where?" asked Mac.

"The sugarcane factory itself.

Chapter 53

Lt. Burkes BOQ

Burke glanced at the clock and fretted over the time. It was 0600 hours and he wanted to be at the sugarcane factory before anyone else. He picked up his sidearm, placing it in his shoulder holster. He put on his suit jacket and looked in the mirror. The jacket hung on him perfectly, precisely as it should. It cost over $200 and reminded him of his high living days. He noted with satisfaction there was no bulge where his shoulder holster was located.

This was the morning he dreaded. Hopefully, burn the damn money without any mishap and face the admiral's music when it was over. The Admiral Johnson was going to go ape-shit when he gave him no evidence of wrong-doing by Kincaid. He realized that the admiral was flush with hate that burned like a white phosphorous grenade.

He turned toward the door and he reached for the knob. He heard a knock and opened the door only to find the crazy ensign who had kept him at the point of a gun for several hours.

"Sir, the admiral wants to see you ASAP."

Burke looked at the ensign wearily. "Don't pull a gun on me, you little prick. I'll break it off in your ass!"

"Sir, I apologize for the last time we met. The admiral told me I was a permanent ensign for letting you out of my sight. So, we are on the same page regarding him. But I must tell you that he wants you in the uniform of the day."

"Fuck the bastard. . . I don't have time to change. Did you tell the admiral I called him a prick?"

"After he said I was a permanent ensign, Sir, I told him you called him a prick."

"You have potential yet, ensign." Burke smiled. "Let's go see the asshole."

They arrived at the Admiral Johnson's office within fifteen minutes. Lieutenant Burke strode by, past the protesting secretary, and burst into Johnson's office.

"Admiral, I'm on a tight time constraint. We are scheduled to burn the money in a little more than an hour. I need to be there."

Admiral Johnson looked at Burke with disgust. "How dare you walk into my office unannounced and in civilian clothes. You are a naval officer, not a civilian. Go back and change into uniform and report back to me."

"Sir, I protest! The money is about to be burned. I need to be there to supervise the destruction of the money. I cannot be responsible if something goes wrong."

"A Treasury agent will be overseeing the destruction of the money until you arrive at the scene." Johnson yelled for Ensign Culver. "I want you to stay with Lieutenant Burke and escort him to his BOQ and back to me. Do you understand?"

Ensign Culver avoided the admiral's eyes and answered, "Yes, Sir."

"Both of you are dismissed."

"They climbed into Culver's jeep. Burke looked over at him and said. "We are not going to my BOQ. We are heading over to the sugarcane factory. I need to check on my men."

The ensign grinned, "I thought that was what you were going to do." He gunned the jeep into a tight turn and headed to the factory.

Chapter 54

Sugarcane factory...Day of the burn.

Kincaid smoked a pack of cigarettes before breakfast. Between that, the coffee and last night's bourbon, his stomach was reeling. He hoped his breakfast would stay down. He took a deep breath and drove up to the gate and the armed Marine. He flashed his credentials and continued to his parking space. He drove around the building to see if anyone was in the immediate area. It was 0530 hours, and Burke and his gang were not supposed to be there until 0700-0730 hours. He opened the garage door and quickly closed it and locked it. He turned on the light and saw the rows of mail bags filled with money ready to be burned. He checked the first twenty bags and saw they were ready to go. The alcohol troughs were filled with 100% alcohol, not 50%, ensuring the bags of paper would burn once soaked, in less than fifteen minutes. The evidence had to be burned.

He went to the elevator and lifted the doors. He pressed the power button and went down into the storage area.

Walking quickly, he went to the truck and smiled as he unhooked the tailgate and peered inside. His heart crawled into his throat. He tried to scream something…anything, nothing but air escaped his throat. He could not believe it. He felt himself falling and he grabbed onto the tailgate to steady himself. The fucking truck was empty! He leaned over a crate and tossed his cookies. He made a wrenching, rasping noise that could have been a cry for mercy or hopelessness. He pounded a sugarcane pallet and let out a curse from hell itself. That fucking Jack fucked him. He sat down and took deep breaths to keep his heart from bursting through his rib cage. He had to think and think fast. He went to the elevator and rose to the factory floor. He closed the metal gates and walked to the garage door.

He opened it and stood outside, gasping in the cool morning air. It was hard to believe that Jack could get into this secure facility. Impossible! Maybe he paid off one of the guards. Where was the fucking money? Just as he started to walk back onto the factory floor, three men in a jeep stopped within feet of him and got out. They were all big men, one walking with a cane. He walked toward them, wondering who in the hell they were and how they managed to enter the secure facility. All three wore sidearms.

"Good morning, Commander Kincaid. It is a good morning, isn't it?"

Right at that moment, Kincaid sensed he was in trouble, and these three men had him by the balls. He just stared at them with a stupid look on his face and answered. "A great fucking morning."

Mac smiled, lightly grabbed Kincaid's arm and guided him into the garage area. "Turn on the furnace now, commander." The words spoken in a quiet, authoritarian voice, almost kindly in nature.

He walked over to the furnace, and with a great bellow and whooshing sound, the furnace started. Kincaid watched as the second man backed the truck into the garage area and opened the tarp covering the opening.

"Commander Kincaid, you are a very bad boy. I believe these belong to you; well, not exactly belong to you," said Mac. Kincaid stared into the truck and saw his 20 bags of cash, and his heart sank. He stood silently as his eyes darted to each man standing in front of him.

"Turn off the furnace, commander, and open the door. Now start taking the bags that you tried to steal from the U.S. government and stack them in the furnace. In fact, we will help you, commander." Mac looked at his watch. If Burke and the Treasury agent arrived early, they'd be stopped until 0700 hours. They had fifty-five minutes to play with Kincaid.

After they stacked the bags in the furnace, Mac walked back to the furnace door and asked Kincaid to start the furnace. With a whoosh, the flames began eating at the bags.

"How long, commander, before those bags turn to ashes?" asked Mac.

Kincaid pulled a cigarette out of his pack and extended the cigarette toward Mac. He pulled out his lighter and lit it.

In between exhales, Kincaid said, "Who are you guys?"

"How long, commander?"

Kincaid took a draw on his cigarette and looked at Mac hard and long.

"Ten-fifteen minutes. Who are you guys?"

Wojo spoke up. "We are the guys who are burning millions of dollars that you tried to steal. That is who we are!"

Padre McCaffery stood in front of Kincaid. "My dear boy, confession is good for the soul. If you tell us everything and do what we ask of you, there is an excellent chance you walk away from this transgression without physical or spiritual damage. If you don't cooperate, you are doomed."

"What is it you want?"

Wojo said, "In mere minutes, a young man is going to walk through that door who you tried to screw over. He believed in you and thought you were an okay guy. But you turned out to be a lying, no good asshole of a thief. Let us help you understand the predicament you are in. You stole 20 bags of money and replaced them with paper."

Mac walked over to the first twenty bags and slapped the first bag. "You are one of the smartest bastards I have ever had the displeasure of knowing. Very clever. But what we don't understand is why? Jack is going hang you by your balls when he finds out you double-crossed him."

Kincaid knew that if he didn't play this right, the admiral would get his wish, and he would spend the rest of his life in prison. . . or worse.

"Who are you guys?"

Mac pulled out his badge.

Kincaid gave a sad, melancholy smile. "So, you guys are with Lieutenant Burke. You fuckers are everywhere. What do you do, multiply during the night like rats?"

Wojo pushed him toward the furnace door. "Check the damn bags, you piece of conniving shit."

Kincaid turned off the furnace and opened the door. "They are they burned up completely.

Wojo looked in and repeated what Kincaid said.

"Looks like our furnace works."

A Marine guard came to the garage door. "Mac, there is a Treasury agent here to supervise the burn. Burke has not shown up yet."

Mac pushed Wojo and the padre off to the side and whispered. "We almost walked ourselves into a disaster. We need Kincaid and the Treasury agent to sign off the bags of money on the roster before they get burned."

He turned facing Kincaid. "If you want to survive, then listen to me. We are not going to soak the bags in alcohol as planned. We are going to burn all the bags. Jack gets zero bags!"

Kincaid's eyes bulged out of his head. "Are you fucking crazy? If you do that, we are all dead men!"

Chapter 55

"You have two minutes, Kincaid. Make up your mind. What are you gonna do?" Wojo asked.

Kincaid was hyperventilating. Wojo didn't know if it was sweat or tears running down Kincaid's face.

"Will you keep your word. I mean, about letting me go if I cooperate with you?"

Mac looked at his watch. "You better hurry, Kincaid. If you tell the truth, and we believe you. You are free to fuck up the rest of your life."

"I figured no one would find out about me taking the money. All the bags were tagged, and none were missing. I thought you guys believed me about the Rose Kincaid story, so I had a reason not to screw up the deal. I leaked out information to certain people that Jack was going to be getting thousands of dollars. Also, the information when and where. It seemed to me Jack wouldn't be around too long after that."

"Who is Rose, and is she Jack's girlfriend?"

"No, she and I were in cahoots together. She fed me information about Jack and what he was going to do. She was going to get half the money."

"So, you set up Jack for a killing?"

"Not exactly, I wasn't going to murder him. Somebody else was."

"Did you pay someone to kill him?" asked Wojo.

Mac walked up to Wojo and grabbed his arm and pulled him next to the padre. "What do you think?"

"I think Kincaid is a very bad man, but the Lord works in mysterious ways," said the padre. He turned away from Kincaid and winked at Mac. Wojo just shook his head as if to show Mac Kincaid was an ass wipe.

"But I think we can figure this out in short order," said Mac. He walked up to Kincaid and stared into his eyes. He tried to figure out what was going through Kincaid's mind. He averted Mac's hard stare.

He turned toward Wojo and the Padre. "Here is something we can do to draw Jack out. We just burned Kincaid's bags of money. There is no proof of anybody stole money and all the bags are accounted for. Here is the tricky part. We must assume a few things. One that Rose will not tell Jack that she is or was working with Kincaid. Odds are that Jack will kill her." Mac waited for a response.

The padre poked Kincaid in the chest. "What do you think, Kincaid. Will she squeal about you two?"

"Why do you guys think she isn't going through with the plan that we devised. Why do you think that she'd send me down the shitter?"

"Do you think she will wait to see who gets the money before picking a side?" asked Mac.

Kincaid looked down at his tobacco-stained fingers and his Naval Academy ring.

Kincaid had a confused look on his face. "Your premise that she is in love with Gentleman Jack could be wrong. Then again, you could be right. My gut instinct tells me she will remain silent about what she knows. I don't think she wants me killed. I can't answer your question with surety."

The padre made the sign of the cross twice.

"Let's discuss what we talked about early this morning," said Mac. "We have Kincaid contact Jack and tell him he snuck the money out last night just as planned. He tells Jack that he will only give him the money and no one else, after Rose is released and out of the sugarcane factory. This will protect our storyline and theirs. He can bring any amount of men to the factory for security. We will nail Jack along with anyone who is involved in this mess."

"Kincaid are you with us on all this?" asked Mac.

Kincaid answered, barely keeping the surprise out of his voice.

"So, you are using me to get to Jack. My ass is going to be hanging out like a target for that homicidal maniac. No deal!"

Mac strode forward and grabbed Kincaid by his shirt collar. "You are dead right! You are the goat tethered to the pole. You are a drunk, a thief, a dishonorable officer, and now fucking goat meat!"

Padre McCaffery chimed in. "And a fornicator!"

Mac fixed Kincaid with a withering gaze. "Wojo, handcuff the thieving son of a bitch. We will deliver him to the admiral trussed up like a butchered goat. He makes me want to vomit."

Kincaid backed up. "Wait. . . wait a second, let me think about this. How are you going to protect me? And what about Rose?"

"Look, Kincaid, I have no clue what the hell is going on between you and Rose or Gentleman Jack and Rose. Personally, I don't give a shit. She's your problem. I don't know if we can protect you, but you'll be as safe as any of us. Once we know Jack is present, and we know for certain we have Jack where we want him, you are no longer needed and free to go," said Mac.

Wojo sneered at Kincaid.

"Look, you piece of shit. Once we have Jack, you are going to be a hero. I wouldn't doubt that they pin a medal on you and promote you," said Wojo.

Kincaid got a dumb look on his face. "Gee, you think so? It's been a long time since I was a good guy. Don't know if it is possible."

The phone rang in the factory. Wojo picked it up and said, "Thanks… Lieutenant Burke has arrived. He is walking in with the Treasury agent. What do we tell him?"

The padre looked at Mac and said, "My dear Mac, say nothing until the money is destroyed and we all get the hell out of here!"

The garage door rolled up. The jeep carrying Burke, Culver, and the Treasury agent drove into the factory.

Mac grabbed Kincaid's arm. "Wait a second. Who in the hell did you leak the information about Jack too?"

"The fat Hawaiian. A competitor of Jack's."

"Will he do something about it?"

"Most likely, when I call him."

"You are a work of art, Kincaid."

He turned away from him and walked up to Burke and shook his hand.

"We were wondering when the hell you were going to get here, lieutenant. You are fifteen minutes late. Everything is up and ready for destruction. The furnace is operating, and the manifest is ready."

Burke took Mac by the arm and guided him over to the side.

"The fucking admiral is on the warpath." He pointed to the ensign standing near the door. "He has attached the ensign to me like a moray eel to a fish. Something isn't right. The admiral wants me out of the way, and I can't figure it out. Anyway, has Kincaid changed his mind? Is he still working with us?"

Mac tried to look calm and collected.

"Yes, he is working with us. I'll tell you all that I have learned as soon as this damn money is burned. Let's begin burning this shit. I never want to see so much money again."

Burke smiled. "I'm with you, gunny."

Burke walked over to the Treasury agent. "Start checking off the bag identification numbers so the burning can commence. Do the first row of one hundred and fifty bags. As soon as you check off the first twenty, we will throw them into the furnace." Burke yelled for Kincaid.

"Is the furnace operating at full efficiency when turned on?"

Kincaid took a deep breath. "I have it set to the highest temperature and opened the air vents. Each burn should take less than fifteen minutes. We can load the first twenty bags."

Wojo brought in four Marines to load the bags into the furnace. The Treasury agent shouted out that the first twenty bags were logged in and ready to be burned.

Burke motioned for Mac to come to his location.

"Have the first twenty bags been soaked in alcohol?" Mac looked at Burke and said. "We had to change our plans. We are burning all the money. We can't afford Gentleman Jack to get any of the money and we can't ensure we don't lose the money."

Mac left Burke with his mouth open.

Padre McCaffery crossed himself and prayed. Mac had sweat running down his face and thought his heart would stop. They were moments away from salvation.

Burke followed. "How about all our plans?"

"Trust me, Lieutenant Burke."

Mac looked at Wojo and gave him the thumbs up.

Wojo looked at Mac and smiled. He looked at the padre who placed his hands together as if in prayer. He closed the door and shouted for Kincaid to press the burn button. Kincaid just stood there. Wojo walked up to Kincaid and whispered.

"Press the damn button, Kincaid, or I'm going to throw your worthless ass in next!"

Kincaid nodded and pressed the button. With a tremendous whoosh, the furnace started devouring the bags. The padre let out a war cry and everyone laughed except Kincaid. He knew somehow these crazy bastards were going to get him killed.

Chapter 56

The Black Orchid

Rose put her arms around Gentleman Jack and kissed him. He buried his nose into her neck and breathed in her perfume. She hung her neck back and let out a small moan of pleasure. He let out a laugh of pure joy and looked into her eyes.

"I have never loved like this before. I feel like I'm eighteen years old and floating on the clouds," he said. She playfully bit his lip and kissed him again.

"I know all you care about is the money," she said.

He let go of her embrace and walked to his desk. He poured himself a drink from the decanter.

"No, you have changed me, my dear. I don't know what I want, except to be with you."

She walked up to him and grabbed his hand.

"If I only could believe that."

"Believe it," he said. "In a few hours, the money will be picked up. I want you and the money."

"We have more than enough money. Let's leave this all behind and forget about the money. Leave on the Clipper. Go back to California. Forget all of this, including killing Kincaid," she said.

"Kincaid has been a useful idiot. Of course, you were the reason everybody thought Kincaid had to help this Burke fellow and cooperate. In the meantime, he steals them blind with my help. Don't you worry. I have a plan for getting rid of him without killing him."

Gentleman Jack started to laugh. "If I told you how, you would laugh your ass off."

She felt a cold shiver go down her spine. Rose kissed him and whispered.

"How, darling? How are you going to get rid of him without killing him?"

Gentleman Jack smiled. He was enjoying this so much.

"First, let me explain. I learned that Kincaid was the supervising officer in charge of burning the money. I also knew he was desperate for money since he owed me over five thousand dollars. I had a little talk with him and convinced him it was in his best interest to work with me. Then through some luck, I found out about a Marine searching for me. In turn, a private detective was seen going into his room, and he was followed to his office. Then more luck headed my way. This Lieutenant Burke was seen visiting the Gunny Mac Detective Agency. It was a brilliant plan to tell everyone you were Kincaid's niece and use the threat of violence against you if he didn't cooperate with me. Just in case Burke didn't believe Kincaid, you told your wop friend Tony that you were being followed. Everyone fell for the setup. My boys helped by giving the shamus a picture of you. The dummies shared their notes and the setup was complete."

"Who filled you in on Kincaid and what he was doing?" asked Rose.

"I'll explain that in a second. You won't believe who. Before we started this charade, I get a phone call from someone and he tells me about a loser by the name of Kincaid, who visits my club every day. He says Kincaid is in a position to steal millions of dollars. He just needs a reason. This person says that he needs Kincaid set up for the fall guy. He says I can have the money, if he gets Kincaid on a silver platter. He even gives me the name of the Naval Intelligence Officer assigned to follow Kincaid. Are you starting to get it now, my dear? The voice on the other line is feeding me all the information. Telling me about Kincaid. Telling me about Burke. Telling me how I can get the money. The best part is Kincaid has stolen the money and is getting it to me very soon. In fact, as of this hour, all evidence of the theft has burned to ashes."

"So how do you get Kincaid without killing him?" asked Rose.

"He is going to be found with some of the money."

Rose swallowed hard. Things were getting complicated fast. She looked up at Jack and forced a smile.

"How?"

"Tonight, after we get the money, Commander Kincaid is going to get drunk with our assistance and need a ride home. Someone will drive his car to the BOQ and get him to his room. We will deposit some of the the money in the trunk of his car and a phone call made. Kincaid will be arrested. That easy!"

"How do you know your source is not setting you up?"

Gentleman Jack laughed. "Because I know who he is and I told him if he double-crossed me, he'd be dead in less than an hour or his career in shambles!"

Rose put her arms around Gentleman Jack.

"I'm dying with anticipation. Tell me!"

"I got a phone call I told you about. . . from someone asking me if I wanted to make some money. The voice said he needed a certain guy set up to take the fall. If I was to say yes, his plan was foolproof for me to have a payoff. After this guy was set up and I got my money, it was over. It had to be someone in the government. I asked Kincaid who he was working for, and then he told me how much the son of a bitch hated him."

Jack poured himself some bourbon and walked back to Rose.

"You would never guess in a hundred years."

Rose now began to understand.

"Admiral Johnson! Kincaid's boss!"

Rose knew she had to wait for Kincaid's phone call and hopefully, it was soon because hell was slowly freezing over.

Chapter 57

While Kincaid was busy burning the money, Mac met Burke in the office.

"We found out that Rose was not a hostage, but a girl-friend of Gentleman Jack. This left no reason to give any money to Jack. So, we burned the money. Easier for all of us."

"What the hell are we going to give Gentleman Jack? What do we do next, Mac?"

"When we couldn't reach you, we developed a plan to lure Jack to the sugarcane factory tonight, arresting him or killing him. The object is to draw Jack and DeVito out in the open where we can take care of them. Our lives aren't worth a plug nickel if he escapes. Odds are his friends in California will track us down and kill us."

Burke tried hard not to shout. "Shit, this is spiraling out of control. Fucked up beyond belief!"

Mac grabbed Burke's shoulder. "I'm not going to be looking over my shoulder for the rest of my life. Either are you."

Mac yelled at Kincaid from the office. Kincaid walked over to Burke and Mac.

"You ready to make that phone call to ole Jack?"

Kincaid shook his head no. "But I guess I have to or that big bastard over there said he would put my ass in the furnace."

Mac said, "That gunny wants Jack bad and I'd hate to be the guy who tries to stop him!"

Mac gestured toward the rows of money. "When do you think we will complete the burning?" Kincaid rubbed his jaw and did some mental calculations. "Every sixty minutes we burn eighty bags. We started at 0715 hours. I figure around 1900 hundred hours this evening if nothing goes wrong. I was briefed that the conveyor belt might not last the whole operation. It was scheduled to be replaced this week. And it's hauling a hell of a lot of ashes away. If we start to have problems, we might have to lessen the number of bags we burn each time. If we must replace it, we will lose a couple of hours. I'm keeping my fingers crossed."

Mac yelled for the head Treasury agent to come over to them. Mac pointed to the office behind them. "We will be in the office for about fifteen minutes with Kincaid. Can you and the other Treasury agent keep things rolling, accountable, and legal?"

The agent pushed back his fedora and wiped the sweat on his forehead. Grinning at Mac, he said, "If you can't trust a Treasury agent, who can you trust?"

Mac looked at Kincaid and smiled. "That's more than I can say for some people."

The padre and Wojo came up to them.

The padre spoke up. "We are ready for the meeting, Mac, whenever you are."

The four of them walked into the office and closed the door.

"Fill me in boys, because I'm in the dark," said Burke. He stared at each of them in the room and settled his eyes on Mac.

Mac looked at Kincaid and spoke. "We concluded that Rose not only is working in Jack's office but has a relationship with him. He watched as Kincaid's body stiffened.

"Therefore, not a hostage situation. This freed Kincaid to work with us without fear of getting her hurt. Isn't that true, Kincaid?"

Kincaid was silent and nodded his head up and down. Mac continued. "We figured out that we didn't need to give him any money. Anyway, giving millions of dollars to the Cosa Nostra was complicated and illegal. We all agreed trying to keep track of the money, Jack and his boys was too daunting of a task. We devised a plan that would force Jack to pick up the money himself. But to get the money, Jack has to meet with Kincaid personally. Kincaid is going to call Jack and say he has the money in a truck ready for Jack to drive away."

The padre handed Mac a cigar and lit it with his Zippo. Mac stared at the cigar band.

"Padre, I see you are giving me one of my very own cigars. Thank you for sharing with me."

The padre beamed. "Don't worry, my dear Mac, I have a full shirt pocket of them."

"Padre, why don't you tell the lieutenant what we devised. Then Wojo, you can explain your part."

The padre took a puff on his cigar. "Mac, I'll tell you these are the finest cigars I have ever smoked. Pure delight. Pure delight."

He turned to Burke; all his levity gone. "He is not going to have to find out. We are going to tell him. We debated where to make all this take place and decided right here at the sugarcane factory. Forty-six acres of grounds, lots of buildings. Even a railroad track with strings of railroad cars. A three-story factory. All forty-six acres fenced in. When he shows up with the girl, Kincaid opens a bag and shows him worthless scraps of paper."

Kincaid let out a gasp.

Burke interrupted. "We are all dead men. He is going to bring lots of men with him. He won't take this."

Wojo walked over to the blackboard and uncovered it. "You are exactly right. Look at the chalkboard." Burke went up and stared at the diagram. After a minute of silence, he turned to the group and smiled. "Simply brilliant. Now, what is Kincaid going to tell Jack to get his ass to personally pick up the money?"

Chapter 58

The Black Orchid

Rose involuntarily jumped when the phone rang. Jack looked at her and smiled. "A little jumpy, aren't we?" He walked over to his desk and picked up the phone. Rose and DeVito watched his facial expressions as the conversation continued. Jack did not seem very happy. He put down the phone and walked to his bar and poured himself a cup of coffee.

DeVito spoke up. "Well, boss, what the hell did he say?"

Jack walked over to Rose and looked down at her on his settee.

"Our plans have changed due to Burke. Last night he told Kincaid they were going to burn all the money and give us bags of scrap paper. Late last night, Kincaid took twenty bags of money and hid it in a truck and replaced it with the twenty bags of money he filled with paper scraps. He says no one knows anything. Kincaid gets one bag and we get nineteen. He fears me and fears a double-cross. He wants me to come to the sugarcane factory at 9:00 pm, give me the

336

money and have us drive the truck out. To show his good faith, I can bring as many men as I want to check out the area before I get there. If I don't show up, no deal."

DeVito spoke up. "Do you believe him?"

"He messes with me; he knows he is a dead man. You will be right at my side, covering him with a pistol. He sounded sober. I will call the admiral about the change of plans and the time; he will ensure the factory is closed once the operation is complete. The admiral will be very pleased when I tell him how we will set Kincaid up. I'll tell him the factory area must be deserted except for Kincaid with the truck. He is going to park the truck under a large light and stand next to the truck. The gate will be open, and our men will be able to check the place out one hour before I show up."

"So, no big deal boss, I get there ahead of time with some men and post guards. You zip in, take the money, and we escort you out, making sure nobody follows you. We grab Kincaid, pour enough liquor in his gullet to get him drunker than a pig, put some money in his trunk, get him in his BOQ, and call the fucking admiral. Everything nice and tidy."

"Get the boys rounded up. Tell Chin he is going with me. Kill the fat Hawaiian. Tonight, when we have the money, we load the Clipper and head to California. I never want to see Hawaii again."

Rose took a deep breath and exhaled. The money was soon going to be in their hands- all that beautiful money. Everything was going as planned. She just hoped that Kincaid knew what the hell he was doing, or her plans had to change.

Chapter 59

Pearl Harbor BOQ

Burke walked into his BOQ, sat on the bed, and realized for the first time that he might not get out of the admiral's grasp. After Kincaid made his phone call and he saw the plan, his head was on fire. So many things could go wrong and when Mac said he could pretty much guarantee things would go wrong because they always did, that's when his hair caught fire. On top of that, he was on his way to see the fucking admiral along with the permanent ensign. He changed into his uniform and fifteen minutes later, he was standing at attention in his office.

Burke could feel the visceral hatred the admiral had for him. He could see each line of hate etched into his face and eyes.

"What time will the 'Operation Torch' be completed?" asked the admiral.

"We will complete burning by 1900 hours."

The admiral sipped on his coffee and didn't look Burke in the eyes.

"I will be there at 1900 hours to supervise the initial closing of this operation. A photographer will be with me to witness this historic event. By 1930 hours, the factory area will be cleared of all personnel and left as we found it. My people will padlock the doors to all buildings within fifty yards. As of that time, your services will no longer be needed. You will go to your BOQ and write up your report if it is not done already. Your report will be on my desk tomorrow morning with evidence of Kincaid's involvement. I'm going to enjoy writing your fitness report. It's going to read like a horror script. Now get your ass back to the burn area until I arrive tonight and watch Kincaid. If he steals any money and gets away with it, you will be cellmates with him."

Burke did an about-face and ran out of Johnson's office. He had to tell Mac about the admiral closing the factory by 1930 hours. The gunny was right; plans were meant to be pissed on.

* * *

Mac watched Kincaid through the office door as he went about his business, herding the Treasury agents around the room. Burke had walked into the factory floor and told him about the change in plans. The admiral was coming to visit the factory at 1900 hours and close the factory down. It posed some problems, but not enough to sweat. After all, it was his Marines that would be closing the area. They would have to ensure that none of Jack's boys infiltrated the forty-six acres before the admiral left. Having his Marines check out the buildings and padlock them helped them. It was a good omen that luck was siding with them.

He glanced at the crude drawing of the sugarcane factory building and grounds drawn on the chalkboard. He saw the spot Wojo would be with his rifle. Wojo was in the corner, checking his .03 Springfield rifle.

"Wojo, you sure you can hit something with this? It will be dark, and you don't know how much light that will be available."

"Just make sure our little transaction is under some light. Damn, you and I shot open sights at the five-hundred-yard line and hit our targets. I'll only be seventy-five yards away using a scope. At that range, I could clobber him over the head with the butt of my rifle."

"I want Corporal Reynolds to be with you. He'll make sure you aren't bothered by anyone."

"As long as it isn't that Sergeant Peterson. Something wrong with that boy."

"He asked me if he could be with you. He feels you need somebody mature to watch you," said Mac.

The padre slapped Wojo on the back.

"Sergeant Peterson has sort of adopted you. He worries about you. Like a little brother." The padre and Mac let out a chuckle.

Mac walked up to the chalkboard.

"This is the first building they will lock. Three of us will be hiding below the elevator that Kincaid used to hide his money. We disconnected the power and will use the pulley system they used before there was power. This also stops anyone from operating the elevator with the power to check it out. We greased it up along with the steel doors, so they don't screech. One man can pull up the other two or lower them. We tried this and it works great. There is a window on each side of the garage door so we can watch what is happening outside. One hundred yards away, twelve Marines armed to the teeth will be chomping at the bit to shoot something. If things get bad, they will be watching and waiting for their signal to join the fun when they hear a shot. They will be coming full bore from three directions converging on the money truck and us. The major problem is how efficient Jack's men search. They will have plenty of men, but less than one hour. The admiral is supposed to be out by 1930 hours. Maybe we can help him leave sooner. That leaves us one and a half hours 'til showtime."

Kincaid knocked on the door and came in. "We are on schedule to get everything burned by 1900 hours. We may even finish thirty minutes earlier. What the hell am I going to do tonight?"

"Listen in on our final plans. Your role is very straight-forward," said Mac.

The padre spoke up. "This area is forty-six acres with one huge building and many smaller buildings. To clear this would take one hundred men a full day to check everything out. The admiral will mostly concern himself with the buildings we used. Those will be locked down. No need to check the rest."

Wojo stopped cleaning his rifle and said, "I agree with the padre, Mac. The bastards will most likely spread around this open area near the money truck, some on foot, some in cars. I'm sure he will be station a few around the gate leading to this compound; the problem is how to keep Kincaid from getting shot. Soon as ole Jack sees paper; he is going to see red."

Kincaid looked around the room. "What do you mean, keeping me from getting shot?"

"The way I look at it, Kincaid," said Mac, "Wojo is the one who will be keeping you and all of us alive. Anyone threatens us at the truck Wojo will take him out."

"You can bet on one thing, that I'm going to blow Jack's balls off, a bullet in each ball," Wojo said.

"Wojo knows what to do," said Mac. "We can guess what Jack's reaction will be when he sees he has bags of paper. He will go off like a star cluster. Odds are he is going to pull out a gun and shoot ole Kincaid through his black heart. Or DeVito will. Wojo's job is to take out the guy trying to end Kincaid's miserable existence on this earth. Then Jack is going to try to get in a car and be spirited away, with everyone running like chickens with their heads cut off. A problem we have is somebody probably told Jack about Burke and his role in all this. What he knows about our involvement is unknown. We must plan on him knowing. At least about Burke."

Wojo let out a long sigh. "Mac, I don't like you locked in the building when this is going down. No way you can get out if we run into trouble. I'd feel better if your somewhere outside the building."

Mac smiled. "No wonder you are a gunny. The more I think about, I should be in the back of the truck where the money supposed to be."

Mac walked over to the padre. "Once that truck is backed in below us, I want a Marine in the driver's seat ready to go. Sergeant Peterson will be the Thompson machine gunner hanging on the running board. You will stay."

The padre nodded. "Ok Mac, will do."

He looked at the clock. Mac began to wonder if they knew what the hell they were doing. It was 1800 hours. In just a few hours, hell was going to break loose. He checked out the truck that he was going to hide in where he could put some firepower down, if needed. They had checked out Wojo's sniper nest and the locations of the assault teams. He and Corporal Reynolds would have clear fields of fire protecting Kincaid. For the first time in months, Gunny Mac felt like a Marine, which made him smile.

At 1830 hours, Kincaid reported to Burke that forty bags were left to be destroyed. Burke walked over to Mac.

"Kincaid says less than forty minutes till this stinking mess is complete. Around 1910 hours. The admiral could show up anytime," said Burke.

Gunny Mac told Burke where he was going to be during the money exchange. He also told the padre.

"That's a dangerous spot, gunny but a good one," said Burke.

Sweat trickled down Burke's back and he realized for the first time how hot it was in the building. He opened all the doors and windows and cool ocean air swept through the room. He hoped all the Marines were in the right positions. Padre McCaffery and his two Marines were downstairs waiting. Gunny Wojo and Corporal Reynolds were in position as well as the response team in four different areas with three men each. He looked around for Gunny Mac. He saw him sitting in the office with a Thompson across his lap.

"Showtime, gunny."

He got up and slung his Thompson over his shoulder.

He was holding onto a lock and chain.

"Follow me, lieutenant."

"You and Kincaid will be in the most dangerous position," said Mac.

As they rounded the corner, a truck was sitting there with the keys in the ignition.

Mac said, "This is the truck with the fake bags of money that you will show Gentleman Jack. You will drive it around to the front of this building, as I showed you before. Once you open that bag and show nothing but paper to Jack or whoever that is the signal for Wojo to shoot someone and the shit is going down fast. I will be in the back of the truck hiding behind the bags. When shots are fired, the padres truck is coming out fast and my Marines will be assaulting from their positions. I will be trying to protect you and Kincaid." They walked around to the rear of the truck. Mac reached in and pulled out a .45.

"This .45 will in the corner of the truck for you to grab if something happens."

They went around the side of the factory where padre and the boys waited inside. He lifted open the door.

Padre McCaffery stood there with a .45 on his hip.

Mac handed him the chain and lock with a key. "I want you to lock this garage door from the inside. As soon as this door is checked by our Marines and the admiral's men, unlock this door."

The padre stepped forward and stuck out his bear claw of a hand. Burke shook it.

"Remember, lad; you have seventeen of us watching out for you. We will have sights on all his people."

He put Mac in a bear hug. "Be careful, my dear Mac."

Mac grabbed Burke's hand and held onto it.

"Tell Kincaid to get that truck under the lights as soon as the admiral leaves. You two will wait by the truck under the lights for Jack to show up. Try to get Jack or DeVito in the open so Wojo can shoot." Mac slapped him on the arm. "You can do it, kid. We have gotten used to you, so be careful."

Mac watched him disappear around the corner. "Padre, you know what has to be done. You stay here once that door is opened and the truck leaves. I don't need you getting shot. Mac handed his Thompson to Sgt Peterson. One of your Marines will drive, and you will be the Thompson machine gunner. You know where I will be. The first sound of gunfire, have your Marines come barreling around this building and take out whoever is in front of you."

Chapter 60

Sugarcane factory

When he left his friends, Burke felt like he was alone in the world. He walked back into the factory and saw the Treasury agents filling out the last of their paperwork and signing the manifests. Kincaid was in the corner chain-smoking cigarettes. All was quiet except for the ticking of the furnace cooling down. Burke wished he had a drink in hand. His thoughts went back to his failure as a son and naval officer. Guadalcanal and Wojo seemed like a lifetime ago. Gunny Mac was fighting hard to survive outside his beloved corps with his unusual friend, the padre. All were working together to stop a gangster who would kill any of them without a second thought. He put a cigarette in his mouth and searched for matches. He couldn't find any. A lighter appeared in front of him. Kincaid smiled at him. Burke nodded back. "Thanks, commander."

"I want to thank you and Gunny Mac." He paused for a few seconds, gathering his thoughts. "You know, stopping me from being a total degenerate. I haven't felt this good about myself in years. I might even make a good naval officer someday." He let out a small laugh.

"If something happens to me. I probably deserve it."

Burke, for the first time, thought of Kincaid as a naval officer. Maybe it was because it was the first time, he saw the commander sober.

"You are not the only person who has changed for the better. You hang around real men; they rub off on you. Wojo, Mac, and the padre are special men. We have to make certain they don't get hurt."

A pang of regret ripped through Kincaid. He would never have people think of him in that way. "The admiral will want my ass handed to him on a platter like it's Thanksgiving dinner. You going to let him have me?"

"No."

"I deserve it."

"Maybe, maybe not."

"Anyway, whatever happens, thanks for not letting the admiral take me like a whore."

Burke watched the headlights of two vehicles approach the factory.

"Just remember to keep quiet and follow the admiral's orders until this thing is over. I have no idea what the hell is going to happen next. But we must try to get him out of here in thirty minutes or so. I'll do the talking."

Admiral Johnson walked over to the Treasury agents and shook their hands. Flashbulbs flared, as a photographer took pictures. The agents talked to the admiral and gave him the manifests and signatures signifying the burning was complete.

He handed them to his aide. He walked back to where Burke was standing. He gave a withering stare at Kincaid, who was standing at attention.

"The Treasury agents gave me the manifests and said all went well. Do you agree?"

"Yes Sir, all is well. The mission has been carried out," said Kincaid.

Burke looked the admiral in the eye, wondering why he had been so scared of him. Not anymore.

The admiral walked toward the furnace and stood for pictures. He then told his chief to take the Marines and padlock all buildings within fifty yards of the furnace building. There were five in total. He called out to Burke.

"Lieutenant Burke... remember I want a full report tomorrow on 'Operation Torch,' and I know it will be a complete report. It better have all the information I need."

"Sir, I think you will be very shocked at what I have," said Burke.

The admiral walked past Kincaid and got into his jeep and waited. Fifteen minutes later, his NCOIC walked up to the admiral and saluted.

"Sir, the area has been locked down except the factory. All personnel have left except Kincaid and Lieutenant Burke."

"Tell them to exit the building, chief."

The master chief walked in and asked Burke and Kincaid to exit the building.

Burke looked at his watch; it was 2035 hours.

The chief ensured the windows were locked and then checked and chained all the doors around the building. At 2045, he walked back to the admiral and told him the building was secure. He hopped into a jeep behind the admiral and they left without a word.

Kincaid walked around the building and brought the truck next to where Burke was standing and backed it under the lights. Kincaid left the truck running as instructed by Mac. They both looked at each other and smiled grimly. They smoked one cigarette after another as they waited in silence. At 2100 hours, Kincaid poked Burke in the arm and pointed toward the gate.

Burke walked to the back of the truck. "Mac, the bastards have shown up." In the distance, a caravan of cars approached the main gate and slowly drove through. Two cars stayed outside the gate, and eight men got out. One car drove a car length behind where Burke and Kincaid were standing and stopped. Burke could see four men were in the car. Another car blocked the truck's forward avenue of escape. Three men got out with pistols in their hands hanging at their sides. The driver stayed in the car. Three other cars stopped in a semi-circle in the parking lot. The men got out and waited. Burke noticed that one of them was DeVito. Burke counted at least eighteen men and seven cars.

Burke imagined Wojo and his assault teams were adapting plans to meet the threat as they saw it.

DeVito barked some orders to check the area out and his men fanned out. Burke watched the beams of light from flashlights shooting off at different angles like a Hollywood premiere. He moved closer to the edge of the truck and the .45. His eyes stayed on DeVito.

DeVito walked up to Kincaid. No cigar was hanging from his jowls. He slapped the cigarette out of Kincaid's mouth.

"I find anything out of order I'll put a bullet in you and your boyfriend second. You got that, commander?"

"You just don't know much is out of order, you bastard," Kincaid thought.

Kincaid managed to squeak out a weak, "yes."

DeVito poked each man with his pistol indicating for them to raise their arms. One of his men searched them both. He kneed Kincaid in the balls and laughed. Kincaid reached down to grab his balls.

DeVito pulled back the hammer on his .45.

"Keep your hands up commander or I'll shoot your miserable ass." DeVito turned his gun toward Burke. "You must be Lieutenant Burke, babysitter to this fuck up next to you. Just shake your head yes or no."

Burke nodded, yes.

DeVito knocked Burke to the ground.

"My boss wanted me to bust you in the face, lieutenant. You might be getting a little more later."

Burke got up and spat some blood out in DeVito's direction.

DeVito went to the back of the truck and looked in.

"Hey, you, fucking babysitter, pull out a bag and let's see what's in it."

"Pull out the bag yourself, fat boy," said Burke.

DeVito started to laugh. He walked over to Burke and put the .45 to his head.

"Your brains are going to be all over that wall unless you pull that fucking bag out."

Kincaid spoke up. "The deal was Gentleman Jack had to be here before the money was to be exchanged. No, Jack, no money."

Burke looked at Kincaid, who had some puke on his chin. He moved closer to the tailgate of the truck. Where in the hell was Jack?

DeVito went up to Kincaid and punched him full in the face. He then kicked Kincaid in the ribs.

"Shut the fuck up, you drunk."

Kincaid started to laugh and slowly got to his feet. Unsteady on his feet, he looked at DeVito and laughed again. "You fucking fat wop. We knew you would try this shit. Go on, open a fucking bag. See how you fucked up."

DeVito opened the bag and out poured scraps of paper, which were soon scattered over the parking lot as the wind picked up. He let out an oath and walked up to Kincaid and put the .45 under his jaw.

"Where's the money. You have to the count of three before I blow off your fucking head."

Burke spoke up. "Gentleman Jack or no money. You can kill that worthless SOB, but we made a deal. We want to make sure Jack gets his money. We are not going to look over our shoulders for the rest of our lives."

A voice from the back of them spoke. "Relax, DeVito. Kincaid, you have more balls than I thought."

Gentleman Jack walked to DeVito's side. "I'm here now. Where is the damn money?"

Burke knew he had to stall for some time. "Is this the real Gentleman Jack or an impostor. Could it be Jack Calamari in the flesh?"

The figure walked up to Burke.

"So, you figured it out. Interesting. Now I'm going to have to kill you both. Before I kill you, how did you find out?"

Burke moved a little back, so Calamari was not blocking Wojo from seeing DeVito.

"We got your prints and sent them to the FBI."

Calamari moved closer to Burke. Burke moved a little further away from DeVito and Calamari.

"How did you get my prints, college boy? Yes, Burke, I know all about you, and what a fuck up you are. As much a loser as Kincaid. I also know where your family lives. In fact, after I kill you, I will make sure I kill all of them."

Kincaid gagged on some blood and spat it out in DeVito's direction. He spoke forcibly. "No, I'm a bigger fuck up. He is a good kid."

Burke turned his head and spoke to Kincaid. "You are right, Kincaid. In some ways, you are, but in other ways, I'm a bigger fuckup than you."

Calamari told them to shut the hell up. "Both of you are fuckups."

He moved very close to Burke. "How in the hell did you get my prints?"

Burke decided to tell him, and he hoped Wojo was getting a good target because if he didn't, he was dead.

"Remember how you got painted up? All those pretty colors. They hid the blue ink we used to get your prints and we had a hell of a lot of fun doing that!"

Burke heard the click and looked down. Calamari had opened a switchblade and held it down by his side.

"Now, I'm going to gut you like a fish."

Wojo stared through the scope and was tempted to kill DeVito twice, but held back. Gentleman Jack was the real target. He set the reticle on the side of DeVito's temple and that's when Gentleman Jack came and stood next to DeVito, blocking his view of his head. He still had the .45 under Kincaid's jaw. DeVito had to be the first one sent to hell. He watched Burke move closer to the truck to get Gentleman Jack out of the way. He moved the scope to Gentleman Jack and saw the knife.

Burke watched Gentleman Jack's eyes and waited for his head to explode from a thirty-ought six smashing through his soft brain tissue. He was getting nervous. Where in the hell was Wojo?

Kincaid exploded. "You hurt him; I swear you'll never see any money."

Jack looked at Kincaid. "My patience has ended. Where is the money."

Kincaid struggled to speak. "Get the fucking pistol out of my throat; I can't talk. I'll show you."

DeVito kept the pistol pointed at Kincaid's head and pushed him toward the truck. Burke yelled to DeVito, "Don't hurt him; I'll get the money."

Wojo saw his opening. He centered on DeVito's head and pulled the trigger. He immediately moved the scope, searching for Gentleman Jack.

Burke saw DeVito's head disappear in a burst of red and grey matter. Out of his peripheral vision, he saw Kincaid fall. His face covered with red and grey tissue mass.

Mac pushed down hard on the bags and looked through the truck opening and opened fire. His first shots hit the driver and one man in the car behind the truck. He rolled out, looking for Burke and Kincaid. He saw what was left of DeVito lying on the ground, his head gone, except for his jowls sagging on the ground. Then he saw Kincaid covered with blood on the ground and Burke struggling to get up. He yelled out to Burke and threw him a .45.

The Marines came charging out of their positions. A Marine with a BAR took out the men at the gate and shot up the cars for good measure. They ran straight into the mass of gangsters, yelling like rebels from hell.

Padre McCaffery threw the young Marine out of the cab and drove the truck through the garage door opening with Sergeant Peterson attached to the running board. He drove like a wild man around the building with Peterson spraying the three cars in front of them. Two of them started on fire.

He shouted to the padre, "Push any truck out of our way."

Wojo searched for Jack and found him through the smoke lying on the ground at the truck's rear tire. He fired and watched Jack's leg jump up. The shot hit him in the lower foot.

Wojo didn't have a clear killing shot. A wrong angle for a headshot. He fired again. He hit him in the forearm. Wojo aimed again, and the round hit Gentleman Jack in the hip. He saw him crawl over to a pistol. He grabbed it and started to aim it at somebody. Wojo centered on his neck and pulled the trigger.

Mac was searching for a target. A bullet passed close to him and he looked around, trying to find the shooter. He heard the padre yell out for him to watch his back. He turned and fired. The first round hit Captain Chin in the right thigh, the second in his shoulder. He fell to the ground shrieking in pain. Sergeant Peterson ran up to Gunny Mac. "You ok gunny?"

Mac looked at him and said, "Yeah, sarge, this is the guy who pissed on my .45."

Chin lay groaning on the ground. Sergeant Peterson unbuttoned his fly. He looked at Gunny Mac and smiled. "Payback is a mother."

A steady stream of piss rained down on a screaming Captain Chin.

* * *

Koholo watched as the Marines attacked screaming like maniacs. Some crazy man chewing on a cigar came around the corner driving like a maniac with a Marine hanging off the side of the truck, shooting a machine gun with one hand. He made a very wise decision at that moment. Get the hell out of the area before those crazy Marines shot him full of holes. Who needed money? They wiped out his competition and for that, he was grateful.

Wojo walked over to the factory where the padre and Peterson joined him. They found DeVito's body with half his head missing.

"The rifle shoots a trifle high."

The padre said a prayer over his body. Next to him lay the body of Gentleman Jack.

Wojo stared at the body. "This man was pure evil."

They went searching for Mac and found him talking with Burke on the factory floor. Mac smiled when he saw the three of them.

"Where in the hell is Kincaid?" asked Wojo.

"I'm here, gunny. You showered me with bits of DeVito. Had to wash the stink of him off of me."

"Sorry about that. I had to take the shot before Burke was fileted."

Kincaid stuck out his hand. "I felt the bullet go right past my nose. Thanks."

One of the Marines came up to Mac. "Want to say good-bye to Chin, gunny?"

They walked up to Chin, who had a tourniquet on his thigh and his shoulder in a sling.

All four of them looked at him. "Piss on him," said Mac.

"Anything you say gunny," said Sergeant Peterson, as he unbuttoned his fly again.

"Let's go home," said Wojo.

Chapter 61

The next morning Burke picked up Rose and delivered her to Mac's office. Waiting for her was Kincaid. She saw him and ran into his arms. He hugged her and then pushed her away. "I'd advise you to cooperate with Lieutenant Burke and tell him all you know. You are too pretty to go to jail."

Kincaid nodded to Burke. "I'll wait for you in the hallway."

Burke told Rose what her options were and pushed the paperwork toward her. She read it and looked up at Burke.

"If I sign this, will I go free?"

Mac spoke up. "Kincaid, Burke, and I have signed statements saying you helped us in this investigation. That is if you cooperate with us and sign that statement. It is a true statement and one we need very much to end this situation."

He watched her as she reread the statement.

"It is true."

She picked up the pen and signed the statements.

The padre walked over to her and put his hand on her shoulder.

"Lord, lead this young lady to live for you." He smiled at her and said. "You are free to go and live a good life."

She walked to the door and spoke to them. "Thank you, gentlemen, for helping me."

"Thank the commander."

Kincaid watched her as she approached him.

"You know I loved you," he said.

She patted him on the arm and walked down the hallway. He watched her until she disappeared and out of his life.

He walked back into the office and said, "Are you guys ready?"

They all looked at each other and smiled. All of them were dressed in suits and ties that Lieutenant Burke had picked out for them. "Damn boys, you all look sharp," he said.

They drove to the Base Operations Center and walked shoulder to shoulder to the front door.

"Lieutenant Burke, you first," said Mac. They entered one by one into Admiral Johnson's secretary's office.

Burke walked up to the secretary and said he was reporting to the admiral. She looked at him and said, "You're not in uniform, lieutenant. He will be very unhappy."

Burke stared down at the ground and said, "Yes, he is going to be very unhappy."

All four of them walked into Johnson's office. The admiral walked from behind his desk and smiled, "You brought the prisoner to me." He walked up to Kincaid. "I get to say goodbye to you, Kincaid, while you rot in prison for the next twenty years."

The admiral spun around on his heels and said, "Get the son of a bitch away from me." Burke took the handcuffs from around his belt and pulled them out. He called out and two Marine guards walked in and stood at attention. He nodded at them. They walked up to the admiral and placed their hands on each of his arms.

"Tell these guards to get their hands off me!"

Burke walked in front of the admiral and placed the cuffs on his wrists.

"You are under arrest, admiral. You'll be given over to the Provost Marshal for an Article 32 investigation concerning operations against the United States of America."

Kincaid watched as the admiral was escorted to the door. He moved to the side.

"You were right, admiral. I am saying goodbye."

* * *

"No, I'm not leaving you guys and my Marines, Mac," yelled Padre McCaffery.

Mac drummed his fingers on the desk. "Padre, you outrank me and it's not like I can order you to go."

The padre beamed. "That is very wise of you, gunny, and very true."

"Look, padre, you will be back in two weeks and I want you to meet my father and tell him I'm all right. And I can trust no one, but you for this mission. I personally will suffer not having your great intellect and Jesuit training to lean on and your great friendship. But this is a cause bigger than all of us."

The padre walked up to Mac. "I know, my dear Mac. I'm being a baby and two weeks is not that long."

"You have three hours before the Clipper takes off and we have to load your twenty bags of bibles onto the plane.

Sergeant Peterson and Corporal Reynolds will be with you so that you won't be alone. Padre McCaffery put his arms around Mac and hugged him.

"This is the Jesuit in me, Mac."

He noticed the tears in the padre's eyes. Mac turned away and ran his hand over his eyes. "Gee padre, you'll be back in a couple of weeks."

Chapter 62

Three weeks later

Wojo poured Mac and the padre a drink. They sat in silence and puffed on their cigars.

"Did you gentlemen, miss me?" asked the padre.

"There has been more bourbon available around here," said Wojo.

The padre smiled.

"There have been many more of my best cigars available for me to smoke," said Mac.

"It's been nice and quiet around here."

Then they burst out laughing.

"Then you did miss me," beamed the padre.

"Now, before we get all sentimental, tell us what happened in Cleveland while we were busy missing you."

The padre got up and walked around the room, thumping his cane.

"First of all, Mac, I stopped and paid my respects to Father Gibbons and all the lovely nuns. We had a grand time talking about your childhood. They are very proud of you, not only at the church, but throughout Cleveland. Father Gibbons said he hopes you will visit as soon as possible. I also left a substantial offering for him and his church per your wonderful instructions."

He thrust his glass forward and smacked his lips, which made Mac laugh.

Mac filled it and asked the padre to continue.

"The amount of money came to $2,750,868.00."

Mac and Wojo clinked their glasses, let out a hoorah, gulped down their drink, and poured more.

"I contacted Lieutenant Burke's father, a lovely gentleman who helped us diversify our assets under several banks and corporations. This includes land and real estate holdings. All our assets are in that big binder in your desk drawer. In that bag, under your desk is $243,000 in cash.

Wojo poured the padre another drink. He smacked his lips, and Mac howled.

"I also did a little shopping for myself, Mac. You did say I could buy a church. I bought an old monastery outside Cleveland. It's rather large and can be our base of operations when we move to Cleveland. Many of our Marines will be served through this. It wasn't a Catholic church, so I had to get it sanctified. Mr. Burke Senior is making it habitable and keeping the character of the building."

Mac interjected. "What do you mean 'we' exactly?"

"Where you go, I go," said Padre McCaffery.

Wojo raised his glass. "Where you both go, I go."

Mac raised his glass. "I was hoping we would be together. Wherever we go, we go together."

They heard a knock at the door. Sergeant Peterson opened the door while Kincaid and Burke walked in the room.

"Well, looky here, boys," said Wojo. "We got ourselves a new commander."

Kincaid looked resplendent in his uniform. They each got up and shook his hand.

"I just wanted to stop by and tell you guys, thanks."

They brushed off his comments and asked the big question.

"Did you get a command?"

Kincaid looked at them, grinning from ear to ear. "Yes, a fast, new destroyer."

He paused, trying hard not to show emotion. "I'll never forget you guys. I must shove off. We are sailing tomorrow morning. The first action we run into will be for you guys."

He stopped at the door. He slowly turned around.

"What happened to the admiral?"

"You didn't tell him, lieutenant?"

"Thought you guys would like to share the news with him."

Mac said, "Fined, reduced to commander and retired."

"Could have been me. Or worse," said Kincaid.

The padre put his hand on the commander's shoulder and prayed.

"May this saved man kill many Japs and end this miserable war. Protect him, dear Lord."

They all got up and shook his hand and wished him happy hunting.

Burke got up and poured himself a drink.

"Gentlemen, the navy is discharging me due to my wounds. It has been my privilege to serve with the finest of men. To my undying gratitude and your health."

"Where are you going, Lieutenant Burke?" asked Mac.

"Going back home and try to earn back the money I lost for my dad, I suppose."

"You're not going anywhere, Alan. We have a lot of work left to do," smirked Wojo.

Mac walked to the large window overlooking Chinatown and ripped down the temporary curtain.

"Well, I'll be damned."

"Well, read what it says," yelled the padre.

"Mac, Wojohowitz, McCaffery, and Burke Investigative Services."

He walked to the window and traced the names with his fingers.

"My dad agrees with you guys. He said I make a better detective than a businessman."

Mac winked at Wojo and the padre. "That better not be the case, Alan. It's amazing what twenty bags of bibles will buy."

Burke got a confused look on his face and then it slowly dawned on him.

"You guys took twenty bags of money."

"Let's just say we have money for our veterans that our government decided to burn and waste. Your father is assisting us, and now you. Welcome to our Board of Directors."

"How did you do it?"

"That's a story for Wojo and the padre to tell you. I must get to the naval hospital."

* * *

Lieutenant Van Deer asked Mac and Seadog to meet her near the benches overlooking Punta Point. A gentle breeze was coming off the ocean and his thoughts went back to the Canal. A deep sense of loss made him involuntarily drop his shoulders. All this started because of Guadalcanal. It was the beginning of the end for him. The island was going to be in American hands soon enough and the end of another Marine Corps campaign flag added to their legacy. The Marines were storming another beach somewhere and dying on an island they couldn't pronounce. He would never be with them again. The Japs started it and it would end, just like his battle with Gentleman Jack. He could only marvel how fast his life changed.

He watched a destroyer cruising out of Punta Point. Maybe Commander Kincaid's ship. He felt good about that man. Planes roared overhead and he waved to them. He stared at Ward D and a tremendous sense of pride overwhelmed him. The courage of those wonderful wounded guys.

That's when he saw them.

She was walking alongside him. He was walking with the aid of a cane in his dress greens. He tried to hold back tears, for the life of him, but they forced their way out and down his cheeks.

"Hello, pecker head," said Jonesy.

They shook hands and embraced.

Seadog was thrilled to be around his friend, his tail bouncing madly off the concrete.

"Semper Fi, Jonesy."

He turned to the woman who saved them both. He kissed her gently on the lips.

He grabbed her hand and said, "I think this is the beginning of a beautiful friendship."

Hi... thank you for buying my book and hope you enjoyed it. If you would like to follow the exploits of Gunny Mac, Wojo, Padre McCaffery and Burke please visit my website: Gunnymac.com and see when the next book comes out: *Gunny Mac Private Detective:Trouble in Cleveland.*

Steven Walker